TOWN & GOWN BOY

A Novel

by Jonah West

Town and Gown Boy
A Novel
by Jonah West

The story is told through the eyes and mind of a boy growing up in Oxford during the 1940/50's. It is a time when homosexuality was criminal but the University – "The Gown" flouted the law with impunity and the law itself sent the "Town" local homosexuals underground. This silence created perfect cover for homosexual paedophile men to exploit vulnerable boys of whom there were many – created by the time and by the Oxford hybrid culture "Town and Gown".

A few Town boys crossed to the Gown world via the 11-Plus intelligence screening that took place during the time. Some of these boys became vulnerable due to the vast differences they encountered between home and school during early teenage years. These boys presented a target for paedophiles from both Town and Gown – out looking for them in the streets of central Oxford.

Could one of these abused boys fully survive this experience?

Jonah West
July 2019

CONTENTS

Chapter 1.

Town and Gown

I didn't expect to be in Oxford in 1960, let alone at St. Giles Fair. Until now I believed my escape in 1954 was permanent.

The annual St. Giles Fair in Oxford is on the first Monday and Tuesday of September following St. Giles Day on September 1st - a couple of weeks before the beginning of a new Oxford University year.

Oxford students refer to this time as "Going Up to Oxford For Michaelmas Term". For Town boys like me, it's just " College starts again". But Oxford University, the Gown, tends to use puffed-up phrases like going "up" to Oxford - as in arriving at a higher level.

Some consider achieving a "place" at Oxford University as a scholarly pinnacle. My place in Oxford was much lower. My place in Oxford was owned and exploited by the Gown, controlled by closeted Masters with grand titles like Extraordinary Fellow, Prize Fellow and Fellow Emeritus.

Collectively the University Masters are known as Oxford "Dons" - historically short for Lord, and as-in Mafia crime boss. Often they can be seen in pompous procession in gold-adorned, black and red silk robes, topped by enormous mortarboard hats, leading some irrelevant Oxford University event, rooted in similarly irrelevant history. Oxford is all about history.

Oxford University owns most of the land and valuable buildings in Oxford. And when students are "up" they occupy the Town. To them Oxford becomes a status possession - accommodating an already advantaged path to even more privilege. Wearing black robes and white bow ties they flout and pout the elitism of the Gown. They speak in a uniquely condescending tone - known as the "Oxford accent". It indicates to all within earshot that you belong to the Gown.

The Oxford division between Town and Gown became a bottomless chasm in 1355, following the St. Scholastica's Day riots – instigated by two college students assaulting an Oxford taverner over the quality of his ale. This resulted in the Town locals banding together behind the taverner and marching into the University areas to kill and injure many of the Gown community.

Following the riots the University Chancellor, who ruled the area for the King, imposed a fine of five shillings and three-pence on the Town - one penny for each of the sixty-three students killed. The fine was to be paid for five hundred years, on the same date, personally by the Town Mayor - who was ordered to remove his hat for the occasion.
One penny for each dead student seems a low price – the higher price was to doff the hat to the Gown.

Town and Gown rime but not when it comes to public harmony in Oxford. The Gown looks upon itself as on a higher level, looking down on the Town people as uneducated and inferior. Thousands from the Town are employed by the Gown as "College Servants" - a term the Gown perpetuates to describe people who clean their rooms, serve their meals and tend to the imposing college buildings and majestic grounds that monopolize the ancient streets of central Oxford.

In early days the servants and choirboys recruited from the Town were paid in "leavings" - the food left over by the Gown. That tradition lives on with choirboys - still the prize of the perverted Gown Masters stalking Oxford's Gents public toilets.

Chapter 2

Oxford St. Giles Fair

St. Giles is the widest road in central Oxford - leading north out of the city center for about 200 yards - where it forks around St. Giles Church, mentioned in the Doomsday Book of 1086. Across the fifty-yard width run four traffic lanes. Along both sides are centuries-old stone buildings housing some of the University's most ancient colleges. St. John's, Balliol, Trinity and Keble College, among them. Other landmarks include the Ashmoleum Museum and Randolph Hotel, the Eagle And Child pub where Lewis and Tolkien gathered with other inebriated Gown Fellows to engage their fantasies.

During St. Giles fair the surrounding streets are closed to traffic for two days. The area becomes jam-packed with thousands of local people. Blaring organ music, barking showmen, whirring ride machinery and pounding diesel generators inhale the atmosphere and pump excitement into the air. The smell of candy-floss, toffee-apples and fish and chips - with the haze of cigarette smoke and engine exhaust, adding to a human buzz so different from the snooty thin air of the Gown - who normally occupy this historic area.

At the south end of St. Giles stands Martyr's Memorial - a stone monument to three early Church of England Bishops who where publicly burned to death during the mid-1550's. They were three of the early University Dons dressed in the black gowns of the Church. They enforced their dress and doctrine on the University community - imparting the title Gown. Because they were Bishops, they were granted favor over others publicly burned alive in the day. So small bags of gunpowder were tied to their bodies in expectation that explosions would finish them off quickly before they suffered the inferno. But as usual it rained in Oxford and the gunpowder failed to explode – inflicting an even more slowly tortuous live cremation. Oxford can be like that - ablaze and dank at the same time. Often a smoldering Town smothered by a damp Gown.

Just a few yards from Martyr's Memorial there is a Gents public toilets. It is housed underground, accessed by flights of steps at either end. Here many of the Town, Gown and tourist queers have sex. In the long row of cubicles dozens of homosexual encounters are randomly and hurriedly performed on a daily basis - right under the noses of the Martyred Bishops. The Oxford Police, who know exactly what is going on, either turn a blind eye or arrest a few now and then and have them reported in the Oxford Mail.

Like other boys in Oxford I was molested here as a schoolboy. This happened because Oxford's warped culture labeled and discarded me at age 13. Now after seven years of dispossessed survival, critically transformed, fate has returned me to Oxford. Before departing this time I plan to settle a few grievances.

Chapter 3

Sent to Wales

I don't remember much before I was eight, but I do remember that's when my problems started. I shared a tiny bedroom with my older brother. The single beds had hardly a gap between them but we were barred from crossing that gap – there was to be no physical contact with each other, or our clothes and beds.

My brother was completely bald at twelve years old – after catching a highly infectious form of ringworm at our grandparent's home in South Wales. It was blamed on the feral cats living in the stairwell coalbunker. My father denied it and said it was contacted at South Oxford School in St.Ebbes. He cursed the school headmaster, the teachers and the local doctors. A lot of kids in Hinksey had ringworm - the South Oxford School clinic was very busy and quite a few boys wore lint caps over baldheads. My father ranted that the Council and the Colleges couldn't care less about poor local families.

The infectious ringworm sores spread across my brothers' scalp. Soon it covered his entire head and reached down his neck. At South Oxford School Clinic his scalp was shaved and scrubbed with stiff brushes and hard soap – an ointment was rubbed in and his head covered in a white lint cap. He was barred from school and contact with children, including me. He received a violet light treatment twice per week at the ringworm clinic and special ointments at home. This kept him completely bald.

Each time my brother went for treatment I was also examined under the detection lamps. Inevitably ringworm was detected in my own scalp. That night my father shaved my head and scrubbed it with hard soap until my scalp bled – during the scrubbing he told me I was to blame – I should not have come into contact with my brother.

My bed was stripped and the bedding burned in the back garden. The bedroom was scrubbed and my brother and his bed were moved out of the house to a neighbor with no children. I knew that the neighbors talked badly about the children in the community who wore the white lint caps – I knew my parents were ashamed and becoming jittery.

For the next three nights my father scrubbed my head raw with the laundry soap –cursing me for becoming infected. Then an ointment was rubbed in and covered with the lint cap. On the third night he pressed his nails into my head so hard I cried. There was huge relief when my next examination showed no trace of infection.

The following morning my parents took me out in front of the house where my aunt Joy was waiting with at a taxi. I had not seen Aunt Joy in a long time - not since Christmas when we had been in South Wales, before my brother got ringworm.

Suddenly I realized I was leaving with my Aunt. For the first time I saw my Mum cry. My father stared at me and said nothing. I felt alone, at the edge of something bad.

In the taxi aunt Joy hushed me and said we were going to South Wales where I would be staying with my father's family. I had no idea why I was being sent away other than my ringworm. I wore a green peaked school cap that had been strapped to my head with a white elastic bandage tied under my chin - under the cap was a lint hat covering my medicated bald head.

We changed coaches at the hub station in Cheltenham and in five hours we were dropped in Penygraig, South Wales. We walked steeply up Tylacalyn road to the miner's cottage on Hughes Street where my father's family lived. The stark difference between Oxford and these surroundings was frightening. The narrow, interconnecting roads of terraced cottages were built on the hillside above a smoking colliery. The grey water struggling through the grimy riverbed was very different than Hinksey Stream. Black dust was settled everywhere. Dustbins were outside each house and sheep were roaming the streets. Raggedly dressed miners leaving the "Pit " had black faces, but white smiles as they walked home after a shift underground.

My grandparent's house had no toilet or bathroom. My aunt Daisy and uncle Dai also lived in the house, along with a strange old man named Jonny who stayed mostly in the small coalbunker off the kitchen, with the cats. With windows only at the front and back of the narrow house there was a dinginess that hung in the air.

The kitchen had a huge fireplace, taking up the entire back wall. Iron ovens were mounted above and to the sides. A metal grating stretched over the fire, supporting black kettles, pots and pans. The stone hearth enclosed two large coal buckets, steel pokers and tongs. It soon became my job to fill and bring the buckets from the outside coalbunker.

For washing there was an outside enamel sink under a metal lean-to. Above the sink was one cold-water tap. At the back of the house there was a toilet shed and a large coalbunker. Inside the toilet shed was a wooden box contraption with a seat and hinged lid. The poop dropped into a dark pit below the seat. The smell inside was putrid – I'd never smelled anything like that before. Also new was the toilet paper, which was torn newspapers pages. I began reading the local newspaper.

Aunt Daisy took me to a small, cold bedroom off the landing at the top of the stairs and told me to unpack my suitcase into the draws of a dresser - the only item of furniture in the room besides the double bed. She showed me a white china chamber pot under the bed that I was to use for peeing, which she called number one. I was to use the pot before bed and during the night. The pot was not to be used for number two – this I would do in the outhouse lavatory in the back garden.

She removed my caps and inspected my scalp. She told me to stay inside the house or in the back garden and keep my lint cap on at all times. She ordered me to use the pot and get into the bed. I asked if I should brush my teeth and was taken back down stairs to the sink. Asking for toothpaste I was told that it was not used here as everyone had false teeth – instead I was offered salt, which my aunt fetched from the sideboard in her living room. I gagged on the salt in my mouth and from that moment on stopped brushing my teeth.

It seemed nobody knew why I was there - I was bewildered by how my life could change so much, in a flash, without any explanation. When I asked about my parents I was told Mum was very ill and may die. I was numbed – she was fine when I left a few days ago - except I noticed she was crying. When we boarded the coach at Gloucester Green, I realized she was crying because I was leaving.

Everyone ignored me except to order me around. I was fed the same every day except Sunday. Breakfast was one Weetabix with sugar and milk, and sometimes jam – dinner was bacon and baked beans with fried bread – tea was a banana sandwich and half an orange with cups of tea at each meal.

On Sunday the family cooked a huge dinner together - it was always local lamb roast and mounds of potatoes and vegetables with gravy. It was also the only time we had pop but the flavor was always dandelion and burdock which made me gag. Listening to the dining table conversation I got the impression that the lamb was sometimes obtained from poachers known by my Uncle Dai, a local miner strongman.

My grandparents spent most of their day sitting either side of the kitchen fire – which my grandfather lit from newspaper, sticks and coal every morning. He would boil the first kettle of the day over the fire once it got going and make tea, which he would instruct me to take to my grandmother in bed.

He never spoke at all except to tell me to do something. One morning I tripped and spilt tea on the stairs – when he discovered it he tried to kick me as I went to run past him.

After the first cup of tea in bed, my grandmother would come down and sit in her chair by the fire. Her first action was to light up a Players cigarette with a match. There was a kind of ceremony to it – she watched the burning match curl into a thin black ash tail before tossing it into the red heat of the fire. Her first drag of the day always produced a fierce coughing bout that drew up long spits of phlegm, which she pursed through her lips into an old jam-jar. After a few drags and a few more spits she would settle down and drink the next cup of tea brought to her.

During the day my grandmother kept her false teeth in another old jam-jar on the kitchen sideboard next to her chair. She put her teeth in when preparing food and put them back in the jar after my grandfather had fallen asleep in his chair – as he always did after eating his dinner - which was ready for him every day when he returned from the pub. Their dinner was about the same as mine every day – except they had more bread which they used to soak up the bacon fat from the tin plates it had been cooked in.

My grandmother's face was pale yellow - her jowly cheeks sagged below huge earlobes. It was impossible to see her eyes behind glasses that were so old the lenses had clouded. Her hair was streaky grey, combed back into a ponytail, greasy and smelled musky, like their bedroom. Her voice was my clue to her mood but she rarely talked, unless a visitor came, or to curse me for something. She rose from her chair only to pee, cook, eat, go to the outside lavatory or go to bed – which she did most afternoons. Aunt Daisy did all the shopping, housework and cleaning.

My grandfather's daily routine was identically repetitive. After making the fire and first pot of tea he would have me fetch the newspaper from the front door letterbox and sit down in his chair by the fire. He used a huge magnifying glass – it was the largest I had ever seen and had to be eight inches wide. Each day he took a charcoal stick to mark the back pages, which carried the horse races for the day. I soon learned that these marks were his to be his bets at the pub - and the results would later tell on his mood.

After three weeks confined to the house doing chores and avoiding my grandfather my hair had grown to a short coverage. Aunt Daisy had washed my scalp daily and all the scabs had finally disappeared - leaving rough scars that could be felt under my hair. During this time I began to think aunt Daisy was my Mum.

One day I was called into the back kitchen by my grandmother – she studied me silently as she took drags on her cigarette and coughed up gobs of spittle into her jam jar. She told me I was to start school on Monday. I was to be ready in school clothes at eight o'clock for her to take me on my first day. She told me I should be like my father who was admired by everyone in the family for his intelligence.

The next day aunt Daisy took me out for the first time since my arrival – we walked to aunt Joy's house about a quarter mile away. We carried a bag of coal from the bunker and a bag of potatoes and vegetables. The house was larger than my grandparents but starkly empty, very cold and damp. Aunt Joy sat in the bare kitchen dressed in her coat, scarf and beret. The house backed onto a dump known as the tip - a smell of rotting rubbish permeated the house.

Aunt Joy instructed me to go the tip and collect sticks and scraps of newspaper. On my return they built a fire in the hearth and added some of the coal we had carried, gradually a crackling fire started to warm and dry the room. After about two hours the back boiler behind the hearth had heated enough water to run a shallow bath - in a real bathroom like at home in Oxford.

First aunt Daisy, then Joy and then me bathed in the warm water. When my turn came the water was cool and grey. I had not bathed myself before - but I felt cleaner and dried with the shared damp towel. This was sometimes the same routine at home in Oxford but my father always washed my hair and body.

The next morning I was ready by eight – dressed in my jeans and a white shirt. When my grandmother saw me she screamed at me to change into short trousers, and to never wear jeans to school. As I stood in protest with my grandmother I heard the door from the lean-to burst open and my grandfather lunged in towards me with a tin mug raised in his hand – I ran to the stairs and under my bed. After a while aunt Daisy entered my room and coaxed me out – she was irritated that I had caused my grandfather to flare up.

Wearing short grey trousers my grandmother walked me to the school. She was dressed totally in black with a black net veil over her face, white hair visible beneath her hat. She led me into the headmaster's office. She spoke at length with Mr. Davies who had been my father's teacher before rising to headmaster of Dinas Boys School. They reminisced about my father's good record at the school. Mr. Davies was the most fierce-looking man I had ever seen. He was over six feet tall and leaned his chest over me as he inspected my scalp. His arms seemed so long that he looked like a Tarantula. I could see his eyes up close – they had white warts on them.

When my grandmother left, the headmaster led me up a long set of stone steps to a dark granite building on top of the hill, housing the classrooms. I was shown into one and introduced to Mr. Roberts who was to be my new teacher. Rising from the chair behind his desk Mr. Roberts appeared stooped and had puffy grey cheeks, flecked with red veins that extended down his neck and spilled over his shirt-collar. His moustache and fingers were nicotine stained – he smelled like my grandfather. He instructed me up wooden stairs between four rows of pew-like desks at which sat about thirty boys on benches. He grunted at me in welsh and noticing my blank face ordered me in English into a seat halfway down the second row. I glanced around at my new classmates – only one smiled at me – the rest stared at me without expression.

Mr. Roberts returned to his desk and the blackboard on the wall. Sums were chalked uniformly and neatly across the board. The teacher recited the sums to the class in English but I had no idea what was being taught because I had never seen this type of sum before.

I understood the instruction to copy the sums into an exercise book with one of the thin sticks of charcoal on the desk. I had never used charcoal to write before – at school in Oxford we used pencils sharpened by the teacher.

Every few minutes Mr. Roberts took a cloth handkerchief from his jacket pocket and blew his nose on it. At the end of each blow he coughed up a wad of phlegm and pursed it out through slobbering lips onto the handkerchief. I had never seen this before - my grandfather and uncle Dai spit theirs into the fire and my grandmother and Daisy had jam-jars. Mr. Roberts put his a handkerchief kept in his pocket.

Halfway through the morning I followed the other boys out to the playground – they continued to stare and me and I wondered if they could tell my head had recently been shaved or if the short crop of new brown hair covered my scars. The boy who had smiled at me in class sidled up and nodded hello. He told me he lived opposite my house and his name was Derek – he had been told by his mother to bring me back home for dinner at twelve-thirty and return to school with him at two in the afternoon for the rest of the day. I felt a surge of friendship for Derek – my first outside contact for three weeks.

At the end of the morning session I followed Derek for the ten-minute walk home – we crossed the tip behind aunt Joy's house and I spotted the door in her back wall where I had gathered scrap wood for the fire. I felt the sadness that lay within that house, the drabness and closeness to a rubbish tip. Derek knew the short cuts through the hillside lanes and gullies – and through the colliery area with the grey water and choking air.

Jonny started to speak to me after a few weeks and asked me to pick up fagends off the street for him– he showed me how he pulled out the unburned tobacco from each and put in a brass snuffbox. He rolled up the retrieved tobacco in a new paper to make a cigarette. He gave me my first drags of cigarette smoke – it made me dizzy but kind of happier. Jonny was a very small man with a bent-over back – his skin was deathly pale and streaked with blue veins - his small head was totally bald. His only hair was two thick tufts that grew from each nostril. His clothing never changed, was blackened and shiny. Everything he had was scraped together including worn-out leather boots. He had no false teeth and his chin kind of disappeared into his mouth when he closed his lips. He placed his hand over his mouth on the rare occasion he smiled and continuously wiped his lips and nose with the back of his wrist. No one in the house had real teeth – except for uncle Dai.

The punishment at Dinas Boys' School was harsh. At Hinksey School we could be slapped on the back of the legs with a ruler if really naughty, but here one teacher hit me on the head with a knotted stick because I got out of line in a queue.

I became familiar with failure – in arithmetic tests I had no idea what was on the blackboard – in welsh classes I just sat and tried to understand at least one word – at the end of classes we sang songs in welsh – these I learned to mime and gradually learned the words.

I was forced to bring home a report each week that condemned me as lazy and stupid – my grandfather started to hit me when no-one else was around – punching me on the arms or thighs for being "bad" at school as he called it. He told me my father would be ashamed of me.

After four weeks at school I was still not grasping the sums or the welsh – but I was slowly being accepted in the playground. A very tough boy named Lyn had made friends and I noticed the taunts and bullying began to lessen. Lyn lived a couple of houses down the street from me and started to call for me to walk to school – on the way home he led me along streets and lanes all over Dinas, Penygraig and Tonypandy.

After school we began to hike up the mountains – Lyn knew many exciting places and introduced me to old coal mine workings and the feeder lakes. We chased sheep and searched for old pit ponies that were often abandoned on the mountain. We explored the chain-driven dram railway that replaced the ponies but decided against trying to board a dram for fear of being trapped in the chain. A year earlier a boy had his leg shredded off by the chain as he tried to jump onto a dram going back down the track.

Things at school continued to slide downhill – I made no progress at all, except memorizing one welsh song we sang every day for five minutes. I learned where to place emphasis in the verses and developed a welsh singing accent but didn't understand a word.

At home I was scolded and ridiculed each Friday when I brought home the test results for signing. My grandmother announced in a smoke hazed, eye-piercing rant that she was not signing any more because I had let down my father and shamed the whole family.

For the most part the local boys gradually accepted me and I spent all my free time on the streets or the mountains, and hiking to other colliery towns with Lyn. We were never questioned as we wandered through the roads and mountain tracks worn in by years of miners walking to work across the mountains - and coming home carrying a sack of coal. Lyn's family had lived in the valleys forever and he knew every town, village, corner shop and mine.

My confidence grew except at school where I felt stranded - the teachers began to ignore me completely - except occasionally to curse me or stare at me in hate.

After about four weeks I had worn holes in my plimsolls – I found thick cardboard on the tip and lined the insides. But the soles wore away completely in two more weeks. My Sunday best shoes were now all I had. My grandmother scolded me for wearing out my shoes and stopped me from playing outside saying they couldn't afford new shoes. The ones I came with were supposed to last – I was to wear them for school only.

I heard my grandparents arguing about why my father had not sent enough money to pay for my keep.

One Friday the palms of my hands were so swollen from canings at school I had difficulty holding my knife and fork at dinner. My grandmother was shocked when she saw the bruises I was hiding and complained to the school headmaster – after that I was punished with isolation from the playground and made to stand against a wall outside the classroom. The most horrible teacher – Mr. Lloyd, kicked me occasionally.

The teachers ridiculed me for ignorance and the way I spoke. A new boy from Gloucester came into the class after I had been there about two months. I watched him struggle to understand and be understood – just as I had. I began to gain a reputation for football and fighting and made friends easily, including another new, and only black boy in the school, whose was nicknamed Darky – he had just moved from Cardiff and did not have a dad. He was by far the fastest runner in the school and taught me how to push myself physically.

At home my grandparents ignored me – and my aunt and uncle were always busy. I roamed the streets and mountains with Lyn and other boys whose parents didn't care. We smoked a lot and were adept at stealing cigarettes from homes and shops. I became familiar with the tips of rubbish and the mounds of coal slag – the blackened world of dust and rust.

My bedroom became my den, where I spent most of my time in the house – often under the bed. I read and reread the comics I had brought with me. They gave me a connection to home so I kept them hidden in my shirt draw. When uncle Dai was home I sat in their living room watching and listening to the conversation with Daisy – they talked of their children and their grandchildren who all lived away and rarely visited.

Uncle Dai worked at a colliery in Gilfach Goch and came home after every shift covered in coal dust caked on with sweat. Just before he came in aunt Daisy would have a small tin bath in front of the living room fire - filled with water heated on the kitchen fire.

On arriving home his first ritual was to sit in his chair and carve small pieces of twist tobacco into his pipe – which he smoked in silence listening to the radio. In five minutes he would stand up and drop all his clothes to the floor and step into the tin bath – the water reached to his hips when he sat down with his knees drawn up to his chest. My aunt would wash his back and hair – pouring clean water over his head and body from a stone jug – he would then stand up again to wash his lower body before stepping out to dry off and put on clean long underwear.

I never tired of watching this ritual – it was amazing to see his transformation from black to white every day. He began to talk to me a little bit– he was the only person, except Jonny, who spoke to me. He told me stories of his days in the Navy where he had been a stoker on board battle ships. His tales included descriptions of the batteries of coal fired boilers and the lines of stokers shoveling coal and trimming the fires - and of how it took many days and hundreds of stokers to manually refuel the bunkers. The stokers, he said were the toughest sailors because of their constant strenuous work. He made his own pipe tobacco, the way he had learned in the Navy - cured leaf weaved together into thin, tarry black sticks called "twist".

The meal after his bath was always the same – a massive mound of mashed potato topped with a thick brown gravy made from the juices of sheep liver and kidneys – occasionally minced lamb or chops would appear alongside the green cabbage or turnip. The meal was enormous and consumed with gnarled, coal-scarred hands grasping two forks. His repeat slow-motion arm movements were stiff from the shoulder and his grip seemed almost ape-like. His shoulders and arms were massive and his fresh complexion stood out. He had a few top and bottom front teeth that were showing the roots and was revered for extracting his own teeth with pliers when it was necessary. A mop of blond hair defied his age.

Not a word was said before he finished eating and sat in his armchair facing the fire. He lit a new pipe and stared at the glowing coals – sometimes he would tell me stories of how he competed in miner challenges, carrying sacks of coal over a three mile mountain track – describing the fit of his shoes and the leather harness he made to support the sack over his shoulders.

At the front of the narrow house was a closed room, never used – it was called the "front room". The furniture was the newest and best in the house and there were framed photos of the family on the walls. I learned from aunt Daisy who went in there to clean that two sons in the family, my father's older brothers, were dead – I was instructed never to ask about them. She pointed to herself as a teenager alongside an infant girl who she told me was actually her son Gareth, now grown up who would be coming to stay for a while soon. I asked why he was dressed like a girl – again I was instructed never to ask that again.

I noticed my aunt sometimes went in the front room stared at the photographs for what seemed a very long time – she told me to just look at the faces and pray for them – the faces all looked very similar. When we came out of the room there was always a downward and pursed look on my Aunt's face – at these times I noticed tears ran down deep groves in her cheeks onto lips that collapsed into her mouth.

Gareth came to visit and I was told to call him uncle. The next morning I noticed my underwear draw had changed and my comics were in a different order. I also noticed my chamber pot had been half-filled with strong yellow pee.

I kept my distance from my grandfather. Jonny came in one afternoon with an old pair of black boots he had found on the tip. He cleaned and polished them and gave them to me to try on – they were a bit big but with two pairs of socks they were tight enough for running. Jonny made me smoke like him and soon after I was sick in the outhouse. But now I had boots I was free again to roam with Lyn.

We started to collect fagends anywhere we could find them - soon I could smoke like everyone else - inhaling without coughing or being dizzy. My grandfather read out a story from the Sunday Echo where a 4 year old boy was smoking 10 fags a day - so smoking must be ok for children he reckoned. We began smoking before and after school every day – the secrecy and enterprise of it gave me a sense of achievement.

One night I woke as the door quietly opened to see uncle Gareth slipping into my room – I clenched my eyes tight and remained still. After a few seconds I heard his breath close to me in bed and then receding. After a period of what seemed endless silence I heard the door closing. The next day I asked him why he was in my room last night – he said he needed to use the chamber pot and was it ok? Uncle Gareth swore me to secrecy.

That afternoon I was sitting in the outside toilet reading a scrap of newspaper when my grandfather came home from the pub. I heard him shout for me to come out – then kicking the door soon after. Half in panic I tried to finish and clean myself as the rant continued outside. When I opened the door he grabbed my hair and pulled me to the ground – pushing my face hard against the stone slab. I struggled wildly and got up but he cursed and kicked me as I fled into the house. My grandmother screamed at me for creating a row then went into an uncontrolled bout of coughing.

I fled to my bedroom and my hiding place under the bed – the close smell of the stale urine in the chamber pot made me choke. After a while I fell asleep and was wakened by the door opening. I noticed uncle Gareth's shoes and saw them move to my dresser and heard the draws opening and closing. Then the shoes remained still for what seemed like many minutes but I noticed his trouser bottoms were shaking. I heard him groan and cough and a gasping sound. I began to feel very frightened and started to cry into my hands.

Uncle Gareth's voice ordered me out - he stared at the me intently and asked me if I had seen what he had been doing at the dresser. I shook my head - he said he had been tidying the draws but to keep it secret between us. He told me my grandmother had taken to her bed very ill because of the upset earlier and that my Grandfather was now sleeping in his chair. But uncle Gareth warned that my Grandfather was very angry and was blaming me for causing an upset in the house. Then he undid his belt and pulled down his trousers – his massive red and purple "billy" frightened me so much I began to cry again. He quickly pulled up his trousers and patted me on the head – he said he was just going to use the chamber pot. Again he swore me to secrecy – this time adding that if I told anyone our secrets he would tell everyone that he had caught me stealing cigarettes, an unforgivable sin.

Later that day, sitting in the living room I felt a sense of dread seeping over me. Suddenly the door from the back kitchen opened sharply and my Grandfather stood in the doorway holding a poker. For a second he halted, staring hate until lunging toward me. I jumped to my feet and instinctively put myself on the opposite side of the table from him. I felt the whoosh of the poker as it passed the top of my head. My only escape was out the front door through the hallway – my fingernails split as I forced the chain off the hook in a panic.

That night aunt Daisy packed all my clothes and we walked to aunt Joy's house. They told me I had to stay here now because my grandfather couldn't stand me being in his house without my parents giving more money.

There was no food in the pantry and no milk outside so Auntie Joy made tea and we went into her bed to get warm. There were fagends in an ashtray, which she put on a hairgrip and lit with a match - she showed me how to suck out a drag. She asked me if Mum gave me "titty" - I kind of knew what she meant and I said no. Then she lifted her nighty and pulled my head toward the large brown nipple on her naked breast. Just before my lips touched her nipple I turned my head and she pulled me closer, saying "You can always have a little titty here".

Lyn and I started a stealing route of ten or so shops - sometimes the bell on the door wouldn't work so we could sneak in and steal ten woodbines. Then we sold them singly to other boys for a profit – then went back and bought more cigarettes at the shop we had stolen from in the first place – sometimes stealing more. Lyn told me he learned the system from his Dad who had done it for years. We took the stuff we had stolen to Lyn's house - his parents didn't care where we got it. We just had to stay out of his Dad's way because he got drunk a lot and would take his belt off to beat anyone in the house that was in reach. I'd never met anyone like Lyn's Mum - she was the kindest most smiling lady imaginable. She washed my clothes once a week and looked at my ears and neck to see if I was washing.

Lyn also got bad reports from school every Friday - but he just signed them himself and handed them back in. His parents didn't care how he did in school - he planned on going down the mines as soon as he left school - like all the rest of his family and most of the neighbors.

Although he was only eleven he could beat any boy on the street in a fight - even boys of fourteen were scared of him. He had fights almost every day but was not a bully - most of his fights were about protecting a smaller boy against a bully.

Chapter 4.

Return to Oxford

When my father came to collect me after six months, there had been no contact from home at all – I had difficulty imagining their faces any more. On the way back to Oxford in the coach I was fiercely sick - my father folded a newspaper bag for me to vomit. At the Cheltenham hub where we changed coaches he took me to the toilets to clean up – very stern and angry, he told me Mum would be upset to see me like this.

After sitting me on a bench outside he went back into the toilets and was gone for a long time – I became very worried and started crying. A lady asked me if I was lost and I said no but my Dad was lost. Just then he returned – as we boarded the new coach he pinched my arm really hard. We travelled the rest of the way to Oxford in silence.

As we walked up Abingdon Road I saw Mum and my brother looking out our back window. By the time we rounded the corner into Bertie Place Mum was rushing toward me with tears streaming – I started to cry and laugh at the same time I was so happy to see her and feel her arms around me.

Soon after I was in the bath with water so hot I couldn't sit down for a long time. Mum was very upset with the state of me – my hands and arms were covered in thick warts - some bleeding – my clothes in tatters. My father stood by the bath impatiently waiting for me to sit down. It was then he saw the sores under my hair – he swore under his breath – something he never did. I heard the dreaded words "ringworm". He used scissors and a razor to shave my head in the bath and scrubbed me all over with a brush. My scalp and the puss-filled warts were pressed with a steamed hot cloth with a slice of boiling bread inside called a poultice. Mum sowed a cap out of white linen and put it on my head - she cut my finger and toe nails and stood over me while I brushed my teeth. Then she put me to bed. Regardless of my problems I felt so relieved to be home.

The next morning Mum took me to the clinic at South Oxford School. They looked at my head under blue lights and confirmed ringworm – the worst part was when Mum sobbed. The ringworm nightmare was starting all over again.

The nurse looked at my penis and tried to pull back my foreskin but it wouldn't go – my Mum became more upset and a doctor came to calm her. The doctor saw my warts and asked Mum what she was doing about them. They talked about the yellow discharge coming from my nose. The smell of the clinic and all the medical apparatus scared me – now that Mum was ill I felt a panic – like when I had bad dreams.

The School dentist chair was the worst – he picked pieces of my teeth away with steel spikes and told my mother I must have some teeth taken out, some filled and to start brushing immediately. The dentist used a big steel drill on my teeth - I was terrified and bewildered by my problems. Then four teeth were pulled out after I was gassed to sleep.

After a couple of days large boils started to appear on my legs and arms – the warts all became crusty and cracked, leaking puss. My temperature rose to 105 and each time I fell asleep my mind faced an endless barrage of nightmares all with theme of an impossible situation – of a brick-house that had collapsed and being told to put it all back together again myself. My Dad's face kept appearing and cursing at me to get it done and then turning his back. Eventually an ambulance came to the house and took me to the Radcliffe Infirmary in St. Giles.

I was placed in a small ward with four beds – only the one next to me was occupied. Immediately nurses started to arrive and take blood from me through huge needles – mostly from my arms, legs and fingers, also there were injections in my legs. I was taken to a large hot bath each morning and left to soak for twenty minutes - then the sores were covered with a sticky mesh soaked in medicine under two layers of bandages. Back in bed I would wait in dread of more blood tests and injections. Every other day I was wheeled to another part of the hospital and placed under a large lamp that gave off blue light. After about an hour my head was bathed and a cream applied to my ringworm sores.

A screen partition separated my bed from the boy next to me. The first thing I noticed was every couple of hours he made sounds that began with loud painful moans and ended in whimpers of despair. I covered my eyes with the sheets each time the nurses carried him to bathe because he had massive bloody holes in his exposed legs. My family did not visit but a cleaning lady stopped at my bed each day and gave me a sweet or a biscuit. She told me I was brave.

In a week my sores started to shrink and the blood tests stopped. My ringworm sores dried up and began to heal - I was very relieved until a doctor came to look at my penis. The following morning I was moved to a big ward next door, with lots of children, some in bed and others moving around. My sores were all healing. But in the afternoon things changed for the worse. A nurse drew the curtains around my bed and I saw a very big injection needle on her trolley – I started to cry when she pulled down my pajama leg and I realized I was to be injected.

I remember being wheeled into a room with bright lights in the ceiling – then a mask flowing gas placed over my nose and mouth. Then I woke up back in my bed – my throat was burning and I felt pain in my penis.

Mum came to see me – bringing grapes and an orange. She took me the bathroom and inspected my penis – there was blood on it and when I peed it hurt so much I shouted out. Mum explained that my tonsils had been removed from my throat and my penis had been circumcised - it would hurt for a while but not for long. I started to feel much better – an end to the pain and panic seemed possible.

A few days later Mum picked me up - she explained that she had also been in hospital all the time I was in Wales. In front of the fire in the living room she took off her blouse and showed me a thick bright red scar that started between her breasts and went down to her belly button before curving around the bottom of her left ribs and ending at the top of her back – virtually cut in two. The scar was from surgery to fix a valve in her heart – she said she was very lucky to have been picked by a famous Oxford University surgeon who had saved her life. My father said Mum had been used as a guinee-pig for experimental surgery - but Mum seemed pleased with her new reputation.

Chapter 5.

Primary School

It took four weeks for my sores to heal and my hair to grow back – there was a week of worry that the treatment would make me bald but I was very relieved that I would not have to wear a cap in school.

When I went back to New Hinksey primary school the boys were much bigger than when I left seven months ago, but I was still the same size more or less. In the playground a bully and his friends taunted me for having scars on my head and legs. On the way home to dinner a boy from Weirs Lane punched me on the nose and lips without warning. After dinner Mum took me back to school and showed Miss Broom my swollen face – the boy said I had pushed him in the playground - it was a lie. That night in bed I was sad - I was home in Oxford but in some ways it was even worse than Wales - I missed Lyn.

I was made to sit in front of the class with my back to all the rest – Miss Broom said it was so that she could give me special attention to help me catch up. But she didn't help me at all and soon I felt out of place again – just like in Wales.

My house on Bertie Place was only a mile south of the city center, the world's heart of education. But it could have been a million miles away based on difference in so-called "class". The city center is inhabited by Gowns floating around in upper class while the working class ekes it out in Hinksey - in estate housing built largely to accommodate the growth of Morris Motors - fast becoming the biggest car manufacturer in England. Men from Wales, Scotland

and Ireland migrated toward the high labor wages paid by the Morris Motors Factory at Cowley. Creating Oxford's split culture of academia and manual labor.

Our brick house was damp and cold. The heat came from an open coal fire in a tiny living room. Sometimes the fire would not start or the matches would run out. During the day the fire would sometimes go out and there was no heat when my father arrived home. This would cause an upheaval, followed by an evening when all conversation was banned and the wireless turned off until I was sent to bed early.

Mum trained me to start the fire. The worst part was going outside in frost and snow to chop the sticks from old orange boxes and get the coal from the outside bunker - but setting the fire was easy after that - the secret was shielding the match with the palm of your hand as soon as it lit - otherwise they regularly blew out before you could touch the flame to the newspaper. Horse and cart delivered the coal and the coalmen carried them on their backs through the house because the side path was so narrow. They didn't care if they unloaded them cleanly into the bunker so there was always one day after coal delivery that I would have to clean up and organize the bunker.

Mum praised me for being "clever" and trained me to clean and polish the house - to clean the windows and the bathroom and go to the shops for food. Every family had books of ration coupons issued by the Government. Ration coupons were needed to buy everything except vegetables - of which there weren't any anyway. Mum instructed me how to make a list, count the number of coupons needed and cut from the ration books - then go to Brown's shop on the corner of Sunningwell Road.

Often several trips were needed each day because the shop would run out of everything except sugar and potatoes - so Mum would have me running to and fro to check on new deliveries. I learned to stay at the back of any queue and soon noticed Miss Brown was keeping things aside for Mum and would produce eggs, tomatoes, biscuits and bread from the back or under the counter - but only if no one else was in the shop and always buried deeply in my canvas bag before I left.

Life revolved around my father working forty-eight hours per week at "The Factory" as Morris Motors car production operation was known. The sprawling complex in Cowley could employ most able-bodied men looking for work in Oxfordshire - and some women. Thousands of workers arrived by train, bus and bike six mornings a week and put in eight hours Monday to Saturday.

Fridays my father brought home his weekly pay envelope and ceremoniously handed it, unopened to my mother as we sat at the tea table. She opened the sealed envelope and counted out the notes and coins onto the table and compared the amount to the hand written account on the envelope. If the amount was ten pounds or more we knew things would be ok for a week - if not we knew otherwise.

There was always a lot of conversation between Mum and my father about what was going on at the Factory. It seemed my father had been passed over several times for promotion to Foreman. He complained that management wanted him to push their message on the shop floor and support them on wages and work conditions - but they had backed out on the promise of a promotion. Morris Factory Foreman was one of the biggest things to brag about in Oxford if you were Town. My father was very bitter and criticized any neighbor that seemed to be doing well at anything.

By far the most important thing in our house was my father's cigarettes. According to my father the brand of cigarettes a person smoked said something about the quality of that person. He insisted on smoking expensive Players Navy Cut and demeaned anyone that smoked a lesser brand like Players Weights or Woodbines. His breath permanently smelled like burned tobacco and his fingers and false teeth were stained with nicotine. I don't remember anyone who didn't smoke.

Mum was always too weak or ill to do anything else but the cooking. My father developed a reputation as the family martyr - singularly responsible for Mum being alive, by virtue of his unwavering commitment and labor. Any time I did anything bad I was threatened with the prospect of causing Mum to die with a heart attack. It became my biggest worry.

In the winter we gathered around the coal fire in the tiny living room. We listened to the wireless - my father demanded absolute silence when the "Dick Barton - Special Agent" program was on. Mum and my father smoked cigarettes and my brother went outside to smoke secretly. I knew because when he came back in I could smell the smoke on him. My parents didn't seem to care or couldn't smell because the room was always hazed in smoke anyway. I sat on a small stool and deliberately inhaled the smoke that floated by. I collected the fagends from the fireplace and hid them in my socks until I could put them in my secret place in the shed, which is where I did most of my smoking.

We ate at a fold down table in the kitchen - often while my father shaved in the sink. His tea would be like dinner and was always the best food. My brother and me ate mostly bread with margarine and jam or banana sandwiches. Our dinner was at mid-day and was usually mince, mashed potatoes and swede. We had lots of liver and sausages. On Sundays we had a roast dinner - usually lamb or pork. My father was not keen on gardening so we didn't have much vegetables or fruit.

After tea on my tenth birthday, while he was in the bathroom, I stole a cigarette from my father's 20 Players packet and hid it in the shed. Mum had made a cake with candles. After we had eaten some my father opened his cigarette packet and before taking one I noticed he was counting them. He looked straight at me and lifted his chin. "You've pinched a fag out of here" he snarled. He put out his hand "let's have it". I was speechless - not knowing whether to risk a lie. "I counted them before I went to the bathroom" he shouted at me. I led him to the shed and my hiding place - he took the cigarette and the fagends and papers I had hidden.

My father ordered me to the bathroom - I knew what was coming. He closed the door and ordered me to remove my short trousers and underpants. He sat down on a trunk and dragged me across his lap. He beat my bum with his bare hands and kept shouting "if you smoke again you get the stick" and "you little thief". He had set a trap I realized and was now punishing me. Mum started shouting up the stairs for him to stop - she always did this after my father had been beating me for a while.

It was my brother who really taught me how to steal in Oxford – expanding on the skills I had learned in Wales. He started by showing me how to steal fruit and vegetables from gardens and allotments around Hinksey. Then how to steal sweets and cigarettes from the shops along Abingdon Road. At Christmas he showed me how to steal presents from Woolworth's, Marks & Spencer and other shops in Town. We stole a lot of things to eat and were always on the lookout for cigarettes.

By the time I was 11 I had a stealing route well developed. I stole from everywhere I could. Mum's purse, neighbor's purses, the shops, church, school, gardens, orchards, cars - anywhere there was cash, cigarettes or food. My brother didn't need to steal anymore because he was making enough money on his paper round - specially at Christmas when the neighbors gave big cash tips. I had friends who stole too - most were able to steal cigarettes from their parents. The first time Mum caught me stealing from her purse my father used his belt on my bare ass for three days in a row. He also made me dig over and weed the whole back garden, which took two weeks - plus clean and polish the house every Friday.

There are lots of university sports fields in south oxford and a friend whose dad worked at one introduced me to a good source of cash. While the players were on the field or pitch we stole money from their clothes hanging in the pavilion dressing rooms. We also knew where cash boxes for club dues and bar proceeds were stored. This was also a good source of cigarettes as most the players smoked and left their fags in their pockets in the dressing room. We took a little from as many sources as possible.

I had a hiding place for the things I needed to keep out of the house. My father regularly had me strip off and search my clothes for anything I could be caught and punished for. Often he came into my room when he thought I was sleeping and searched my dresser and wardrobe - so I knew not to hide anything there.

I had a place under Hinksey Lake bridge needing climbing over a spiked fence and crawling under an earthy silent foundation. I went in there sometimes after cubs or scouts - as a safe place to smoke. One night I was about to climb the fence after scouts when my father came out of the darkness on his bike. He looked at the high steel spikes and at me - luckily he guessed wrong and accepted my story that I was there to catch a train-spotting number. But it warned me that he was following me.

It was during this time my brother started to molest me. He started by tossing off in front of me and told me to do it too. I did but although I got stiff there was no feeling or spunk like my brother had. He tried to put his billy in my bum but I got really scared and cried - so he choked me to stop me crying. He threatened if I told Mum he would drown me in the river and held my head under water in the bathroom sink to show me he meant it.

Some of my friends at church and school were into openly tossing off and sometimes doing it to each other. One boy kissed me on the lips when were sitting up on a willow tree by Hinksey stream - I didn't like it but I let him toss me off.

I played football for the school team and we got into the city semi-finals - my father complained when I asked for new boots because the ones handed down from a neighbor had worn out. Another neighbor gave me an old pair that fitted and Mr. Harris the cobbler on Wytham Street put in new studs. I felt like a new player in those boots. My father never came to see me play. I realized I could do sports well and as I was gaining size and strength. I started to stick up for myself around school and the neighborhood. I noticed that if I acted a bit like Lyn the other boys backed off. I also learned from the sports master Mr. Hayes that trying hard at physical training was good. He also taught to brush your teeth – he said if you didn't you would get stomach ulcers.

I began to believe I could be like Lyn. I volunteered for boxing, it had a natural feel to it as I danced and bobbed throwing multiple shadow punches. The trainer made me stand orthodox and jab with straight lefts - but as soon as a real sparring session started I switched to southpaw and full on attack - just like Lyn - with ferocious intent to destroy. The bullying at school stopped when it became known I would fight anyone.

My brother and I were distant, like with my father. My brother picked on me every day, and incited his friends to pick on me. I was always scared of them - one of the worst things I remember is when he and my older cousin stuffed a rotten apple with ants on it into my mouth. It was blamed on me for being "cheeky". My father laughed at the bites on my lips and said I had been taught a lesson.

My brother and my father did everything together - they went fishing, did carpentry and bike repairs, they raised and raced pigeons and bred budgies. One day my father brought home a springer spaniel whose name was Rex. He was kept outside and had a basket in the shed.

My brother didn't want to take him out and was even more put off that he had to take me too. Soon I was taking Rex every morning by myself, across Hinksey Lake bridge to let him run in the fields along the lakes by the railway. It was late in the year and cold with frost on the grass some mornings. Rex sat outside hoping to get in but Mum didn't like him and said he growled at her.

On Guy Fawkes Night we had a bonfire and fireworks in the garden. After, I went to let Rex out of the shed - but he wasn't there. I ran to my father to tell him but he said Rex had gone back to his old owner because Mum was scared of him. I was shocked and really sad - I could not believe this had happened to Rex and me. That night I cried under the bedclothes. Never a word was ever spoken about Rex again - when I did ask about him my father told me not to bring Rex up again.

Around that time my father started to train me for the eleven-plus exam. Every night I practiced spelling, composition and arithmetic that he brought home on paper from the factory. I practiced puzzles with different shapes and letters and problems about distances and time. Each night I had to write a composition about things like how to make a cup of tea, what to take on a picnic and how to darn a sock. There were books of puzzles and lessons about the Royal Family and Parliament and places in England.

My father told me that he had passed an exam to go to grammar school in Wales but his parents were too poor to buy the uniform so he had to leave at fourteen, when he was old enough to work. My brother's chances to pass the eleven-plus had been hindered by his isolation for ringworm so my father drilled into me that it was up to me to pass - for the family.

In March the eleven-plus exam was nerve racking - especially the week of constant training set by my father before the exam. On exam day we sat at desks moved into the school hall. The Headmaster and Miss Broom walked up and down and looking over our shoulders. Not a word was spoken during the two forty-minute sessions. My father asked me questions about the exam for a long time that night. He was angry because I had left out some important things in the composition about gardening and incorrectly spelled some words.

At Cubs I was a Sixer leading my patrol and I earned the most money in the Oxford Bob-a-Job week competition. For a week I left the house at daybreak and rode around South Oxford in my Cub uniform, knocking on doors asking if any jobs were available for a shilling, "a bob", contribution. I earned three pounds, seven shillings and six pence for the six days I worked - it was an Oxford record and I got a shield with a Wolf head painted on it - presented at a parade in town on Remembrance Day. My father said if I could work that hard for the Cubs I could do more work around the house and wrote out a list of jobs for me to complete each week before I had free time after school.

I went to the Baptist church on Wytham Street every Sunday for the morning service and Sunday school in the afternoon. Mum and my brother went to the Sunday evening service. My father never went - except on Christmas morning. While Mum and my brother were at church my father would take the News of the World

Sunday paper to the bathroom and be gone a long time. Sometimes he would leave it in the bathroom and I read some of the stories, which were mostly about men kidnapping and harming girls and boys - and prostitutes and queers in London.

One evening I went up and kissed him on the forehead - like I did to Mum. I was shocked when he glared "never kiss me again". Whenever Mum and my brother would get home after church my father would leave for an hour on what he called his "walk to clear his mind" – he meant the problems he had with me. I didn't know what they were.

One May morning at school assembly the Headmaster announced that two pupils had passed the 11-Plus - me and a girl who lived in the second-hand shop on Abingdon Road. At dinnertime Mum showed me a letter that said I had passed and I could choose from three grammar schools in Oxford. At tea time my father said I had not done so well because I was not offered a place at Magdelen School. My father decided it would be City of Oxford High School (COHS).

That weekend we went into Town and my father bought me a green Raleigh Lenton Sports bike at Halfords. That was my 11-plus reward - for years it had been promised if I passed.

At the schools Gala at Temple Cowley pool I won the 25 yards breaststroke and came second in the diving. I also raced in athletics, boxed and played cricket for the school. On my last day at Hinksey Primary School I won a book for the best all-round junior sportsman. My father complained that I had not finished top in my class at exams. He said coming third was not good enough and he couldn't care less about how I did in sports.

A large envelope arrived from my new school. There was a long list of all the clothes and supplies required. The compulsory uniform was chocolate brown blazer with the school's Oxford emblem sown to the breast pocket, a matching brown tie with red and blue stripes and either a white or grey shirt. Trousers could be long or short - either matching brown or grey. A brown peaked cap with a central school emblem rounded it off.

There were lists of sports clothes for rugby, cricket, athletics and gym. A leather satchel for carrying books was mandatory as well as compulsory rulers, geometry sets, a fountain pen and ink, pencils and painting supplies. All the clothes had to have a silk nametag sown inside each item. The lists went on and on, and each teatime my father complained about the cost of it all.

There was a big upset one evening when the cost of rugby boots came up. The school insisted on black boots with aluminum studs and no nails - my father wanted me to wear my old football boots - even though the studs were nailed in and the nails were coming through into my feet as the studs wore down. My father said he never had rugby or football boots so why was it necessary for me?

Chapter 6.

City of Oxford High School for Boys (COHS) - Years 1 and 2

I started at my new school right after St. Giles fair in September. I rode my new bike up the Abingdon Road to Carfax, along Queen Street to New Inn Hall Street and down to the school side gate. I'd never seen so many eleven year old boys before - there were three classes of thirty called Forms One A, One B and One C. I was in One B and this really got me into trouble at home because my father said I was not in One A because I had not done as well as I should in the 11-Plus exam.

The teachers were called Masters. Form One B Master was Mr. Glee who taught Latin - his nickname was Shaggy for some reason. All the Masters had nicknames. Every morning began with School Assembly in the Main Hall. Prefects herded us into lines with the juniors in front and the seventh form at the back. We stood silent and straight as the Head and Masters filed in seniority onto the raised stage at the front of the Great Hall.

Prefects were chosen from the sixth and seventh forms, they never seemed to smile and watched like hawks for any misdemeanor like whispering or eating sweets. You could get punished by having to write a hundred lines like "I must not speak in assembly". One day my prefect caught me flicking a cardboard pellet with a rubber band and punished me with writing a composition on the uses of copper. For this I had to go to the Oxford Library at the Town Hall after school. When my father found out he was very angry - after punching me on the arms till they were numb he told me the prefect was using me to do his own homework.

Just after I started at COHS my brother was expelled from his School for stealing - I wasn't supposed to know. He started work as an apprentice joiner - something my father was very proud of - that his son had got an apprenticeship. Apparently my father had been able to pull strings somewhere.

During the hurried change I was forced to take over my brother's morning newspaper round. The papers were delivered to the house and Mum arranged them in the order in a huge shoulder sack that I took along Wytham Street and the side roads. The sack was so heavy on the day when the Radio Times and the weekly magazines came out, that I had to split the round in two. The pay for the round was one pound - I was given five shillings and the other fifteen shillings was given to my brother. My father said it was so my brother could cover his cigarette cost while he served the first week of his apprenticeship without pay. I was forced to do the paper round for four weeks with the same pay. Five shillings a week was a tenth of the amount I was stealing in money and cigarettes. Mum and my father had no clue about my school subjects. In my first year there was two hours homework every night and after tea I was sent to my bedroom to do it. Occasionally I would get stuck on a maths problem. My father sometimes could get an answer that was right but he guessed or did it in a way that could not be explained to my teacher. When I tried to point this out he became angry and so I stopped going to him for help. He urged me to study languages and often recited "Amo, Amas, Amat which were the only three words of Latin he knew. He had no idea of the meaning.

I did well in all subjects - Latin, French, English, Maths, Religious Knowledge (RK), Science, History, Geography, Music and Art. I excelled in gym and sports. I played rugby for the first time and was chosen as captain of the under 13 School Team. The rugby Master was a very large flabby man we called Dumbo - he was also the Biology master. He asked me if I was Welsh - I told him my father was - he said I should be able play rugby well because of my Welsh blood.

The only other boy from Hinksey, Swanny Chivers, was in Form 3A. Sometimes he caught up with me going back to school after dinner - he had a racing bike like the one I had wanted. He was kind and gave me tips on how to go about things in school and Town. He had a reliable source of cigarettes and cash.

Swanny was a much more experienced thief than me. He was a helper in the school Tuckshop that sold donuts and sweets at break-times. He taught me to come to the window where he was serving and buy a donut with half-a-crown that he had already given me. For change he would give me ten shillings or more and we would split it on the way home to dinner. He said the prefect in charge just watched for anyone putting something in their pocket so he would never look for money being stolen in the change.

Most of the boys were from North Oxford, Cumnor and the City and spoke in a way my father and brother called "posh". There were two other boys in my class whose fathers worked at the Factory - this seemed to bond us and we became good friends. One of them Anthony was repeating year one because he had failed year-end exams. He lived in Florence Park and had much more freedom to come and go than I did because his Mum worked too. He was a very loyal friend and stood up for smaller and younger boys in our class. We often went to his house after school because there was always something to eat and cigarettes. Anthony was also connected to a gang of boys in Cowley who broke into shops and businesses. He always had cigarettes and cash.

At Christmas Swanny and I roamed around the shops in the center of Oxford. We stole from most of them - a of lot pens, propelling pencils, staplers from the stationers - cigarettes, tobacco and pipes from tobacconists, sweets and chocolate from Woolworths. In one week we stole all the presents for his and my family from Marks and Spencer. I told Mum I was studying at school or in the stamp club or chess club or other clubs I made up.

Swanny became more adventurous - coming up with a scheme to steal money from tills in the many bookshops around town. On the way back to school after dinner and after school in the afternoon we rode around all the bookstores, waited until there were several customers being served and then went in to check out the location and type of tills they had. We decided on Blackwells in Broad Street as the best target. There were three floors, all with a single button release till that could be opened almost silently. I stood watch at the stairs or distracted a staff member while Swanny triggered the till and extracted up to a limit of two pounds. We never took more than two pounds each time and always stayed clear of the shop for two weeks after a successful take.

We also had a scheme where we stole foreign stamps and sold them to collectors at school - also train-spotting books and pens were easy to steal and sell. We expanded the idea of stealing from shops by looking for the staff rooms in the large shops like Ellistons and sneaking in to steal from the ladies handbags left inside. Between the three of us - Swanny, Anthony and me we had a reliable and steady supply of cash and cigarettes. Our diet was mainly chocolate, sweets and fruit pies - we stole cakes and fruit from the Covered Market. As our cash stealing grew we started eating at Crawfords Cafeteria on Queen Street where Swanny knew all the ropes.

Swanny, Anthony and myself were in Crawfords one dinner time - I had told Mum I was playing cricket away so I wouldn't be home that day. As we ate I noticed one of the school porters, Noddy, looking across at me from another table. Halfway through the French lesson in the afternoon the secretary entered and informed Sarge that Anthony and I were to go the Beak's study.

We looked at one another - wondering why we were here as we stood waiting to be called in. The Beak informed us we were seen in Crawfords Cafeteria during dinner hour and not at home as was expected. It was against school rules for boys to eat dinner anywhere but at school or at home. We knew this but didn't expect any Master would frequent Crawfords - we had not thought about a porter seeing us and reporting to the Beak. It was my first caning.

The Beak was a very big man - well over six feet with a hefty appearance under his long black robe. He picked up a thick whicker cane about four feet long and ordered Anthony to bend over and touch his toes. The Beak raised the cane above his head and with a grunt delivered a lash that caused Anthony to squeal like a dog. The Beak began to put more force into each stroke – his breath became loud and on the fourth stroke the cane hit the ceiling.

Anthony jumped up and started dancing around rubbing his backside as the Beak ordered him out.

I was determined not to squeal but the first lash was like a slice being cut from my ass. It arrived with a nauseating swoosh and scorching impact. The final stroke was preceded by a momentary pause and hit me behind the knees. I released the breath I had been holding for twenty seconds and bolted upright frantically rubbing at my buttocks and trying to walk. But my body began to jump and jerk across the room – I saw the Beak's disdainful gaze before he turned his back. I jaggedly danced to the door clutching my buttocks and squeezing back the tears.

I was selected for the under-13 cricket, athletic and swimming teams. When the school said I should get running spikes my father went mad again but did give the money. When I failed to win in my race at Iffley Road he said it was a waste of money. I came third in my class in Exams at the end of the year. The top two boys in my class were promoted into Form One A - my father had expected and pushed me to get promotion and was very angry that I had failed. He gave me letter to take to the Headmaster.

Later that morning I was summoned to the Beak's study. He asked me if I thought I should be in Form One A - I didn't know how to answer. He picked my father's letter and said "your father thinks you should" - I still didn't know what to say. The Beak asked me if I would like to be in One A and I said yes - and to "why?" I answered that I wanted to learn Greek and it was not available to One B boys. My father had told me to say this if I was ever asked - now I knew why. I really had no clue about Greek or why I should be interested. Later that afternoon I was summoned back the Beak's study and the secretary gave me a letter to take home.

My father opened it at teatime and announced I would be in Form One A after all so he and Mum were very happy and talked about sending me round the neighbors to tell them of my success. I was not happy that I would be loosing my good friends in One B but even less happy that I would be in One A with all the posh boys.

In my second year I did well at the start. I excelled in Latin, French and Greek and did well in most other subjects except history and geography. The masters for these subjects were nicknamed Curly and Wingnut. Curly was completely bald and physically shriveled - his method of teaching history was to have boys read out passages from the text book while he read a novel or the Oxford Mail - the emphasis and the homework was memorizing the dates of battles and reigns of kings. He chain-smoked Woodbines when not in class - each cigarette hung limply in his lips as he breathed in the smoke through his mouth. His chin, lips and hands were stained brown by nicotine and coming round a corner in the passages you could smell him before you could see him.

Wingnut was named for his huge ears - accentuated by a flat Frankenstein forehead and a vanishing chin - plus a pair of horn-rimmed glasses. In a full year of geography I had learned nothing except how to draw a map of Britain and list the counties. Wingnut was also a very short man - some of the boys were already taller than him. To compensate for this he used a snooker cue as a pointer on large hanging maps. Most of the time in this class I drew cartoons of him and passed them around - my image of him was a pair of ears mounted on horn-rimmed glasses flying through the air over Britain on a snooker cue.

Latin and Greek consisted of memorizing the vocabulary and structure - we did a lot of reciting out loud of the rules of grammar, clauses and tenses. I found this easy and the French even easier because the master, Sarge, engaged us in French conversation throughout the class instead of copying words from the board and the textbook. Sarge got his nickname because he was the master in charge of the monthly school parade where we all lined up in military formation in the playground and stood to attention for five minutes.

After Christmas my second year I got my first detention. Detentions were periods of time after school when instead of going home, the boy must report to the detention room and remain seated at a desk writing lines for forty-five minutes - known as an "evening" detention. Wednesday afternoon was for sports so there were no school classes. For persistent or more serious offenders a "Wednesday" detention could be handed out - which meant spending three hours in the detention room while the rest of the school went home or to the sports fields.

If you were handed a detention slip the boy had to take it to Hitler the deputy head master, a very sour man with bulging eyes magnified by thick glasses, who never smiled and smelled of mothballs. He always wore a long black gown - like the Headmaster. Hitler made boys wait outside his classroom for at least ten minutes, then would sign the detention slip and enter their names in a record book and on a list given to the master in charge for that detention.

I started to collect more detentions for fooling around, talking and eating in class. In spring term I got my first Wednesday - for shoving a boy who tripped me in the passage. Mole the Greek master saw the argument and gave me a Wednesday for fighting. He gave the other boy no punishment. After that Mole moved me from a desk in his class to a chair right alongside his desk. He kept three chairs there where he placed boys he wanted to keep a close eye on. Mole was a pipe smoker and had a constant cough - he encouraged boys to bring him cough sweets, which many creeps did. He gave off a smell of tobacco and medicine and often had a drip of saliva on his stubbly chins.

Some masters like Curly and the art master Dogend were the nastiest in detention - they would make boys stay longer while they smoked their pipe or a cigarette and read the paper. There was always a sneer and a rebuke when they signed the slip. Standing next to Curly as he reviewed the slip was extra punishment – his breath stunk so badly of Woodbines – and had a body smell like vegetable soup.

I brought home a mediocre report at Easter. My marks in history, geography, science and RK had dropped. My father was very angry and punished me by making me stay at home every day of the holiday until I had dug over the entire back garden for planting. That took a week and the next week was Scouts Bob-a-Job week. I went out for six days and won the Oxford Scouts first prize by earning four pounds ten shillings - a new record. My father said he had taught me how to work successfully - I knew I had done it all myself. In the third and last week of Easter break things went badly.

My aunt and uncle from Canada were visiting and Mum caught me early one morning stealing money from my aunt's purse. I had sneaked into their bedroom, picked up her handbag and was outside opening the purse when Mum appeared from nowhere. She grabbed the handbag and rushed into the bedroom dropping it next to the bed. She mumbled something about a mistake and came out glaring at me and almost crying. For the first time I felt like I had done something really bad.

The next day my aunt and uncle left and Mum told my father what I had done. I was in the back garden waiting for what would happen. My father stormed out the back door, went into the shed and came out with an axe - he kicked me as he went past to the apple tree and hacked off a thick branch. Carrying this branch he herded me into the house and down into a corner by the front door - there he beat me with the branch across my arms, shoulders, legs and back. When I cowered and covered up he kneed me on the thighs and shook my neck in a vice grip. Mum screamed at him to stop - my brother watched from the kitchen.

At this time I started to have very bad experiences with my teeth. In our house looking after your teeth was not important. Mum and my father both had full plates of false teeth and my brother already had a partial plate for missing front teeth. My father said it was because of the war and the food rationing people didn't get enough calcium so their teeth rotted out. Mum and my father shared a brush for false teeth and we all shared the same tin of Gibbs Dentifrice. I rarely brushed much except the front teeth now and again. I noticed places of decay showing up between my teeth and getting toothache in the back teeth. The toothache got gradually worse until it became impossible to sleep. Smoking helped during the day but the nights were hell. Finally I had to go the dentist whose appointments I had been skipping for years.

I dreaded the appointment I'd been evading for over two years – but at thirteen, in constant pain and under scrutiny by schoolmasters I had been forced to show up. Glancing around the austere waiting room I could not escape the thought of what I would soon have to deal with - pain and terror – both were going to be extreme – I tried to cling to the thought that in an hour it would be over.

The dentist appeared through his office door – shoulder to knee in a white starched coat. He seemed surprised and irritated that I was there. He specialized in older patients requiring extractions and dentures like my parents. He looked and acted harsh. I followed him into a square, high ceilinged room – in the middle was a steel dentist chair with a black leather seat, back and arm pads. He applied leather belts to constrain my arms, shoulders and lower legs to the chair - commenting this was a precaution against involuntary muscle spasm. This was new to me and I surmised because of the struggle that took place at my last appointment. He applied pads against my temples and strapped them together across my forehead. Instructing me to open my mouth he inserted two rubber- encased metal blocks between my back teeth forcing my mouth wide open. He told me to bite down on them if the pain became unbearable.

I felt the dentist's body against the chair and noticed the musty odor of his white grimy hair, as it got closer to my nose. His sharp voice asked why I had missed appointments for over a year. I said I had been sick and smelled his putrid breath as he warned that any further skipped appointments would result in me being banned as his patient. I blinked acceptance as he pushed a long, sharp pointed steel probe into the decay in my upper right teeth. The pain sent me rigid as I strove to contain it by biting down on the rubber blocks in my mouth and straining my arms and body against the belts. The dentist reversed his instrument and used a pointed hook to pull out a decayed filling – I felt a large piece drop into my mouth.

I sensed the dentist readying the drill as I felt what remained of the tooth with my tongue. The electric motor started and with it a whir of the pulleys and cords driving the drill. After attaching a steel drill piece he started to grind out the inside of the tooth.
I smelled my tooth burning – nausea adding to the panic and building despair. The dentist became agitated and increased the force and speed of the drill. I tried to close my mouth causing the drill to bang into a lower molar breaking into the top enamel.

The dentist cursed and stopped drilling - I could tell he was drained by the physical effort needed to stop me moving my head. He cursed and blamed me for the accident as he attached a smaller drill to grind smooth the cracks in the lower molar. This time he turned my head and pressed his elbow into the side of my neck – this new constraint and the agony from the drilling finally made me cry – I was very ashamed. I was released from my constraints and instructed to rinse my mouth with strong antiseptic liquid. I could not evade the sight of the ghastly instruments - I prayed the drilling was over for now.

The dentist mixed two types of metal – filling the hollow tooth with a grey core followed by harder outer material that was polished. To the chipped lower molar a white paste was applied and shaped – the dentist explained that this was temporary because he was late for his next appointment.

I felt euphoric relief that I had completed the first ordeal – at least for a while I hoped that raving toothache would cease and give way to at least one night of sleep and some energy to get through the next day. It was over for another month at least I thought as I attached my satchel of schoolbooks to the crossbar of my bike. The pain in my mouth was now a pulsing throb – touching the tooth with my tongue produced a paralyzing head spasm – guilt and shame persisted when the tooth pain ebbed momentarily.

I took Blue Boar Street, past the library and onto St. Aldates to pedal the one mile down Abingdon Road to my house. My school uniform had become threadbare – the stretch in my socks was long gone and my elastic garters had worn out, so they hung around my ankles – there were cardboard pieces in his my shoes to cover the holes in the soles. At home things were getting worse - my brother had stopped molesting me and turned to beating me up regularly - sometimes twice a day. Mum was taking his side in arguments and so my father was bearing down on me more and more. He said I was responsible for Mum's chronic bronchitis, which made her cough continuously. He said it was worry over me that made her sick all the time.

Our minister, Rev. Parkins suggested I take the voluntary religious exam set annually by the Oxford Baptist Church Council. He coached his son and me for four hours a week in the church vestry. For six weeks we were tutored and tested on New Testament passages before the exam, which was sat by three hundred plus thirteen-year-olds. One evening the tutor session in the vestry was attended by my school Biology teacher Dumbo - he told us what to what to expect as exam questions. After excusing myself I was in the church bathroom peeing when Dumbo came up next to me. He said nothing but through the side of my eye I saw his exposed huge, stiff cock that he stroked while looking at me. I was petrified, and paralyzed for a few seconds then turned and ran from the bathroom, across the street to my house.

This was the third time I had experienced this - the first had been from Swanny. We were at his house in his bedroom looking at stamps when all of a sudden he dropped his trousers and waved his cock at me. He asked me to toss him off and got shirty when I hesitated and then refused. I told him I was scared. He then tossed off in front of me until he shot onto the floor. He never mentioned it again for weeks until one day we were at the school cricket field and he asked me to go in the showers with him. Again I got very scared and he got more aggressive - putting his hand on my cock, and trying to kiss me. I started to get stiff when he tried these things and eventually let him toss me off - but I didn't shoot. He kept asking me to suck him off but I gagged at the thought.

The other time I was going to pee at Hinksey Park swimming pools when a man came up close next to me and started tossing off. I had never seen anything like that before - it was so massive and red that I froze, then panicked - I didn't know what to do - too scared to move. The man smiled at me and looked down at my hands covering my cock - peering down directly. He started to move his hand toward me and I ran out of the toilets and hid in the bushes by Hinksey Lake. After this I often saw him walking through the park and going into the toilets. Walking home one day I saw him going into a house on Sunningwell Road.

In the summer term I sat the Religious Exam with the minister's son and several hundred other thirteen-year-olds. The minister's son came in top place and I was second - with one percentage point separating us. My father said they gave top marks to the minister's son because they couldn't stand a factory kid taking first place. The church congregation was very pleased that we had done so well - a feather in their cap. There were lots of announcements and congratulations.

My end of second year report was quite bad. My marks in exams were poor except in French, Greek and Latin. I almost failed history, geography, biology, chemistry and english, and had low mark in all other subjects. A letter from school came in the post - stating I was to be returned to the B stream and would therefor start next term in form Three B. My father was furious and ranted every teatime about my poor performance. Each day he gave me different punishment - sometimes a fisting on the arms - sometimes cleaning or gardening - and a new one of standing in the shed with the door locked.

Because my brother and me were almost in continuous argument my father built a wall down the middle of the main bedroom making it into two small bedrooms. We moved into one each and Mum and my father moved into our old bedroom. During the work I did all the hard scraping and cleaning. After work each night I cleaned up the shed and managed to get in a smoke while my father shaved in the kitchen. One night he crept out and caught me in the act - he grabbed the dogend from me and shoved the lit end into my lips. My father had never sworn in the house and he and Mum talked badly about neighbors who swore. But now he started to call me a bastard as part of my routine punishment. He said I was a bastard because it was impossible I could be his son.

My hidden life was becoming more my routine life. I lived like a stranger in my house. Mum had started hitting me on the head when I answered her back and making me spend hours sitting on the stairs. One day I complained at dinnertime that I didn't want to eat the pasty Mum had bought at Barton's Bakery. My brother grabbed it from my plate and in doing so tipped his own plate into his lap. Mum started screaming and hitting me on the head. I raised my arms to protect my head, which caused welts on her wrists. That evening my father ransacked my room - tipped everything on the floor and threw me on top of the pile. Then he lashed me across the back and ass with his belt. Mum came up to my bedroom and told me to put everything back together. With a long, hard stare she told me she was ashamed of me and wished she had never had me.

In the last week of summer holidays Swanny introduced me to a new way of getting money. He reckoned that if you earned money you didn't need to steal so much and suffer the punishments - plus you could smoke and eat what you wanted. His plan was to get money from queers - he said he knew some places where queers would pay you for tossing off in front of them or letting them toss you off. They were public toilets or toilets in shops, pubs in the City, Gloucester Green, St. Giles, Banbury and Woodstock Roads, Abingdon Road and along Cowley and Iffley Roads. For two days we rode around Oxford and stopped to observe these lavatories. Swanny called it mapping - like in the bookstore tills.

We started out each day at the public lavatories on Abingdon Road at Hinksey Park. There were four cubicles that required a penny in a slot to get entry. I used penny cubicles in public lavatories for safe places to smoke. All the toilet walls were covered with drawings and messages. The walls were green plaster and high enough you couldn't look over - they all had holes of various sizes that enabled viewing between cubicles. The first thing we did was plugging the holes with wads of toilet paper before we lit up.

At Hinksey Park the messages were advertising for choirboys, cubs and scouts - suggesting meeting for what the writers called "cock-fun". There were drawings of cocks and naked men and women. There were poems and compositions about cock-fun - and offers to pay for it. We noted different messages with dates and times. The toilets at Gloucester Green were particularly graphic and had big enough holes in some of the walls that a cock could pass through. There were notices about other public toilets in Oxford to meet for cock-fun.

Swanny planned my first experience at Crawford's Cafeteria. He showed me the viewing hole in the cubicle door and told me to sit on the toilet with my cock showing. He said someone would spy through the hole and slip money under the door if I tossed off.
That's what happened - as soon as I had sat and got my cock out there was feet at the door and someone looking in. I asked him how much he would pay - he said four shillings to see me toss off. He passed the money under the door and I tossed off while he looked through the hole.

I waited for a few minutes and went back down to the table where Swanny was waiting. I showed him the money and gave him the details - he pointed to a man sitting nearby as the queer who had followed me to the toilet and paid the money. My normal feeling of fear turned to self-loathing - I felt really low and degraded - I knew I had done something much worse and riskier than stealing and smoking. I had a feeling of despair – of going down.

Swanny's plan was to follow queers into the toilets and go into a cubicle next to him - leave the holes open and flash his cock. Hopefully there could be some payment then to see him toss off or more. I was to stand at the urinal after he had entered the cubicle, watch anyone else entering and cough a signal if that happened. The first time it worked perfectly - behind me I heard both cubicles open and close. We met up around the corner - Swanny flashed a ten-bob note. He kept saying it was much easier than stealing.

Pretty soon it was obvious that certain men came each day at about the same time and did the same things like locking their bikes to the railings and spending a long time in the toilets. We did the same mapping at Gloucester Green, Crawford's Cafeteria, the Oxford railway station and St. Giles underground toilets. A lot of the same men were using all the toilets daily.

One dinnertime we rode to Florence Park and checked the men's toilets, hiding our bikes at the back. There were three cubicles with holes in the walls and many drawings of cocks and adverts by queers to have cock-fun. We took an end one, plugged the holes with toilet paper and lit up cigarettes. Soon someone came into the next cubicle and gave a couple of exaggerated coughs – it sounded like my father. I froze and looked at Swanny – he could tell I was scared to death. We stared at the plugged holes and very soon one plug was pushed into our cubicle. Swanny bent to look through the hole – after a second he motioned me to look. In the next cubicle a man was tossing off a huge cock an inch from the hole. I saw the same wedding ring my father wore and his unmistakable fingers. My stomach rolled over to the point I thought it was going to spew.

Chapter 7.

City of Oxford High School for Boys (COHS) - Years 3 and 4

The first few weeks in 3B were easy. The A class was way ahead in all subjects so I excelled without trying. In third year we played Under-15 rugby in the Oxfordshire schools circuit - COHS was always considered the team to beat. Dumbo was our coach and had started to ignore me in class and on the rugby field - since the time at our church bathroom. Although I was the best fly-half he played me on the wing - and although I was the best place kicker he nominated another boy. I could feel him bearing down on me in class and as soon as I lost concentration or looked at another boy he gave me a detention. I felt his pressure on me as soon as I walked into class.

I learned to sit motionless, staring at him or my books. I learned nothing except how to survive the class for another day.

Swanny now in the fifth form became a supervisor in the Tuck Shop and made me a cashier - we developed a scheme to steal sweets from Woolworths and other shops and sell them in the Tuck Shop - as well as several methods of stealing cash from the till. Also we had unlimited donuts and sweets - my teeth decayed even worse. Swanny got a girlfriend and became obsessed sexually with her - he talked about things I had never heard of. One day after school at Crawford's he bought a new boy from One B. He was to join our team on the stealing rounds. His name was LaRouge and known as Pinkey. Pinkey took over my old role in the Tuck Shop change swindle and we introduced him to the bookstore till thefts.

My father had decided that we could no longer afford the school uniform - he said it was too expensive and was an example of the Gown taking advantage of working class people. So in year three I started as a boy out of uniform. I wore normal trousers and jacket with the mandatory school tie and cap. COHS boys were forbidden to be in central Oxford without a COHS cap. Boys out of uniform in third year were considered inferior - in my case it was obvious that my parents were not going to spend much on my clothing.

A few weeks into first term things went downhill rapidly. Pinkey had tried the bookshop till theft himself and been caught by shop staff. The police were called and Pinkey spilled the beans on Swanny and me. I first learned of the situation when a policeman called at the house one evening. Referring to his notebook the policeman described the arrest of Pinkey and his statement against me as one who had taught him.

The policeman asked me for a response to the charges. My father seethed "tell the truth - it'll be worse if you don't". I confessed to the thefts with Pinkey and reported that Swanny was the one who had set up the whole system. The policeman said that if I were to confess to other thefts "it would be taken into consideration" - meaning that the penalty for those thefts would be reduced. He stated that Blackwell's, Boswells and Ellistons had all reported till thefts and some shops had reported thefts from staff room handbags and pockets.

Thinking it would be impossible for me to deny any of these thefts once Swanny was questioned I confessed to three thefts I had made with him and two on my own - In total I admitted to stealing eleven pounds ten shillings. The policeman wrote a statement in his notebook that I was made to sign. I was instructed not to talk with Swanny or Pinkey. My father was furious when the policeman left. His first act was to throw me down and kick me in the ribs and legs then lock me in the shed.

He began locking me in the shed every evening after that. I had started to explore the shed on these occasions - standing in the dark I imagined I was blind and relying on touch and smell. I opened draws and boxes and discovered loads of tools and supplies my father was obviously stealing from the factory.

After my time in the shed one evening my father handed me a pair of boxing gloves and put on a pair himself. On the concrete pad by the shed he instructed me to box him - as soon as I raised my gloves he hit me with two hard punches in the face - as my eyes blurred he hit me two more times in the stomach. It seemed a long time before I could inhale and then a sledgehammer punch to my stomach sent me down onto the concrete. Then all of a sudden my brother arrived, also with boxing gloves. They pulled me up to my feet and made me square off - I smelled the sawdust in my brothers clothes and remember crying and swinging at the same time for a long few seconds before I gave way to pummeled blackness.

A few days later Swanny came to school with a black eye and bruises on his face. He ignored me completely acting as if I was not there. I learned from Anthony that the policeman had also called on Swanny's house and his father had beaten him up as a result. He also said Swanny had denied all involvement in the thefts and not given a statement.

At home I was detained in my bedroom until teatime and then after doing my homework, sent to the shed. My father pushed me away even further - refusing to speak to me - occasionally I could feel him staring at me - I knew he hated me - my brother said the whole family hated me. I looked forward to leaving in the mornings and delaying my return as long as possible. I started to operate on my own for supplying cash and cigarettes.

I lost my place in the Tuck Shop but had developed a number of the shops in South Oxford as good targets. I also discovered all churches were left open and mostly unattended. There were lots of things lying around to steal - including cash from collection boxes, and food. The vestries often yielded cigarettes and cigars. I thought about the Gents toilets thing, looking for money from queers but decided against.
I still used the toilets for smoking on the way to and from school and sports and saw lots of men and boys who routinely went into the cubicles. I always plugged the holes with paper but sometimes it would be poked back or pulled through the hole - that was time to leave quickly.

After three weeks of house and shed detention with two hours daily gardening, a letter came in the post with a Summons for me to appear in Oxford Juvenile Magistrates Court on five charges of larceny - a separate charge for each theft I admitted. My father was ballistic - not only that I had been summoned to court - but on five separate charges. He said the police were picking on me because I was a COHS boy and the Oxford Police hated grammar school boys. My father was also furious that Swanny was not charged - he said the boy behind it all had escaped by lying - so the Police decided to charge me as the leader that got Pinkey involved.

The court date was three weeks ahead and between time there was to be an investigation into my home and school life and some sort of psychological tests. An older woman came from the Probation Department to the house and interviewed my parents and me - she gave me intelligence tests and asked me if I was sorry for what I had done. Mum baked cup cakes and served tea - the woman seemed satisfied that I was in a normal home and had strayed off path out of character - perhaps influenced by an older boy.

When she left my father took me to my room and slammed me into the wardrobe door. He opened the door against my head and forced my head inside - he fished into a pocket of one of his old suits and brought out a piece of paper. He gave it to me - it was a dirty poem about a nurse sucking off a boy. My father accused me of hiding the paper in his old suit - I had never seen it before. I had seen poems like this at school and I had seen my brother with one. I protested that this was not mine - my father said it had to be me because my brother would not do such a thing. As punishment he set me to write one thousand lines per day of "I will not steal from my family" and "I will obey my father".

About a week before the court date I was summoned to the Beak's office. He told me he had received papers from the Oxford Juvenile Probation Department regarding charges of theft from bookstores in Town. He said I had brought disgrace on the school and had enlisted a junior boy further disgracing the school. He gave me six lashings with the cane - I remember thinking this stings more than anything my father does. The Beak also banned me from the playground and instructed me to stand in the hall outside his office during all breaks. I was also banned from morning assembly and made to stand outside the main doors as the masters and prefects filed in and out - every morning I was reminded of the shame I had brought on the school as the eyes of the masters scorned me. At breaks standing outside the Beak's office, masters glared at me and visitors looked at me inquisitively.

The English master Mr. Frost, "Jack" - was a shriveled, rat-faced scot with grey whiskers and green teeth. He never looked me in the eye but I knew he was always watching me. Before lessons one day he took me outside the classroom and informed me he didn't want me in the class and I was to remain outside from now on. He said I didn't deserve to be in the school – I felt very isolated and could hardly believe my life was in such a mess. I started looking into the classroom through the glass in the door and making faces at my friends. Jack saw me and came out - he handed me four consecutive Wednesday detentions - something unheard of.

Sarge also decided I should be split from the rest of the class. He placed a wooden chair at the side of his elevated desk and made me sit without a desk and with my back to the class. He stopped asking me to read aloud like the others and ignored my raised hand to questions. He started giving me detentions for not completing homework - which made it harder for me to complete homework. Homework was not allowed to be done in detention. Sarge caught me copying homework from Anthony and once again I was sent to the Beak for six lashes.

Dogend the art master also banished me to the passage outside the classroom - as did Wingnut and Curly. Soon the only lessons I was actually receiving were Latin, French, Maths and Music. I lost my place on the under 15 rugby and cricket teams. I started going to the toilets instead of just standing outside classes. Every twenty minutes or so I would go and have a smoke around the back of the toilets or in a cubicle. Occasionally I just walked off and into town. If the master asked me where I was I said at the dentist or the chiropodist or the doctor's.

I had friends who played truant now and again and needed sick-notes. I started forging sick-notes for Anthony and it had worked well. Then a few other boys asked me to write for them. Looking back it was a bit foolish - I almost wrote the same each time and was not careful to disguise my handwriting. But it seemed to work and before long I was forging three or four a week for two shillings each.

On the date planned I attended the Juvenile Magistrates Court with my father. There were three magistrates in black gowns sitting at an elevated bar. The Chief Magistrate read out the charges and asked me why I had done it. As my father had instructed me I said I was led by an older boy and was very sorry for what I had done. The Chief Magistrate said he was a shop owner in the city and for what I had done he could send me to reform school. He said because my parents had given me a good home he would suspend that sentence and put me on probation for two years. If I committed any offense during that time I would go immediately to reform school. I was also fined one pound ten shillings for each charge and ordered to pay back the money I had stolen. At home the mood was very bad.

My father came up with a new punishment. I was to be barred from eating with the family or from entering the living room. My meals would be on a tray that I had to take to my bedroom. I was confined to my bedroom, the shed or the back garden.

On the following Saturday my father instructed me to follow him on his bike to the bank. I had a savings account with twenty-one pounds which my father closed and confiscated the money to pay the court. He vowed to never give me any money in the future and stopped all pocket money completely. Home was now a bleak place - a punishment house. School was getting worse by the week. I started to play truant - to avoid the banishment from class I just didn't show up and began writing my own sick-notes - mostly for dentist appointments that I made up.

Just when I thought it could not get any worse the Oxford Times printed a story about me. Because at fourteen I was a juvenile the story could not name me but referred to a boy from COHS who had been caught stealing from tills in the town and had led other boys to do the same thing. That evening was terrible. My father read the story from the paper out loud in front of Mum, my brother, my aunt and uncle and two close neighbors. They all stared at me at me and shook their heads. The feeling of disgrace turned my stomach upside down.

The story went round Hinksey rapidly - pretty soon I was the most despised boy in the area. A lot of boys from the Weirs and Wytham Street wanted to fight me. At Hinksey Pools boys from Donnington and Florence Park challenged me to fight - boys I had not even seen before. My punishment at school continued and I spent almost every evening and Wednesday in detention - writing lines. My brother was becoming the biggest bully I had to deal with.

Some of the neighbors came up to me and told me to keep away from their house and family. At church the minister called me into the vestry and told me I was a disgrace to my parents and the church and barred me from the youth club. Every master and prefect at school was out to get me for something.

My exam results were very bad and my behavior reports were even worse. Dumbo wrote I was "a menace to society" despite finishing second, with honors, in the Oxford Youth RK Exam. Each master wrote negative comments about me - being disruptive, disobedient, and cheeky. I was quickly becoming isolated and shut-off from normal life.

Another dreaded letter arrived from school - summoning my father to make an appointment with the Beak. During English lesson the next day I was ordered to the Beak's office from my standing duty outside the classroom. My father was there in the Beak's office. The Beak handed me a sheaf of paper - all the sick-notes I had forged going back three months. The Beak asked my father what would be appropriate punishment and my father said I should be caned. The Beak gave me six full-force lashings witnessed by my father. That day I was all but expelled - but sentenced to a form of continuous surveillance and detainment - and banned from all sports and youth activities. Reform School started to sound ok - it couldn't be much worse than this.

Every teatime there was an argument about something I had done - nothing really wrong but like not strictly sticking to times I had to be home or getting bad marks at school. I had tests with electric apparatus connected to my head and interviews with psychiatrists and probation officers. At one appointment a psychiatrist asked me a lot of questions about what different words meant to me and why I stole. I told him it was because I wanted to smoke and this was the only way for me to get cigarettes. He smoked throughout the interview and left his cigarettes on the desk when he left for a few minutes. While he was gone I stole a one out of the packet. After, I realized it was a trap to see if I would steal from him.

It was decided that I needed a physical outlet and "tumbling" in the gym would be an ideal example. My father decided it should be Judo and I was signed up at the Oxford Judo Club headquartered on Polstead Road in North Oxford. It was also recommended that I be given more freedom and allowed to play sports. The restrictions and detentions in school continued but I was allowed back into the living room at home.

I started Judo twice a week from six until seven-thirty. My green-belt instructor Allan was the son of one of my father's friends at the factory. I soon became competitive among the two or three other boys my age. Allan started assigning me to practice with older boys training for their first grading. They were all much bigger and stronger and generally did not try to hurt me unless I became too ambitious and aggressive.

One boy would always throw me down and attempt a hold-down - while doing this he would place his thigh against my cock and rub as I got stiff - I just couldn't help it. I didn't want it or welcome it - it scared me but there was nothing I could do - it was under the mat supervision of Allan and he seemed ok with it. Each practice session it got worse until the boy grasped my cock in a floor grapple. Later in the bathroom he appeared next to me and flashed a massive cock - he forced me into a cubicle and closed the door. He turned me around and pulled down my judo pants - he reached around and grasped me. As I felt him between my ass cheeks I screamed and jumped up, hitting him under the chin with my skull - I heard bones crack - the same sound that I had heard playing rugby when a boy broke his ankle so badly a bone jutted out.

I never saw that boy again at Judo practice. About two weeks later as I cycled home through Town I saw him talking to the man that had paid me to toss off in Crawford's. He had a wire brace around his jaw and chin. After the incident Allan treated me differently - he gave me less time on the practice mat and less hands-on instruction. His attitude toward me changed from friendly to indifferent - as if I wasn't there - I could also sense this from others quite easily now. I also noticed that I was often followed by men I knew were queers on my bike or walking through Town. I saw the same men in all the toilets I visited to get away and have a smoke. All the toilets had view-holes in the walls and doors - and drawings of naked men and women - and advertising for boys.

One teatime my father suggested I should think about joining the Navy - he said I should take the exam for Engineering Artificer apprenticeship. An application was sent in and the exam papers were sent to the school. I completed the exams in two hours and scored forty-eighth in the five hundred boys that sat the exam in Britain. A train ticket and meal voucher arrived at the house for me to attend interviews and medical exams in Portsmouth - I would stay one night there in the process.

The first day was traveling to Portsmouth by train and being housed in Royal Navy barracks - a short walk from the station. The next day was interviews, tests and medical exams. The paper tests were like the intelligence tests I had become accustomed to but there were manual tests like bending wire to the shape of a drawing and questions about engineering. Toward late afternoon I was called into an office by a Navy Officer - he informed me I had failed the aptitude tests and was dentally unfit. He told me I was on the younger end of the possible entrants and six months delay would be better for me – during which time I should get my teeth seen to.

At home my father was angry I had failed the aptitude tests. He demanded minute detail on the whole experience - particularly the engineering tests. He and my brother ridiculed me when I told them my answers to some of the engineering questions. He made me draw the shape of the wire-bending test and brought home wire from the factory. He ordered me to make one shape per day from one piece of wire and hand it to him at teatime. It was a test that I just couldn't learn to do well. Each day the wire was either not exactly to the drawing and had many kinks from trying to undo bad bends. After about five days my father was so exasperated he jumped up and pulled the tablecloth and all the things on the table onto the floor. Some cups and plates broke and there was a big mess from spilt tea and milk. I was again banned from the living room.

I went to the dentist's office in Town and begged him to take me back as a patient to fix my teeth so I could get into the Navy. I could no longer play truant so I planned dentist appointments around the times of classes I was banned from or couldn't stand the teacher. During the next four months I endured fillings to every one of my teeth. The front teeth were the worst - the dentist used a small rotary saw to cut off a piece of each front tooth in the middle. The pain was unbearable and I strained against the belts until I blacked out. When I came round there were plastic strips attached to my teeth with cement between them - the dentist holding them very forcefully in place. Eventually all the fillings were completed - in time for my second attempt at the Navy apprenticeship aptitude tests.

The last term of my third year at COHS was hell. Coming up to exams I knew I was in deep trouble on every subject except languages - plus I had become the most caned and detained boy in the whole school - banned from normal activities and now hounded daily by every master and prefect. At home I was also isolated and kept inside constantly. My only escape was cycling to and from school, visiting my hiding spot and smoking in the public toilets. I recognized most of the queers by now - there were dozens out in South Oxford and all the way through Town and out into Summertown. They also visited the cinemas in Town - the toilets in the Ritz next to St. Giles were very active. I knew how to get in the back or side doors of all the cinemas in Town - something Swanny had taught me. Some men would motion me to follow them into a cubicle or go into the next one and look through holes in the wall. I was always scared at first but it became so common and no-one tried to touch me - they flashed at me and smiled then went into a cubicle leaving the door open. I never followed - my one experience in Crawford's had been enough.

I was experiencing intentions from a few girls from church - where walks on Sunday morning after service included kissing and feeling. There was a numbering system that went from number one, kissing, to number ten, all the way - each rising number getting a bit more cooperative. Walking along Susan asked me how far I went - I said number two which was feeling tits outside the blouse. She led me into the field next to Hinksey Stream and we sat under the bridge. We kissed and she placed my hand on her tits - then she grabbed my cock, which was the first time a girl had done that. I had my first shoot from a girl - just by squeezing outside my trousers.

Sunday was the only day I was allowed outside and only for a few hours after church in the morning. The house was filled with smoke on Sundays with my father, brother and Mum chain-smoking - it drifted up the stairs into my bedroom where I was confined after dinner. I was able to open a window and hang out on the ledge to have a smoke - they wouldn't come up to my room anyway - they preferred me out of the way. Mum and my brother went to church in the evening and my father went to the bathroom for an hour as usual - by now I had figured out he was reading all the dirty stories in the News of the World and tossing off. I also knew he went through all my draws and clothes in the wardrobe - and looked under my mattress and pillow. I always felt better on Sunday evenings because I knew my father would be in the bathroom and I could creep down into the living room - also it meant the next day I could escape the house to go to school.

I went to Portsmouth Navy barracks again and through the same type of tests - but some different from the last time. The same wire bending test was given and I was able get a better result but still not as good as those around me. In the medical exam the doctor kept me naked for a long time and spent a long time examining my privates - until I started to get stiff. I was very embarrassed. Later in the afternoon I was called into see the recruiting officer. He told me I had failed again, but I might be able to gain entry as a Boy Seaman at HMS Ganges - he said my exam results and medicals were acceptable for that type of entry and as soon as I was fifteen they would take me. He gave me the papers to take home – just needing my parents' signatures.

My failure was not taken well at home or at school. My father and brother took to ridiculing me at every opportunity. My father lectured me daily after his tea - he said I was a failure because he had given me everything he never had and now all I could achieve was getting into the Navy as a Boy Seaman - the lowest of the low in his mind. I had no idea of what a Boy Seaman was - but I knew it would mean that I would leave my house and home. Apart from the lectures my father ignored me deliberately - we were like strangers in the house - Mum was sick with something new each day and was always more ill than anyone on earth. Her problems were blamed on me - part of my father's daily lecture was that Mum was close to death and unless I stopped stealing and misbehaving she would die because of me.

Good Friday came around and I was still on full restriction at home and school - now for almost a year. Most of the kids in Hinksey went up to Chiswell Hills on Good Friday and generally got up to mischief. Picnics were set up in the fields and bonfires were lit, often the dry grass was set on fire. Groups of kids from South Oxford inevitably got into arguments and fights and there was a lot of flirting and showing-off. My father told me I was not allowed to go with my friends up the hills.

On Thursday evening when I was supposed to be in my bedroom I crept into my brother's room and stole his scout rucksack, groundsheet and sleeping bag. I took a pound note from my parent's dresser draw and packed underwear, socks and a pullover. I took a towel and blanket from the airing cupboard and made them into two rolls that I placed in my bed under the clothes. My parents and brother were watching television and didn't hear me as I slipped out the front door and into the night. I stopped at the off-license of the Berkshire Arms for ten cigarettes and at my hiding spot by Hinksey Lake where I picked up a lighter and more money.

Pretty soon I had passed through a darkened South Hinksey village and onto the allotments off Chiswell Lane. I wandered around the allotments until I found a suitable shed and organized my sleeping bag on the floor. After about two hours I woke to the sweep of car headlights and the sound of distant voices. It was a Police car moving slowly up the lane with two policemen walking alongside with torches. I wondered if they had been called out by my parents or someone had seen me walking through the village.

At daybreak I packed my sleeping bag and hid the rucksack at the back of the shed. I was the first kid onto the Chiswell Hills that Good Friday, but soon lots of kids arrived in groups and set up their camps in the woods. No one knew I had run from home. I didn't know what to say because I didn't know what I was going to do when Good Friday was over. A plan had been forming in my mind that

I could hitchhike to South Wales to meet up with Lyn and live rough in the mountains like we had sometimes before.

Bonfires were started and bread sticks made in the embers. By mid-afternoon a hundred or so kids were running around in the fields and the woods - all smoking, drinking pop and acting crazy. I was back in the woods with Mary, hoping for a hand-job when all of a sudden my brother and two older boys I had never seen before came running down the hill toward us. Before I could stand up and run they were on top of me. The two other boys grabbed my arms and twisted them behind me so hard I had to kneel over on the grass before my shoulders dislocated. My brother kicked my head like a football and then again on the other side - my back teeth cracked as his foot smashed my clenched jaw. The walk home was a blur - they kicked me around in the shed when we picked up my brothers rucksack - calling me a sneak thief and a bastard.

At home my father ordered me to strip and searched all my clothing. He pushed me around naked in front of Mum and my brother. He then ordered me into my school clothes and had me follow him by bike to the main police station on St. Aldates. There he reported me as violating my probation order by stealing from the house and running away when forbidden to go outside. He asked that I be retained in Reform School, according to my suspended sentence in Juvenile Court.

The Sergeant was a Judo brown belt who had visited our club and he recognized me. He asked me how I got the huge lump on my forehead and the bruises on my face. I looked at my father and was ready to say the truth when I chickened out and said I was in a gang fight on Chiswell

Hills. The Sergeant asked my father if he would give me one last chance to stop misbehaving - he suggested if I was given more time to practice Judo I could change to a better path. My father reluctantly agreed but complained to the Sergeant that according to the Magistrates sentence I should be detained.

At the end of the next week I was summoned to the Beak's office. He said a report had been received from the Probation Department that I had violated the terms of my suspended sentence. He also told me I had been seen leaving school before the end of the day and smoking openly in Town. He said I was a disgrace to the school and jumped up throwing back his chair - he grabbed the cane and came the round the desk toward me as usual. For some reason I snapped - for a moment I saw him as my grandfather, intent on causing me pain and disgrace every day of my miserable life.

He motioned me into the bend-over position and I moved to obey - but instead of bending I turned, standing in front of his towering figure, looking up into his contorted face. I shouted "no" - "no more" and watched, as he looked confused and then even more furious. He screamed at me to bend over again and then threatened if I defied him one more time I would be expelled. By now any excuse to be away from COHS was a welcome thought - even if it meant the disgrace of expulsion - a very rare punishment and a noted disgrace throughout the city.

I continued to stare at the Beak in refusal to bend over. He thundered at me "get out boy". Before I left for school the next morning a telegram arrived from the School stating I was permanently suspended and not allowed on the school premises. Mum went into a crying and fainting fit that was so realistic Auntie Shirley from across the street said she must go to bed. I sat in my bedroom waiting for my father to come home. I knew it would be a very bad evening. I pondered whether to run again and this time to get clear of the Town - into a place where no-one knew me, or cared who I was and what I was doing. I knew there was going to be a very bad beating - I knew my father knew that my brother had held my head under water several times. My stomach was turning over so fast I couldn't focus on anything except not vomiting. I had nowhere or no way to run for the moment and if I did it would be just until they caught me again - and then what?

Chapter 8.

Expelled

I decided to wait - but I also decided I was going to resist being beat up again - and I would not strip off again to be beaten by him or anyone else. I had become accustomed to a life of dodging through the system - not caring - addiction to cigarettes was my daily priority. I was totally outcast from my family and now that I was expelled I was a confirmed Town and Gown disgrace. The idea of becoming a Boy Seaman in the Navy was the only positive notion on my horizon - it was an escape, an end to torment and punishment, and a new place - to be free of the Town and Gown.

I heard my father come home and muffled conversations coming from downstairs. I expected him to beat me or to put my head under water with the help of my brother. But he didn't come into my room. I waited until they had been in bed for an hour then crept down the stairs into the living room. I stole a cigarette from Mum's handbag and crept back up to my bedroom. Sitting in the open window frame the smoke was instantly soothing and gave me back a sense of hope. Suddenly my father burst into the room and in a split second shoved my legs over the window frame. I tried to grab something as I fell, smashing into the glass, breaking it and opening up gashes in my arm. No sooner had blood splashed into my face I crashed onto the grass in the front garden - my shoulder hit first and then whipped my head onto the ground with such force that it knocked me out.

I came round being loaded into an ambulance that drove off with a loud siren. An ambulance man and my father were with me – they were talking. My father said I was hanging out the window smoking when he came into my room and surprised me. He said this caused me to slip back and out of the window - smashing the glass and lacerating myself in the process.

At the Radcliffe Infirmary on St. Giles I waited for several hours on a trolley until a doctor sewed up the gashes on my arm. I could see the open wounds reflected in the chrome centre of the light over the operating table. I saw the doctor inject a huge syringe into my arm and then red-hot spasms of pain until numbness set in. It looked as if my arm had been severed completely with bone and sliced muscle visible - the sight caused me such panic I felt like I was passing out.

I began seeing double and a doctor examined my head and eyes - he said I was severely concussed and must stay in hospital overnight. I thanked god that I did not have to go home as I was now convinced my father would kill me if he could. Overnight in the hospital I had nightmare upon nightmare - dreaming I was buried beneath a crumbled house of bricks and following one dead-end after another trying to escape.
Each dead-end lead to more panic, panic on panic - until wakened by the starkness of facing impossibility. In hospital the next day the psychiatrist doctor visited me. He asked me what had happened in my "accident". I told him my father's version - leaving out the fact that he had pushed me. He asked me why cigarettes were so important to me that I would give away all the opportunities I had been given.

I told him all I knew was that cigarettes got me through each day. Without smoking I felt like nothing, I was on edge and reckless - with a few cigarettes a day I could get by. He asked me why I wanted to join the Navy. I told him because I was interested in seeing other parts of the world – but we both knew it was for the tobacco allowance provided by the Navy. It was always a dance with the psychiatrist - I knew, that he knew, that I knew, he knew what was going on at home.

No one from home came to visit. I was released to Mum after two days but she acted so frail that an ambulance brought us both home. There were other passengers and it went round Botley and several villages before we got to Hinksey.

Mum coughed almost continuously but as soon as we got home she lit a cigarette and her cough disappeared. Like my father she had taken to ignoring me totally - never looking at me when we passed - never speaking or asking anything. Just ordering me to do things or get things from the garden that I was tending. I pleaded with her to ask my father to sign the Navy recruitment papers for Boy Seaman. She said he was against it because of all the money spent on me going to COHS for the best education and now it was to be all wasted by signing for twelve years at the lowest level of entry into the Navy. She said I was a disgrace to them and she was ashamed of me as a son. I suggested it would be better for her if I was gone and couldn't bring the public shame on her anymore. She screamed that a boy should not be locked up at fourteen and the shame I had brought would kill her soon. I begged that she sign the papers rather than see me go to Reform School - I said I would run away again and this time they wouldn't catch me - she said she wanted me away and didn't care.

I realized all the people I knew bullied, punished or detained me - the thought "what do I have to lose?" kept ringing in my head. I decided I would defend myself against further beatings and physical punishment. I moved my bed against the door and lifted my dresser on top of it. With my arm in a cast and already in constant pain I thought the only way to defend myself was to barricade. Several hours after my father got home from work he had not come to my room. I started to feel stupid and hungry, although getting a smoke was more pressing so I got a few dogends out of my stash and rolled a cigarette with a page ripped from my new testament. As soon as I opened the window my father was at the door - he must have been waiting to catch me again.

He was astonished I had built a barricade and shoved the furniture away. He stared in at me through the opening - in his hand I saw my cricket bat. He kept shoving until he was able to squeeze into room past the bed. I was down to my last small space with no protection now and about to get a cricket bat beating. I picked up my bedside chair and shouted at my father - "I'll throw this through the window if you don't leave me alone".
He stopped and stared at me with hatred I'd never felt before. I realized then that he just wanted me to be punished and no punishment was enough. He knew I was trying to escape by joining the Navy - he didn't want that - he wanted me to go to Reform school so he could prove I was bad and beyond control and had to be locked up - so he was the victim of a bad son.

I pleaded with him to sign the Navy recruitment papers. Mum appeared next to him, crying and sobbing. He turned and rushed down stairs - a minute later he forced open the door again and threw in the signed papers. He shouted "the sooner you're out the better - stay away from me." I felt a huge sense of relief - a surge of hope - a way out. I posted the papers immediately.

For three weeks I got up at five every morning, before my father, and cycled twelve miles to Harwell. The stitches in my arm eventually rotted out because I didn't have time to go to the doctor. I picked blackcurrants for five hours - which paid me seven shillings a day. I worked with a group of gypsy ladies that were expert pickers. After a couple of days they invited me to eat some of the dinner they brought each day – and then they gave me something to eat every day. At home I was basically being starved except for Weetabix and banana sandwiches. I had enough to buy cigarettes and food at the off-license. My father surveilled and restricted me down to a specific space that he could search and destroy at any time he felt like it. My fifteenth birthday came and went - it was the first one that nobody said happy birthday.

I also got a job at five on Sunday mornings, unloading newspapers at Oxford Railway Station. This led to an offer by the man that had the South Oxford paper rounds. So after unloading the papers I would fill up a special bike carrier with about two hundred copies of the most popular papers and sell them door-to-door in Hinksey, Abingdon Road and the Weirs. It was a great job because there were many tips and the boss had no idea what was being sold. I was making enough money for everything I needed – including food and cigarettes.

On my third Sunday my father and brother cornered me and stripped me of all the cash I had made that day. My father questioned me as to how I was able to get so much cash for delivering newspapers – and all in silver coins. So he decided I was stealing the cash and ordered my brother to return it to my boss. My brother returned saying that my boss had given him the job and I was no longer needed. They had stolen my money and my job. It was a feeling of all-time despair, guilt and self-hatred.

After three weeks my bike tires were almost threadbare - as well as my shoes and jeans. On Saturday morning Mum took me to a rumble sale at church and bought me a jacket, trousers and shoes - I hated them. Mum said it was a waste of money to buy new clothes, as I would soon be in uniform. I prayed for the Navy papers to come soon. On Sunday morning I was embarrassed to go to church in the clothes from the rumble sale because I knew they may be from people I would see. So instead of going into church I sneaked around the back of the outside crèche and sat smoking by Hinksey Stream - waiting until the service ended. When everyone had left I came from the back to leave through the gate and my father was standing there. "Where the hell have you been?" he screamed and herded me back to the house.

He shoved me down the side passage and into the shed. "Where the hell were you?" he shouted, standing in the doorway. I told him I was by the stream behind the church because I didn't like my clothes. His face and neck started twitching, a sign I knew he was going to swing at me. As he did I instinctively raised my arm to block his and at the same time stepped forward to his side and tripped him up in a simple Judo leg throw. He fell back onto the concrete outside the shed in shock and disbelief. Mum opened the window from her bedroom and screamed "Call the police on him Dad".

I realized right away that my father would be wary of beating me himself now but with my brother it would be different he was bigger and stronger and between them it would be a serious and methodical beating with fists and knees and possibly having my head pushed down the toilet as it is flushed. And my arm was still weak from the deep cuts. I also knew they would bring in my older cousin to give me a kicking for good measure. I also realized right away that I would have to run again. I decided to go right now. This time I left with just the rumble sales clothes on my back and my duffle coat, grabbed on the way out the back door. I knew instinctively that I needed to get out of my house now – and fast. As long as I could survive and hide I may avoid getting locked up or tortured.

Making my way to my hiding place under the bridge I thought about my options for shelter and sleep. From personal experience I knew all the churches around were easy to get into and had many safe hiding places inside. There was also food and loose change hanging around if you knew where to look. I picked up my hidden money and cigarettes. I crossed over the bridge and into the field leading past the Railway lakes. With knowledge I had gained in five years of roaming Hinksey for food and fishing in the lakes and streams, I crossed the water under the train sidings using the concrete foundations supporting a steel bridge. Soon I to ended up in the field at the back of South Oxford Baptist Church on Wytham Street, close to my house in Bertie Place.

I watched, hidden in the long grass, from a safe distance until all the congregation had left the evening service. As it grew darker the lights went out and I saw the caretaker Bert West leave from the back door and enter the boiler room next to it. This was his last check before leaving the property and was his hiding place for the key to the church back door. I was scared of the way West looked at me sometimes and I knew he spied on me at church. He also followed me into the toilets, so I never used them if he was there. I also knew he told my father of anything I may have done. But at home my father said he never talked with Bert West and called him a woodbine idiot. The rumor among the kids was that Bert West was a ringer, and after your bum.

Twenty minutes later I crossed Hinksey stream over a plank put across by the people next door to the church, and crawled along the bank until I came out behind the crèche. I got the key from the unlocked boiler room, opened the back door to the church before replacing the key. I ate left overs from the refreshments after the service. I decided to sleep in the crèche that had a couch and blankets. I went to the Vestry to get the key from the main keyboard.

As I was about to leave the Vestry I heard the side door to the church open. I froze as a light went on in the hall. I very quickly left the Vestry through the door into the church worship area and immediately up into the pulpit – stooping to hide under the lectern – completely out of sight. I tried to control my breath and sink into the silence of the sanctuary.

A sliver of light cast over the lectern as the light went on in the Vestry – I heard the door close as the light disappeared. I waited. Soon I heard the side door open again and footsteps through the hall – two men were talking – the voices were unmistakably my father and Dumbo.

A third voice, Bert West welcomed them by name as they entered the Vestry through the back door. The conversation became hard to hear, as if the voices were lowered deliberately. I thought they must be here to decide how to look for me. I crawled out to the side of the pulpit to hear more if possible. I was adept at listening to the hushed conversations of my parents in the living room as I perched on the stairs.

What I heard changed my life forever. They were discussing how difficult it was to get me to accept sex offers. Dumbo suggested that his priest friend Roger was interested in "having a go" at me – he said the priest could bribe me with food, fags and stamps. My father said "I don't care how you do it – just catch him doing something – I know he's always in the toilets – I've heard he's all over Oxford but doesn't do anything – just smoking. "Just catch him in the act and the police will nab him" – and that will be him gone – and finish him around here".

Then I heard the church film projector start and conversation stop. As the projector clicked, after several minutes I heard grunts and muffled groans coming from the Vestry. Soon after the projector stopped they went into the toilets, and about ten minutes later left the church in silence.

I sat on the steps to the pulpit all night. As the dawn crept through the high church windows the sanctuary took on a feeling of damp, grey misery. I felt paralyzed – completely and totally stunned. I went into the crèche behind the church and laid down on the old musty couch.

After some fitful sleep I hiked back over Hinksey Stream and through the fields to Hinksey Lake bridge. I collected everything I had hidden there for two years. Among my things were a sheath-knife, compass, groundsheet, billycans, a frying pan and a water bottle - all stolen from the Oxford Scout Shop on Turl Street. Also there was a fishing rod, reel, float and hooks.

It was early dawn as I hurried along South Hinksey footpath through the village, across the bypass and up into Chiswell Hills. On the way I stole carrots and swede from some allotments. I went to a tramp camp I knew was abandoned, close to the shallow stream running along the valley formed by the hills. There was an old blanket on the dirt floor and a car seat at the opening. I sat on it to look out on places I really enjoyed, but the sense of freedom soon gave way to despair.

Approaching dusk I roused from another restless sleep – feeling very hungry, thirsty and scared. I thought seriously about going home, but I remembered the hate that was waiting there for me – hate which would torment me even more than living like a tramp. Plus I now realized my father would do anything to get rid of me and wanted me locked up.

I cut up the carrots and swede and ate some raw. Then filled the water bottle from a pebbly little pool in the stream. As the darkness settled I left the camp with my fishing tackle. I reached Hinksey Lake bridge without walking through the village, by crossing the allotments and fields beside the church and cemetery and reconnecting with the footpath on the other side.

Once across the bridge I got into Hinksey Park by climbing over the spiked fence. The area was so familiar that I could have navigated with my eyes closed. I knew there were always one or two bikes left in the swimming pool area at the end of the day. People left them overnight occasionally thinking they were safe in the locked park. I found one right away and rode it to the Marlborough Road gate – which had no spikes – and lifted it over. I had done this many times – coming home from judo - taking a short cut through the park after it closed – stopping for a cigarette by the lake before stashing my take for the day under the bridge.

I rode down Edith Road and stopped at the pub off-license where I bought crisps and lemonade. From there I rode down Abingdon Road to the entrance to Eastwick Farm – where I could see the Gentlemen's toilets. I noticed the curtains opening a little in the side window of the Vicarage opposite. Soon one of the queers I knew used the toilets rode up and propped his bike on the fence.

He walked up and down the pavement by the park until a boy I knew from school who was queer rode up and went into the toilets. The queer followed him and soon a man covered by a thick coat and beret also went in. I couldn't see his face.

I rode to St. John's church at the end of Wytham Street and after hiding the bike in the bushes I climbed over the fence to a door at the back that was always open. I made my way into the inner sanctuary where the vicar hung his robes and sat on the small couch.

After a while I decided that riding to Harwell every other day I could earn seven shillings that would pay for food and fags. I would contact my friend Beesley to ask the postman, who was his dad, if my letter from the Navy was in his bag.

Next morning I hid in the vicarage garden until Beesley appeared on his way to Bonners Grocers where he worked delivering. He was shocked to see me – he said the Oxford Police had called at his house last night to inquire if he knew were I was. We agreed to meet every morning about nine by the Guild Hall to get an update. I realized that I had now really run away and had nothing to gain by going home – that would surely result in the police taking me to Reform School. Once that was on my record, the Navy would reject me.

The ride to Harwell on the rusty bike was exhausting and miserable. Five hours of berry picking was even more miserable but provided food during the work. The ride back to my camp was even more exhausting but I had seven shillings more in my pocket – I realized this plan would not work for long. I stopped at the Red Bridge, hid the bike in the bushes and took my fishing rod down through a secret trail I knew – getting to the end of the lake by the side of the railway lines. Using a stick I unearthed a small red worm and baited my hook. No sooner had the float settled from my first cast when it dipped. Quickly reeling in a plump roach about a foot long I repeated with two smaller roach in a few minutes. When I'd gutted and descaled them with my sheath-knife I wrapped them in a few big dock leaves.

Back at the camp it was dusk as I lit a fire and washed in the stream without soap, using my only shirt to dry off. In Wales Lyn had taught me how to have a shit in the mountains and keep it hidden – also how to use dandelion leaves and grass instead of paper. I fried the roach and some cabbage until it was almost black – it tasted really good and specially to have hot food. I was a tramp at fifteen. That night I decided to fight – no matter what. I imagined fights of impossible odds – as the bullies drew in with knives I decided to always fight back – never surrender – fight to the death.

At dawn next morning I rode furtively toward Oxford along the side of the railway line. It was Wednesday, the day of the weekly cattle market at the Oxpens. The stalls were being raised by the merchants as I wandered around looking for food. A baker selling day-old bread gave me two rolls for helping him unload his van. It was easy to steal apples and pears from the many fruit stalls.

There were no money prospects so I rode down Abingdon Road and noticed an early cricket practice happening at Queens College sports ground. The pavilion door was open and all the cricketers' clothes were hanging on pegs in the changing room. Pretty soon I had picked a pound in silver from a few pockets and was well clear by the time the players came in for lunch.

As I waited at the end of Lake Street next to the Guild Hall, Beesley came through the Cut on his way to work. He told me that a letter from the Navy was in the postman's bag today – that meant it would be delivered to my house about now. Risking everything I rode down Wytham Street looking down the side streets for the postman Mr.Beesley. I found him on Oswestry Road. Riding toward him he looked up and said immediately "you're a bloody disgrace to your family". I asked him if he had a letter for me from the Navy. He shook his head at me saying "it's at your house – the Navy won't want you anyway when they see you".

Getting to my house there was no sign that Mum was home. Taking more risk I crept up to the front door and looked through the letterbox. I could see the letter on the floor inside. My stomach was churning as I climbed through the kitchen window - one my father didn't think I could open from the outside. I snatched the letter and ran upstairs. I grabbed my scout rucksack, all my underwear and socks and my toothbrush a bar of soap and a towel – I didn't care if they knew I had been inside. I decided to take my bike too and hand-towed my stolen bike away. Glancing down Abingdon road I saw Mum walking up from the bus stop with her shopping bag.

After dumping the stolen bike at the Duke of Monmouth pub I rode as fast as possible back to the Vicarage at the end of Wytham Street. Carefully I opened the letter with the official stamp of HM Government on the front. It was addressed to me and my parents or guardians, and said I had been accepted as a Boy Seaman entrant for training at HMS Ganges – ordering me to report to the Royal Navy liaison officer at Guildford Railway Station between 1200 and 1800 on September 6th, 1954. There was a list of items to bring and not bring, and a warrant for a train ticket from Oxford to Guildford.

It was Wednesday – I had four days and nights to elude anyone looking for me. That seemed easier now but my big problem was how to obtain some decent clothes and the items required in the Navy letter. Specially football boots, jockstrap and swimming trunks, a pen, pencil and ruler.

Monday was the first day of St. Giles fair so the city would be jammed and the last thing on the mind of the police would be me. Casual labor jobs were available on Saturday and Sunday for anyone strong enough to fetch and carry pieces from the trailers to the set-up crews. A plan was developing in my mind.

I tried to sleep in Hinksey Park that night, on the stream bank close to Abingdon Road. Again I saw someone watching the Gentlemen's toilets from the vicarage window. And again someone left the house through the back door – this time disguised with a cap and scarf covering his face and a long raincoat. He walked briskly to the toilets and disappeared inside. For an hour I watched as men and youths entered and left the toilets. A man riding a bike pulled up to the railings and walked into the toilets. In the murky light of the entrance I saw a frame and walk that looked a lot like my father. I scrambled up the bank and sprinted in the dark across the grass to the railings – it was my father's gold colored Rudge bike.

My mind churned all night – I wished I could make time go forward to Monday and be on the train leaving Oxford. At about four in the morning it was still pitch dark as I rode into Oxford next to the railway lines, to avoid the Police Station in St.Aldates. Making my way from Botley Road to Walton Street via Park End Street I rode to the Judo Club on Polstead Road. Using the gutter drainpipe I got to a bathroom window that I knew would open from the outside and squeezed through into the building. The door to the office was always open and I knew the hiding place for the money lockbox and the key. Dawn was filtering through the windows as I counted out six pounds – about half of the total.

I rode to Gloucester Green and bought tea and toast at the café, waiting for the shops to open. There was a used copy of the Oxford Mail left on a chair. One report was from the

Assizes Court sentencing eight men to prison for gross indecency. The charges had come about from a surveillance operation at Gloucester Green Gentlemen's toilets by the Oxford Police. Two of the queers were college professors and one was a local teacher that I knew. More than prison was the crippling public contempt and shame. My father always ranted about queers doing this, but he was doing it himself. I hoped the police would watch Hinksey Park or Florence Park toilets.

The sports shop on Turl Street opened at nine and in ten minutes I had bought football boots, swimming trunks, a duffle bag and a jockstrap for four pounds seven shillings. After that I rode back to my camp in the hills, hiding my new things under the Hinksey Lake bridge on the way. Exhausted and dirty I collapsed on my groundsheet. It was late into the night before I woke.

Thursday afternoon I hiked back down over the bypass and through the fields and allotments to get back behind the Baptist Church on Wytham Street. I knew the Women's Own group would have met and left food in the kitchen. I also knew where the jumble sale clothing was stored in the crèche.

All the clothes smelled musty and felt a bit damp. I found a pair of grey trousers, a cream shirt and the only Blazer which was much too big. There were lots of ties, I picked a green one and a pair of beige suede shoes.

Friday morning it was raining hard – I stripped off, stood out in the pelting rain with the soap and under my shelter tree to dry off. After brushing my teeth for the first time in days I sensed a feeling of hope. My arm was healing but I noticed where the muscles were sliced a full stretch was not possible, forming an unusual hook at the elbow. The muscles above and under the deep lacerations were getting bigger and stronger as I naturally compensated for the loss. The thought the Navy would reject me at the final entry medical exam flashed into my mind – my bastard father could have robbed me of my last chance, at the last moment.

On Saturday morning I hiked back down to the bye-pass, and in the first layby found a line of long trailers and caravans, parked ready to be towed into Oxford on Sunday – for St. Giles Fair. There were men, women and children working on cleaning and painting pieces of the attractions and stalls they would operate at the Fair. My first conversation got me a job wiping old grease off dodgem-car bearings. In an hour my hands and arms were covered in black sticky film. I noticed all the men and boys working on the rigs were stained the same way. I made five shillings for five hours work and hiked back to my camp. My bath in the cold stream was long and laborious – the soap was almost useless in removing the grease stain. Exhausted to the point of delirium I collapsed on the dark floor of my camp – thinking how to survive one more day to see a new horizon. I decided to leave for Guildford on Sunday and sleep in the train sidings overnight – in case the Police expected me to leave on Monday as the Navy travel warrant anticipated.

During the day on Sunday I started by getting all my things together needed to appear normal at the Navy appointment at Guildford Station. All the rest of my possessions I hid in the roots and branches of trees of trees I memorized. By early afternoon I had completed the cover-up and spent another hour trying to remove the stubborn black grease from my arms and hands.

The riskiest problem now was to find a place to hide my bike where it could be easily retrieved in the future. It also had to be a place where I could get a bath and properly clean myself for the Navy entry medical. I decided on the COHS sports fields on Marston Ferry Lane. I knew several ways to get into the changing rooms with hot water in the showers.

I arrived there late in the afternoon, having took a long route along the Oxford canal, through Port Meadow and over to Banbury Road via Wolvercote. I hid my bike in the open beam attic above the old cricket pavilion and laid a rotting cricket net over it.

The shower was so welcome it was hard to get out. All the time I worried that Jock the groundsman would show up. My memory flashed to Dumbo walking past and peering in through the steam. – rubbing his stiff crotch. I used laundry powder to scrub the grease from my arms and hands but it stuck firmly to the skin around my nails. By now it was six o'clock and In the cracked changing room mirror I looked better than I had imagined. My face was much thinner – my shoulders almost skeletal, but there was an inner feeling of strength and survival. Two hours from now, if my plan worked, I would be leaving Oxford on a train to Guildford.

Stepping out of the changing rooms it was a perfect Oxford evening in late summer. The sun was dropping over Wolvercote, releasing a faint glow into the still atmosphere. On a different night I would have been In Port Meadow, on the Thames bank – gazing across the darkening flatness of the river – looking for the slightest ripple and casting a red worm into the still surface upstream.

Emerging from the footpath at the Plough pub in Binsey I walked briskly up Binsey Lane to Botley Road and in a few more minutes reached Oxford Railway Station, on the Great Western Line to Paddington, London.

Chapter 9.

1954 - Escape from Oxford

Sunday September 5th, 1954 at 7.15 pm I handed my Navy Rail warrant through the window opening. The lady looked at me closely – and asked for my recruitment papers. I handed over the Navy letter with the travel instructions – after a long pause she issued the ticket. I was half-expecting her to phone the Oxford Police. I crossed Platform 1 and boarded the waiting train. Walking down the carriages, glancing into the dimly lit compartments I saw only one person in third class – a boy about my age.

I threw my small duffle bag onto a faded upholstered seat. The station was almost deserted except for the Ticket clerk and the Platform Inspector. At 7.25 pm the Inspector closed the steel gates and strode across the Platform. He raised his green flag toward the engine driver and blew a shrill blast on a silver whistle.

The train's wheels crossing the rail connectors took on the familiar rhythm that I knew would soon bring me within view of my house. I got up and moved into the passage as we passed through Hinksey – the Park, allotments, and the swimming pools – under Hinksey Lake bridge, along the length of Wytham Street. My house on Bertie Place had the curtains open and I saw the outline of Mum through the window. I had done it - escaped from home and from Oxford.

The train increased speed as we passed through South Oxfordshire. The open fields, bush-rows, tall woods and streams I knew intimately and loved – every pasture, footpath, bridge and farm gate, to left and right, were part of my life. As the rail skirted the Thames back-streams these sights gave pleasant feelings and memories of fishing, exploring beyond the fences and ditches – climbing trees to collect bird's eggs – running from people, dogs and horses – raiding orchards and gardens – swimming in private lakes – snogging in the long grass, feeling a number of the local young girls while receiving their delights.

My short life flashed by - but the image of Mum obsessed me. She was waving - seemingly forced flat against the glass of my bedroom window, as if trapped in a nightmare. How did she know I was on this train? Did I imagine it?

I looked at the letter that came with the train warrant. It was from the Royal Navy, Recruitment Branch – instructing me to report to Seaman's Charity house in Guildford by 9.00 pm the next day – a liaison officer would meet me at the Guilford station.

I was free of Oxford, and my family – but a feeling of fear and panic started deep in my stomach. I had achieved my goal – to get away from them and the rest of the Oxford punishers and bullies, who had hindered my freedom and stunted my life for years.

But now I was just hours away from signing on in the Royal Navy for the next twelve years – I reminded myself I would be twenty-seven when I finished my time. Our church minister had told Mum that boys should not have to sign on for so long at fifteen years old. I prayed he would not convince my parents to rip up the recruiting letter – which my father wanted to do.

In the end, my parents wanted me out of the house as much as I did. Sitting silently on the stairs I heard them talking about me every night– my father wanted more punishment, more beatings, more restriction, more hard labor – Mum cried and sighed often and wondered occasionally if I had a brain disorder or damage from the forceps birth delivery – my father thought I was born evil.

If the Royal Navy wouldn't take me I decided I would run to South Wales and live on the mountains in the Rhondda Valley with Lyn and other boys I knew there. My mind snapped back to the present realizing that last-ditch possibility was no longer needed. But, now I was totally alone with no idea what to expect from the Navy and the future. I felt like I might cry but I choked it back fast and inhaled deep on my last cigarette – where would I get my next one? A deep dread set in - a dread of life itself - I had felt it before in delirious nightmares – but never awake.

About forty minutes later the train pulled into Didcot. I changed Platforms and boarded the waiting train to Guildford. In just over an hour I stepped onto the Guildford Platform. It was approaching 10.30pm and the café was closed. The station appeared deserted as the last train left until early morning. Only a couple of black Taxis were outside the station. The Seaman's home was very close and I thought about knocking on the closed doors. But I decided to do my original plan and find an empty train carriage to sleep in until morning.

As a keen train-spotter I knew the layout of the big southern region stations and where the "sheds", or repair shops were. In the sheds there was always a couple of old carriages parked in unused bays. I headed back toward the station and skirted the fence boundary until I found a way through. On my way along the spur to the sheds there was an old sleeper carriage that looked downgraded. A window in one door was missing and reaching through I opened it. Right in front was a stinking clogged toilet and to the right a passageway with sleeper birth doors every six feet.

As soon as I touched the first door handle, a female scream erupted from inside 'fuck off". Moving swiftly down the passage bangs from inside and curses kept me going. Almost at the end a massive man in underwear came out into the passage. "Who the fuck are you?" I told him I was looking for a place to sleep one night, before I reported to the Navy Officer at the station in the morning.

He snatched my bag and looked through it, reading the letter from the Navy. Looking at me very intently. "Are you on the run?" I said I just needed a place until tomorrow morning. He asked me if I had any money. I shook my head and begged him to let me stay one night – to sleep on the floor inside somewhere. He motioned me to follow him to the last door and led me inside. There was a double bunk bed with dirty mattresses. He asked me my name and said his was Acid – I was even more scared of him now. As he left the cabin I locked the door and collapsed onto the lower bunk.

It was about four in the morning when a knock on the door woke me – for a moment I didn't know where I was. Acid's voice replied "let me in a minute". Dread ran through me when I saw his massively fat body clothed in a white net negligee with red silk pants and bra. His face was made up in bright colors with thick red lipstick and purple mascara. His closely shaved scalp glistened with sweat on the black stubble. Forcing his way in I stumbled back. He closed and locked the door.

Acid opened his mouth to reveal rows of rotten teeth as he attempted to kiss me – the stench from his mouth was like cow-dung. As I pulled away he shoved me up against the cabin wall and pulled down his pants – I had never seen or imagined such a sight. His gigantic penis was jerking in his hand. "Take this boy" he sneered – "or get kicked off here with nothing". My plan of over a year seemed destroyed – without my Navy letter I had nothing.

The overwhelming size and enormity of Acid defeated all my remaining resolve. "What do you want?" I asked. "Suck my cock" I realized that I was close to fighting for my life or surviving by being raped and assaulted. I had never sucked a cock before and automatically felt so repulsed that I gagged and would have vomited had anything been in my stomach.

Acid reached his hand to touch my cheek and waved his huge bulging cock. I started screaming at the top of my lungs "No, No, No". Acid's caress turned into a huge slap against my head, sending me to the floor, I felt blood flowing from a gash inside my cheek. Without thinking I started fighting back still shouting "No". Grabbing his balls in one hand I came off the floor from crouching to jumping straight up. Acid lowered his face toward my hand just as my skull smashed into him. Knowing it was now or never I kept head-butting him with all my strength – on the third strike his nose was flat and gushing blood. A woman shouted outside "what the fuck is happening – Acid are you in there?"

Acid was now on his knees, holding his face in his hands. I grabbed my bag and shoes and opened the door. Two women were standing outside – one was swaying as if drunk and had a vacant look on her face. The other's arms were covered in stick-like tattoos with safety pins through the skin on her wrists. "What the fuck is going on boy?" she shouted through cracked, bleeding lips around a black hole mouth. "Acid tried to rape me," I shouted back as I ran up the carriage and jumped through the open door onto the gravel outside. I stumbled to get traction on the gravel, grazing the backs of my hands as I fought to hold onto my bag and shoes.

Clambering through the hole in the fence the sun was just beginning to shed some light over Guildford. Keeping my head down I crawled into some long grass about fifty yards from the station and waited.

My Navy letter was beginning to look grubby, my clothes were looking more and more tattered and dirty and for the first time in my life I became personally aware of a foul smell coming from my own body, so bad I could taste it. At about nine I walked back up to the station and showed my ticket stub and Navy letter to the Inspector, who directed me to an office marked "Forces Liaison" on Platform 1. On the way I visited the Gentlemen's Toilets to get properly cleaned up and take a crap – it had been a while I realized. It was black – like fox shit. In the dull steel mirror a cut and bruise between my right eye and ear was obvious.

The Liaison Officer on duty was an Army Sergeant with polished brass badges and gold-braid stripes. He looked closely at me and at the letter, backwards and forwards went his head – each time a frown more obvious. "What happened to your ear?" "I was in a fight with a tramp that tried to steal my bag." "When did you get here?" "Late last night." "Where have you been all night?" "Just walking around waiting to come here". With a big sigh the Sergeant looked at me sternly and said "OK take this chit to the Merchant Seaman Home across the street".

Feeling massively relieved I handed my chit to the attendant at the Seamans Home. I would be staying here tonight and then transported to HMS Ganges in the morning with other boys joining up. The shower water was hot and cold at the turn of a lever. After drying off I discarded my filthy underwear and socks in the rubbish bin and put on the last of each I had left. I was so hungry and tired that being clean and fresh felt like a hallucination.

I fell onto my bunk and into a deep and long sleep, interrupted by nightmares of collapsing houses and being chased by Acid. About four I woke up as boys arriving took the other five bunks in the room. We all sat there saying nothing – staring out at nothing. Finally the boy above me looked down and asked, "Are you going to Ganges?" "Yeh are you?" "Yeh, my brother joined there before". Immediately I felt out of depth – realizing I had no idea where I was going or what to expect. The other boys started talking – they all were going to Ganges and knew they wanted to be a seaman or a communicator. On the other hand I had no idea what I wanted to be – except not in Oxford.

An Attendant came in and called my name. I followed him to a small office close to the entrance. A slight, grey suited man motioned me to sit in a chair opposite him, the Attendant closed the door. "I'm a Doctor" he said "How did you get the injury to your face?" I told him the story of fighting off a tramp. "'I would like to examine you – please take off your shirt and vest". I complied as my heart rate was going rapidly up. "How did you get these grazes?" I kept lying about the fight. "How did you get these cuts on your arm"? I kept it up, lying that I fell from a window while doing bob-a-job Scout work. "When was your last meal?" Feeling dread I lied "Yesterday". "Are you hungry?" "Ah yes a bit". "Do you have any money?" "Not really – just half-a-crown I'm saving until I get to Ganges." The doctor rose and left the office – I waited – it felt like the last minute of my life.

About fifteen minutes later the Attendant returned. He gave me food vouchers to use in the cafeteria and a paper bag with a toothbrush, toothpaste and soap. The smell of cooked food in the cafeteria was intoxicating. I collected a tray of bacon, sausage, chips and beans. Sitting down with that food in front of me was like a miracle – a new world. The conversation at the tables was about when we would get our uniforms and hats. Some boys like me had no idea and hadn't even thought about things like that – they looked a bit like me, listening, a bit confused but accepting everything without comment.

Eating this cafeteria food was like an enormous feast. I noticed my worries starting to fade. A kind of troop spirit seemed to exist. Like we were all in the same boat and no one really knew what to expect.

Chapter 10

HMS Ganges – Annex (Boot Camp)

We were woken at five - breakfast in the cafeteria was buzzing. All the boys going to Ganges were instructed to assemble outside the front door. The Army Sergeant from the day before marched up and led us all up to the station and onto a waiting train to Ipswich.

There were about thirty boys sitting in the mostly empty carriage compartments. I noticed the boy who was on the same train as me from Oxford. When I got a chance I spoke to him. He was signing up as a boy signalman – he asked me what I was signing up for? I had no idea. He also asked if I knew when we got hats. He offered me one of his Weights. The first drag made me dizzy – I hadn't smoked in thirty-six hours. Also I was seeing double and had blurred vision. His name was Eddie Williams – he said anyone named Williams was nicknamed Bungy in the Navy.

Soon there were groups of boys talking about where they were from – the accents were   broad. There were boys from Wales, Scotland, England and one boy from Ireland. All were smartly dressed except me and some boys from Glasgow. I could tell they were looking at me – my suede shoes were now very dirty. With my battered face and weird clothes I felt embarrassed and slid into the background.

As the train pulled into Ipswich there were about thirty boys already lined up on the platform. An older boy in Naval Uniform with white gaiters was standing in front of them. Another boy dressed the same herded the new arrivals into a similar formation – I stood in the back row. One of the uniformed boys shouted "Pay attention – my name is Junior Instructor Thomas" "From now on you will call me Sir". 'Whenever I order Class Fall In! – you will assemble as you are now" "Is this understood?" "Yes Sir came a few nervous voices".

Sir Thomas collected the recruitment letters - looking at my tattered paper he asked, "What's your name?" "Hudson Sir" "What's your christian name - Rock?" a few giggles were choked. "You are a scruff aren't you – are those dancing shoes?" "No Sir" "What happened to your face Hudson?" "I was elbowed at rugby" "At rugby what?" "At rugby Sir." "You will need to buck up really fast Hudson – if you're going to survive the Annex". He stared at me until I murmured "Yes Sir".

The Junior Instructors were much younger than my prefects at COHS and strutted around mechanically. Their uniforms were immaculate with brilliant white fronts against the Navy blue tunic. They wore white gaiters into which the navy blue bellbottom trousers were tucked precisely. The royal blue collar with white striping stood out beneath their gleaming white caps - a black silk band with gold thread spelling "HMS Ganges" surrounded the rim.

Suddenly the JI's snapped to attention in unison, with a loud click of heels as, an officer in different uniform approached. His uniform was a navy blue suit, white shirt with a stiff collar and a black tie. His double-breasted jacket had two rows of gold buttons and one row over each sleeve at the wrist. On his lapels were miniature red silk badges of crossed guns under a crown – and two stars under the guns. Under his right arm he carried a black polished stick about thirty inches long – his right hand grasped the stick in the crook of his thumb with fingers pointed straight upward in stiff overemphasis. His hat had a black polished peak under a brilliant white cloth top with gold a gold braid badge in the middle. His lower legs were covered in high black, polished leather gaiters. His pink shiny face was stern and eagle-like.

"Junior Instructor Thomas reporting Sir – Number 242 New Entry Fallen In Sir". The officer nodded and strode into a spot in font of us. He snapped to a halt and turned toward us in one impressive move.

"I am Chief Gunnery Instructor Soames – you will call me Sir." "In a few minutes you will be transported to HMS Ganges Annex – you will be there for four weeks – where we will decide if you are up to snuff for the Royal Navy." "From now on you will refer to yourself as your surname followed by initials – for example if your name is John Smith you are now Smith J – understand?"

Three dark blue buses with RN painted in white on the sides left in convoy to Shotley at noon. The half hour ride was almost silent – except for the odd whisper about what to expect.

We arrived at a bleak looking wire-fenced enclosure. A sailor in full uniform and white belt and gaiters emerged from a guard hut. We passed through the huge gates under the sign "HMS Ganges – Annex". The place seemed totally without color – everything was grey or black.

We were soon lined up in four squads, with about thirty in each. There were now six JI's out in front. They looked identical almost except for their faces. Their uniformed presence was stunning to all of us. Another gold-buttoned Chief Petty Officer stepped out front – to the side were five others. "You will call me Sir" "You will call all Chief Instructors Sir" "You will call all Junior Instructors Sir" "You will now be assigned to your mess" "Your mess is where you will be whenever you are not under organized training". "There is no free time here – there is no leave – there is no entertainment or places to go". "It's very simple – you are either in a class or you are in your mess or the galley". "You are now standing on the Parade Ground – you will not enter the Parade ground unless ordered." "When ordered onto the Parade Ground you will move at the double – which means running."

Each boy was assigned to a mess, which turned out to be one of the long dark huts surrounding the parade ground. My mess was named Explorer - my JI was Sir Thomas. I found my bed about half way up the mess on the right. The mood was quiet and expectant. JI Thomas entered through the double entry doors and up a couple of steps to the floor of the mess. His bed was at the front and had a stack of bedding folded precisely on the mattress. He snapped to attention with clicked heels, yelling, "Stand by your beds.

"Place all your belongings under the bed – hop to it – speed up!" The orders were starting to flow. "Place all your bedding on top of your locker." Look at my bed – this is how you will fold your bedding each morning." At the head of his bed was the neatest set of bedclothes I had ever seen.

"Now take one blanket and fold it like this". He demonstrated an eight-step folding method that left the cream, hairy blanket with four identical pleats at the front and two on the sides – reduced into thirty inches square and seven inches high. He instructed us to fold one blanket each and hold up a hand when finished.

JI Thomas inspected the first boy to put his hand up – he was not impressed. "This doesn't look a bit like my blanket does it?" "It's falling over and loose." He picked up the blanket and threw it at the boy. "Do it again" he turned away abruptly in full swagger, without raising his voice.

There were twenty-one boys in Explorer mess. Following the bed–making instruction JI Thomas ordered " Place your towel and toilet items on your the bed". I retrieved my ragged towel from my duffle bag and placed it on the bed, I didn't have anything except the toothbrush and toothpaste I had been given at the Seaman's Home.

"What is this toothpaste Hudson?" "Ah I got it the Seaman's home Sir". "I lost mine Sir". "Pipe-down Hudson – I'll tell you when I want to hear you – until then keep silent." "Where's your soap Hudson". "I think I left it at the Seaman's Home Sir". I realized this was going to be an intimidating experience but remembered instantly how bad it had been before – I was hundreds of miles from my father and brother – and out of their control – I had to make this work. JI Thomas ordered "Fall in outside".

JI Thomas herded us into a squad of three lines. The tallest boy was placed at the far right of the first line. "What's your name?" "Brown Sir." "Brown what?" "Uh Brown Sir?" the boy stuttered. "What's your initial Brown?" "Michael Sir." Some of the other boys chuckled. "Keep silent you idiots!" JI Thomas bellowed as he walked up to the boy next to me in the front row. "What's your name?" "Angles Sir, sorry Angles J. Sir." The boy replied in a broad scots accent. "Angles, what kind name is that? – how do you spell it?" "I-n-g-l-i-s Sir." "Not any more Englis – what did you think was funny Englis." "Nothing Sir." "Then why were you laughing E-n-g-lis?" The boy remained silent and lowered his head.

Returning to the tall boy Brown, JI Thomas asked, "Are those plimsoles you're wearing Brown?" "Yes Sir". "What's your name?" "Brown M Sir." "Where are you from Brown?" "London Sir." "London's a big place – where in London?" JI Thomas mocked. "Brixton Sir." "Is your old man in prison then?" JI Thomas jeered?" Brown remained silent and also lowered his head. "Look up Brown – from now on your name is Lofty." "Every time we fall in or muster like this you will go to this exact spot – understand?" "Yes Sir." Turning to the rest of us "Lofty Brown is your Marker!" "From now on you will fall-in in the exact same lines – you will look for Lofty Brown and line up on him just like now and always the same. "Got it! - line up outside the galley" he pointed to another long grey hut.

The JI's policed the long line of a hundred and twenty boys as we filed into the dining hall – a barn with a stainless steel servery at one end. There were other boys in uniform that looked our age who were keeping the queue orderly and showing the places for picking up a steel tray with compartments and a steel soup bowl, knife, fork and spoon. They acted in a superior manner – giving instructions as if orders.

The food did not look very good to some boys, who I heard complaining. To me it was at least real food. The runner beans and boiled potatoes were tasteless. The meat was a baked pork chop that tasted like cardboard, with gravy that tasted worse. Better than the roach from the Hinksey railway lake I thought. For afters there was jelly with blancmange on top.

As I sat down with my food the first Annex fight broke out. Apparently a new boy objected to an order from one of the boys in uniform. A shouting match led to the new boy, a very burly boy with a Glasgow accent, head-butting the monitor boy in the face – the monitor boy went down bleeding. Immediately the rest of the monitor boys and the JI's were on top of the Scot – he was hustled out faster than the eye could see almost. We never saw him again.

After dinner we were ordered back to our messes. As we filed in Chief Petty Officer Soames – who had met us at Ipswich station handed us each a large brown military kit bag with instructions to stamp our names in black ink on the bottom. My first item of kit. The boys hung around their beds – a few words exchanged before JI Thomas arrived. "Stand by your beds." he thundered. "What just happened in the galley will never happen again." "The boy has been taken to the cells at the Main Establishment and will be punished. "Don't ever think of hitting a superior in the Royal Navy – you'll be thrown out!"

We were ordered to strip naked and take our toilet gear and towel to the washroom – off to the side of the mess entrance. It was concrete room – including the floor, walls and sinks of which there were about fifteen. A single brass tap stood over each one. Standing just inside was Chief Soames. He looked very closely, up and down, at each boy. A boy just ahead of me had his towel across his shoulders – "Take the towel off boy." The Chief ordered. When the towel came off there was the most disgusting sight of infected blackheads imaginable. "When did you have a bath last boy?" "Ah last year sir" the boy replied in a thick scots accent. The chief motioned for JI Thomas and whispered an order. The boy was led out of line and back to his bed. When we returned he was also gone without any comment.

As I passed the Chief he looked at my arm "What's your name?" "Hudson R. Sir." "What happened?" "I fell through a window Sir." "Where was that?" "At home Sir." "How did it happen?" "I fell through while I was sitting on the window sill Sir." "What happened to your face boy?" "I was elbowed at rugby Sir." "You seem to be a bit knocked about." Turning to JI Thomas "take him to the sick bay." My deepest dread was happening. The JI led me across the parade ground to another long grey hut with "Administration" over the doors and a red-cross emblem.

After a while a quite old and wispy white-haired doctor, almost invisible beneath his gown, examined me in a small office. I had to recite over the cause of the injuries but he was more interested if I could move my arm properly. I assured him I could do anything with my arm – in fact it was stronger now that it had healed. He looked at me a little strangely "You really want to join up don't you boy?" He wrote something on a piece of paper and gave it me. "Take this to your JI." JI Thomas looked at it and said, "Fit for Entry." I had made it under the wire.

Back in the washroom I was at the end of the queue. "Scrub your toggle and two and where the sun doesn't shine." the Chief ordered – wash between your toes and up your nose." The Chief had a sense of humor. I felt that things were getting better at last – although I still had no idea what to expect next.

We stood rigidly "at-ease" back in our bed spaces, dressed in our civilian clothes again we were ordered, "Fall in outside." – again! I noticed the strange appearance of the group. Some boys were smartly dressed, looked strong and eager to respond. Other boys looked ragged, dazed and confused at the barrage of strange orders. For myself I was beginning to think I had made a very bad decision – and one I could not escape from for twelve years.

JI Thomas barked orders at us over and over until we could come to attention and stand at ease, almost in unison. This drill continued for an hour until we were marched over to the Admin Huts. Lines of boys led to two doctors who gave a very brief physical examination to each. From there we were ferried to another hut with long rows of tables stacked with kit.

Each boy was issued with two white towels, two pairs of pajamas, four sets of underwear and four pairs of socks. A bar of soap, a toothbrush, a small tube of toothpaste, a black comb and a sewing kit, called a housewife.
A small brown cardboard case was issued for writing gear and personal items. A tin of black shoe-polish, two brushes and a yellow cloth duster were inside the case. Two pairs of dark blue trill trousers and two cobalt blue shirts were issued as daily drill clothes – called No. 8's. A broad, blue canvas belt with a silver buckle and a money pouch was mandatory through the belt loops. One pair of black leather ankle boots and one pair of black leather "deck slippers" for inside the mess were also issued.

Back in the mess we were ordered to bring our gear up one at a time to a marking table where the Chief and JI Thomas stamped our names in ink on each item except the socks.

After this we were allowed half an hour to meet and chat with our fellow messmates. But most boys stuck to their bed spaces looking at the kit and wondering when uniforms and caps would be coming.

After another hour marching and standing drills we were dismissed to the galley for tea – the food was even worse than dinner and the monitor boys were even more obnoxious and authoritative.

Back in the mess we were ordered to sew over our names marked in ink. Each name was to be embroidered, in chain stitch, in red silk thread. R.Hudson was a lot quicker to sew than O.M.Macphearson, the boy in the bed space opposite me. Each completed item had to receive approval from JI Thomas. Many names had to be unraveled and re-sewn – at his whim. The power of this officer boy was above anything I had ever witnessed. I was fortunate Mum had taught me to darn my socks so I knew a little about sewing

We were ordered to make up our beds and prepare for the night. We looked around at each other – everyone was pretty tense. The order came from JI Thomas 'Turn in – keep silence." As the night closed in the moon cast shadows against the exposed steel rafters - creating a feeling of prison bars. There was hardly a whisper – soon a few snores.

My uneasy sleep was shattered by the sound of two steel dustbin lids being smashed against each other. "Wakey, Wakey, rise and shine – hands off cocks and into socks." JI Thomas stood bellowing at the head of the mess – as immaculate and powerful as the night before – brandishing a massive pair of cymbals. A large plain clock at the head of the mess was at 4.45 am. "Get moving on your bedding." He swaggered up and down the mess looking into the progress in each bed-space.

"After you've washed, dress in your Number 8's and boots." – he repeated up and down the mess. Occasionally he picked up a blanket and threw it on the bed "Do it again – you'll keep doing it until it's right – are you blind, deaf or what?" The intricate folding was easy for me. Mum had taught me to wash, hang to dry and iron since I was eleven. I was soon in the washroom ahead of most of the boys.

Chief Soames was standing in his usual position just inside the washroom door as I arrived in the first group. I knew from the day before that if you were among the last to arrive there would be a wait until a basin freed up. There was a rush by two boys to get to the basin next to me. They bumped into each other and immediately it escalated into a fight. One of the boys, named Starrat smashed the other boy with a vicious straight right and down he went, blood pouring from his nose. In a flash Chief Soames was on the scene and had Starrat in a headlock. JI Thomas was soon there and together they hustled him off to the Admin hut.

The boy Starrat punched got up and started washing in the basin, which filled quickly with a blood red dilution. His nose was twisted and swollen – the blood kept flowing. We all went on washing and getting back to our bed spaces.

The Chief and JI returned to the mess as if nothing had happened. Except for the boy still bleeding over the sink in the washroom we were all standing silently at ease. The Chief strode onto the mess center. Looking toward the washroom he roared "Talbot get by your bed". The boy emerged from the washroom holding a towel to his face and walked slowly up the mess. As he passed me I could see the towel was soaked in blood.

The Chief followed him to this bed space and ordered, "Drop the towel Talbot". Looking straight ahead I couldn't see what happened next – but I heard the Chief. "Hold your head up – put your thumbs against your nose – straighten it out boy – push!

JI Thomas ordered "Class Fall-in outside." We shuffled out into the place and formation of the night before. "Class" he yelled – "Hhaww". A second or two passed until all the boys were standing at attention. So three boys who had disappeared quickly from the scene. Judging by the amount and volume of earsplitting orders there were boys in the other messes in the same boat.

After about fifteen minutes we were dismissed to the galley for breakfast. The food was even worse than tea last evening. Bacon and egg was my favorite - until now. I could not detect any lean part of the bacon and the egg was like rubber. There was a mysterious looking brown mush that the chef called grilled kidneys and pieces of fried bread. A large urn of sweetened tea sat next to a table stacked with white tin mugs. One of the boys who had been in a navy orphanage announced that the kidneys on fried bread was known in the Navy as "shit on a raft".

Half an hour later we were back on the parade ground learning to turn right, left and about. The squad looked like a shamble of convicts, all dressed in detention center clothing and all with a kind of blank, inward look. JI Thomas attempted to march us off to the right but we started bumping into each other almost immediately. "Class Halt" he screamed.

We were milling around when he shouted "take ten minutes stand-easy - if you want a burn – do it now". Most boys immediately reached into their trousers for their cigarettes – I hadn't smoked for a day. But now I knew if you were in the Navy you weren't subject to UK Law that sixteen was the permissible age and it was a "burn" not a smoke.

I looked around for a boy who might offer me one. Right away the thinnest boy I had ever seen walked up and held out ten Woodbines. I accepted one and lit it from his as he held it up. "Where you from?" he asked. I immediately noticed his Welsh accent. "Oxford, what about you?" "I'm from Pontypridd". I was a bit shocked – "I know Ponty" I smiled. My face felt like it was cracking – a surge of kinship came over me.

We started to talk about the Rhondda Valley when JI Thomas shouted. "Fags out – fall in." We were marched again to the kit hut, with our kit bags, and issued with the rest of our uniform. There was a navy blue serge bell-bottom sailor suit with white-fronts and navy blue wool sea jerseys, two blue and white sailor collars, two black silk top collars and three white cord lanyards. A further set of black leather ankle boots, designated as dress-boots, two pairs of white gym shoes and two sailor caps were issued. Also two black silk cap-bands with HMS Ganges embroidered in gold braid. Two complete sets of white cotton shorts and gym shirts and a full length navy blue Burberry completed the initial kit issue.

After another revolting dinner we were ordered to the mess to continue sewing names on our kits. We were also provided with brown paper and labels to parcel our civilian clothes for return to our parents. I feared how my father would react when he found out I was actually in the Navy. I wrote a false address – hoping it would get lost in the postal system.

After tea and back outside again, lined up into our ranks JI Thomas called us to attention "Class Hhaww" – I was wondering how that was supposed to sound like "Attention". "Move to the right in threes" he barked, "Right taarn". We were starting to get the idea behind the orders but the precision and timing were awful. "By the left – Quick Maaarch". "Left-Right-Left-Right-left Right-Leeeft". The boy in front of me started off with his right foot but swung his right arm too – this caused me to trip on his left foot and fall into the boy on my right. The whole class milled to a stop. JI Thomas was furious but most of the boys were laughing or smiling. This made him even more furious. "Get in the mess and stand by your beds" he fumed. "On the double".

JI Thomas stamped onto the center space of the mess. "Strip down to your underpants –leave your socks on". "Stow your clothes in your locker". He was now yelling at full throttle - "Do it Now! – or sooner!" I sensed all round me that the boys were reacting but still somewhat amused.

About a minute of scrambling took place before we were all lined up at ease and standing in our new issued underpants. "I am in charge here – you will call me Sir," he yelled. "If you think it's funny you'll get a chance to find out". "Pick up your boots – one in each hand".

"Mess Hhawwhh" We shuffled to attention with boots at our sides. "Raise both arms in front of you – stand still!" JI Thomas stood motionless staring up the mess. Total silence slowly set in. After a minute or so there were a few grunts as the muscle fatigue started in the shoulders and upper arms. After three or four minutes there were loud sighs and moans. JI Thomas remained motionless staring up the mess. The first boots began dropping after five or six minutes and by now all the boys were grunting and moaning at the pain in the shoulders.

Each time a boot or arm dropped JI Thomas ordered the boy to remove a sock and then return to the position. After about eight minutes I could not hold it any longer and released my shoulders. "One sock off Hudson – get back in position". Soon the weakest boys had removed both socks and their underpants. Now as those boys returned to the torture position they were ordered to bend at the knees also – intensifying the muscle fatigue and pain. All the boys were now looking worried – the amusement had disappeared.

When every boy was naked JI Thomas ordered us back into underpants and outside in the colonnade between the mess and the parade ground. The dusk air was cold and breezy. JI Thomas called us to attention and marched us shivering up and down the colonnade for ten minutes. The sound of bare feet padding against the concrete in unison was eerie. Many of the boys were sniffing and panting. My body was freezing – I definitely got the message on obeying orders seriously. I could hear orders being barked at other classes undergoing the colonnade march.

JI Thomas paced onto the center of the mess – "From now on there will be no fun and games – there will be no time for anything except training and getting your kit together". "Tomorrow I want more effort – more speed – more silence". "Make your beds and turn-in – you've got five minutes". I glanced at the mess clock - 7.30 pm as the lights went out.

Silence fell on the mess quickly but soon a joker made a fart sound which set off some giggling. Immediately the lights were on – JI Thomas was screaming "Turn out – pick up your boots – hold them out – "Mess HHawwhh". I could not believe we were back in the same spot because of one boy.

This time JI Thomas ordered us into the knees-bent – arms out position immediately. Then he added a level – "The first boy to drop a boot will scrub out the heads tonight."

It was the first time I had heard of the "heads" but I guessed it was the bogs. Pretty soon there were moans and grunts coming from all the boys – for me I was beginning to think again that I had made a big mistake. The thin boy from Pontypridd was the first to break – sinking to his knees and sobbing after about a minute. "Jones! Get up! Get up".
JI Thomas came within an inch of the boy's face and yelled again "Jones you are a maggot – get down into the heads and wait for me."

Sleep came rapidly but so did "Wakey Wakey rise and shine – don't turn over – TURN OUT!" – all accompanied by a bashing of the steel dustbin lids. Day two was underway at 4.45 am – we all turned out fast and began stripping and folding our bedding – in total silence. Then into the washroom, past the Chief, wash in freezing water and back to the bed space, into No.8's – stand by your bed – at ease.

After breakfast we were marched to the Admin Hut. Four teams of two sick bay attendants were processing the boys through injection stations. As my turn was approaching I felt a huge shove in my back. Turning to see what was happening a boy fell straight to the floor in a pale-faced faint. Two attendants dragged him to the side and started slapping his face. When the disruption had ended I stepped into the injection station. One attendant gave a vaccination on the right arm while another gave an injection in the left arm. Neither spoke or gave any information on the jabs.

Back in the mess working on our name sewing we were soon ordered "Fall in outside – leave your caps off". After forming up we were marched to the galley and ordered inside the dining hall. Half a dozen chairs were set in a row with a khaki coated barber behind each. Nobody was smiling – the dreaded entry haircut was about to happen. It was the quickest haircut ever – the barbers went straight over the top, reducing each boy to a layer of fuzz on top and shaved back and sides. A minute and a half in the chair at most.

Back in the mess JI Thomas demonstrated the skill of spit and polishing boots. Following another hour of name sewing we marched to the Admin hut again and into a hall with a stage and film screen. The Chiefs and JI's stood at the back. An officer with two and a half gold bands on his sleeves walked onto the stage – "My name is Lieutenant-Commander Dodge, RN, SD, brackets G." "I am the Annex Divisional officer". "I am a special duties officer and my special duty is Gunnery". "You will call me sir and salute every time you see me outside". "If I walk into your mess you will snap to attention". "I was once a boy entry like yourselves – I am proof that your are on course for a successful life in the Royal Navy."

Films and lectures followed for two hours. The history of HMS Ganges as the toughest and most admired boys training establishment in the world was graphically presented.
We were informed that we would be in the Annex for four weeks and depending upon individual appraisal would move to the main establishment at that time. There were lectures on uniform, saluting, personal hygiene, kit upkeep and paybooks. We were informed that an "official number" would be assigned when the paybook is issued – that number would identify us throughout our time in the Navy.

The paybook was the most important item of our kit. If it was lost, stolen or damaged a stoppage of leave, stoppage of pay and additional punishment would be levied.
We were to be paid two shillings per day. Five shillings per week was to be paid as pocket money – the remaining nine shillings per week was paid into a Post Office Savings account. This money was used for extra pay during leave and for kit replacements. There was one free kit, the entry kit – after that any replacements had to be paid for by the boy.

A medical officer lieutenant gave a lecture on venereal disease – including films of the most devastating effects of syphilis. We were instructed that any diagnosis of syphilis would result in immediate dishonorable discharge. We were also instructed that the Royal Navy treatment of gonorrhea entailed daily doses of a very unpleasant medicine called 'mespotsit". The medical officer explained that the Navy treated this disease as self-inflicted injury and therefor a slow, painful treatment by ineffective oral medicine was ordered when injections of penicillin would provide an instant cure.

A Chief Sick Bay Attendant announced, "You may have heard the navy runs on Rum, Bum and Baccy." "Well there's no Bum here and you won't get Rum and Baccy until you're in the Fleet." "Do not be bashing the bishop boys, doing a five-fingered widow or creaming your jeans." There was laughter from the boys – the first for a while. "If you're caught doing anything lewd or lecherous you'll find out it wasn't worth it." "The punishment for that type of conduct is twelve cuts and immediate discharge." A hush fell when the Chief added, "Cuts are punishment by flogging."

A Chief Physical Instructor informed us there would be sports trials, swimming tests, assault courses, compulsory boxing and a mast-climbing challenge in the next four weeks. Each boy would be required to climb "over the 142 foot mast" in the main establishment. There would also be an Annex boxing tournament in which every boy must box.

There were more jabs and x-rays. I became friends with Jones from Pontypridd – he had a seemingly endless supply of Woodbines. At burn times I would light up and take three drags before nipping it off. That way a fag lasted almost all day. Jones was nicknamed Jonah by the boys. He struggled with everything that needed focus or coordination.

We were instructed on the exact methods of folding each item of uniform. There was also an exact method of stowing each item in our lockers. Every item had an exclusive place in the locker with the sewn red silk names lining up vertically and visible when the doors were open. A locker improperly stowed could be turned upside down by the Chief or JI.

There were daily classes on how to use the laundry tubs and how to wash each item of kit by hand. A big bar of "pusser's soap" was issued to each boy. Large drying racks were assigned each mess and a shared table for folding dry items. The central laundry was in constant use – rotated among the six messes. In Explorer Mess we had two very old electric irons and two ironing boards for twenty-one boys. As the items of uniform and kit grew in number the laundry and ironing load outgrew the demand. Fights broke out in the iron queues daily – at times the scramble for space in the laundry was like a rugby scrum. If you couldn't command your space – you lost it and ended up last and dragging behind the rest of the class.

Starrat returned to the mess after two days. He reported that he was detained in a cell in the main establishment and had received six cuts that morning. In the washroom he showed us his ass. Crossing the crack were six red, black and blue streaks about half and inch wide and extending well into each cheek. Starrat said his ass was numb but he was very relieved he was not booted out. He said his Dad would kill him if that happened.

At the end of week one we were paid five shillings each. This involved the entire entry of boys falling in on the parade ground. Then one by one marching up to a folding table behind which sat two petty officers – behind them stood a lieutenant. We were instructed to hold out the left hand bent at the elbow with the upper arm held tight to the side. With the right hand we were to salute and at the same time state our name and official number – as in "Hudson R. Sir P/057381". One petty officer placed a small brown envelope in the left hand and the other entered the payment into a ledger. Jonah was in front of me and got his hands mixed up – he kept trying to correct it but got more and more confused.

In the second week all boys were assigned to sports teams for trials. I hadn't played football for five years but it came back well and I surprised myself. A petty officer Physical Instructor, PTI, took my name after the trial and asked me if I played any other sports. After that I had a rugby trial and did equally well – the same PTI stated he would be in touch with me when and if I made it out of the Annex and into the main establishment.

The boxing tournament started at the end of the second week. A temporary ring with a thick canvass mat was set-up in the dining hall. For about three hours there were twenty or so bouts of two, three-minute rounds. These preliminaries went on for three consecutive days, by which time every boy had fought once. We were paired against boys from other messes, based on height and weight. Most of the bouts were extremely hard fought. In my first fight I was able to move around easily and stay out of range until my opponent from Yorkshire lunged in. Then I would pick him off with a counter punch – usually my powerful overhand right cross. The PTI referee raised my hand on the bell. Jonah all of a sudden showed his unlikely hidden talent – boxing. He possessed an amazing half-uppercut into the solar plexus. His first opponent fell to the canvas in agony as Jonah looked around at our surprised faces.

Semi-finals were fought on the fourth day. My opponent was a very tough, bigger and stronger Geordie, he caught me with a couple of head-buts – the referees were extremely forgiving. However I prevailed in the end as he ran out of steam and I was able to pepper him with jabs in the second round. "I'll get you later" he sneered at me as we left the ring. The finals were at the end of week three and I could tell I was getting stronger each day with all the drill and exercise.

In the third week we marched through the huge iron gates Of the Main Establishment and were faced directly by the towering mast. The Ganges Mast was 142 feet high, rigged as it would be for sail. Scalable rope shrouds led to the "half-moon", a steel grill capable of supporting three sailors at about 100 feet up. From there a rope ladder led to the last crosstree about 12 feet below the "button", an 18-inch diameter disc at the very top. The last 12 feet had to be shinned up like climbing a pole.

A large, rectangular safety net was supported by telegraph poles about 15 feet above the ground. The net was made of one-inch sisal rope knotted together in squares of about a foot. It looked as if anyone falling from high would be shredded. As we waited for the PTI to give us instructions the word went round that last year a boy had fallen off the rope ladder at the top, bounced off the safety net and landed on the roof the nearby post office building.

We were lined up in pairs and ordered to climb to the half moon on the starboard side and descend on the port side. About 50 feet up was the "devil's elbow", where the shrouds flared out at forty-five degrees to support an observation and working deck. We were told to climb out over the elbow but if too scared a hatch called the "lubbers hole" allowed access to the deck without climbing out over the elbow. All of us took the risky path except one, Starrat – he was embarrassed by Chief Soames who called him a coward. Starrat was quiet for a few days after the mast test.

In the boxing tournament finals I came up against Paddy Roony, the lad from Ireland who said nothing on the train from Guildford. His head seemed to come straight out of his shoulders – no neck, like a prop forward. He just kept coming at me taking all my punches and walking through them throwing haymakers with both arms. I managed to survive the first round but could not hold him back in the second. He was like a machine, a robot that was mowing me down. I had come across strong fighters in boxing and judo but nothing like Paddy Roony. I sunk to my knees, thoroughly beaten just as the final bell went. After that fight and the tournament Roony earned the nickname Rocky.

Jonah met a much bigger boy in the final – the fight lasted about a minute before he landed his devastating liver punch. He had confided in me that his dad had taught him this punch as a way to fend off bullies and over the years he had perfected it.

Starrat reached the finals also, beating his early opponents easily without raising a sweat. But in the final he came up against a boy from Aberdeen who was much fitter and faster. Starrat looked slow and ponderous as the scot reddened his face with jabs. Starrat was again embarrassed and angry.

That evening in the mess, spit-polishing, Chief Soames stopped at my bed space on his routine inspection. "Good scrap today Hudson – you represented Explorer mess well. The Irish lad is a promising boxer who'll be boxing for Ganges". "Thank you sir" I felt encouragement for the first time I could ever remember.

Going to sleep each night I was more and more aware that I had made a pretty bad decision. The cost to escape my family and Oxford was proving to be high. The boys around me were mostly much rougher and tougher than me – and no one had the equivalent education. It began to sink in that this was not the exciting life I had imagined – but at least I was free to some degree and controlled by men that were different than my Oxford masters.

The fourth week in the Annex was a dawn till dusk constant demand in training and kit preparation. By now we had dressed in full uniform on two Sundays and paraded in front of the Annex Divisional Officer. Our boots were beginning to look very polished and our uniform pressed to the correct pleats with crisp collars and pristine white lanyards. We were beginning to get used to the caps and the constant need to wash the white top. Marching as a squad and completing changes of direction and formation on the march were now executed competently, even Jonah was beginning to fit in.

Without warning, one morning in the fourth week we were ordered to fall in outside in gym gear, carrying our swimming trunks and a towel. We were then doubled the half-mile to the swimming pool building in the main establishment.

Once inside we were ordered to the showers and then to line up at the shallow end of the pool. Most of the boys were quite confident by now – having survived the mast, the boxing and the parade ground. There were a few though that had been talking about not being able to swim – these boys were mostly from Glasgow. Jonah came along side me "I can't swim" he said. I laughed at him – he must be joking.

We were ordered five at a time into the shallow end with instructions to swim to the deep end, thirty yards away, and then tread water for two minutes. This was easy for me and I was first to the deep end. Treading water, all of sudden there was a boy grabbing my neck and wrapping his legs around my body, from behind – using me to stay above water but forcing us both under. As I sunk deeper he stood on my back as long as he could. When I surfaced he came up alongside and tried to grab me again, it was Jonah, grabbing at my neck - but then came a boat hook crashing against his arms and sending him under again. The PTI's ordered me away while they waited for him to surface. It seemed an age but he finally came up spewing snot and water from his mouth and nose. One PTI extended the boat hook and dragged Jonah to the side. This boy was going through hell. Drying and changing back to gym gear Jonah apologized. I told him he had scared the shit out of me and never get near to me in the water again. Six boys, including Jonah and Starrat were labeled "backward swimmers". If able to pass out of the Annex a backward swimmer was required to report to the pool Monday to Friday at 0500 for an hour of swimming instruction. This continued until the boy could pass the first test. Chief Soames sometimes referred to Starrat as Rat. This led to the nickname "The Rat" – which infuriated him.

I noticed my body had filled out a bit and was getting stronger and fitter.

The final kit inspection was performed by the Commander, one rank below the Captain of HMS Ganges. He asked where I was from. "Oxford Sir". He picked up a couple of items and checked the cleanliness. "Well done Hudson – are you enjoying your time in HMS Ganges?" "Yes Sir". "Hudson it looks like you could use some dentistry on your front teeth – report to the dental block after you've transferred to the Main establishment." "Yes Sir". I had been dreading such an order and since there had been no dental examination so far I thought I was clear.

At the passing out parade on our fourth Sunday Chief Soames took me aside "Hudson you've done well here – keep up the good work when you get to the Main Establishment." I was stunned – for four weeks I had kept my nose clean and applied myself as ordered – it had worked. I still realized that I was in a place that I had totally not anticipated and was ill equipped for on face value. Somehow I had done well in this environment. It was strict to the point of brainwashing but it succeeded in converting one hundred and twenty unruly, fifteen-year-old boys escaping from home into one hundred boys with new identities. Now wearing an official Royal Navy uniform and having passed the toughest boy's entry initiation in the world, the famous HMS Ganges Annex.

We had collectively come through a very tough experience and had individually achieved a new discipline and identity. The next day, after breakfast, we fell-in with kit-bags and marched to the Main Establishment. Exiting the Annex gates forever, I felt apprehension, what lay ahead as a "Nozzer" – the term given new boys coming from the Annex. Nozzers were the lowest form of life in the Ganges culture.

Chapter 11.

HMS Ganges – Main Establishment

The surviving New Entry assembled in Nelson Hall, the massive indoor drill shed adjacent to the vast Main Parade ground. Each boy was assigned to a mess, which became his class number and main identity. I was assigned to Anson Division 20 Mess - with twenty-five or so other boys – some of whom I'd known for four weeks – most I'd never met. Two Petty Officers introduced themselves as our new class instructors.

We were marched across the parade ground as a new squad "Anson 20" and down the Main Covered Way, under the downhill colonnade to the mess. It was a rectangular brick barn about a hundred and fifty feet long and thirty feet wide. The only way in was through the double doors off the colonnade. As you entered there was a washroom to the right – same set-up basically as the Annex – twenty stone sinks, each with one cold tap. To the left was the "night heads" – a single urinal and toilet – no privacy enclosures. Further to the right was the only heated room in the mess – it was called the drying room. A system of steam pipes fed from somewhere circulated heat through the room – clothes hanging racks covered the walls.

Two wide steps led down onto the main mess deck – a hundred and twenty feet of wood-block floor with a few steel framed windows. The brick walls were painted white. Along each side were fifteen steel frame beds, end to end. A set of bedding sat on each. At each bed-space there was a polished steel locker. By the time I got onto the main messdeck with my kit there were only beds at the back available. Right there I knew this new place was going to be very competitive.

Our Instructors, Petty Officers Stimpson and Bone were very different. They strode up and down the mess as we unpacked our kit bags and loaded them into the lockers. P.O Stimpson smoked and cursed. His face was red and puffy. He moved jerkily and occasionally whirled around as he walked up and down the mess. His lips and fingers had nicotine stains – and his uniform was very average. P.O. Bone, who was quickly assigned the nickname Doggy, was immaculate in his uniform, when he smiled he showed white even teeth, clear eyes and a sense of amiable control.

When he got to my bed-space Doggy Bone addressed me "Junior 2nd Class, what's your name?" "Hudson R. Sir" – the usual sniggers were audible. Doggy looked down at his clipboard – "You need to report to the Dentist Clinic". I felt ashamed in front of my new mess members – being called out for bad teeth. Looking up and down the mess I knew there was going to be a lot of competition in the washroom the drying room and for the two ironing boards. All the boys were looking around the same – eying each other up.

After falling in outside we were marched to the CMG – Central Messing Galley. Outside the huge two-story brick block we were discharged to dinner and ordered to return to the mess after.

A long queue of boys stretched up the stairs to the dining hall and around the walls until arriving at the entry door. Once inside the queue was even longer – snaking around three sides of the hall. We all wore khaki gaiters but here there were a few boys with white gaiters, as worn by the JI's. They were a strong symbol of the Ganges culture, known as Badge Boys. These boys did not queue - they went straight to the front. They were in charge of their mess and class - responsible for marching the squad around the Establishment and for discipline in the mess. It was the only rank a boy could gain in Ganges that privileged him above the others. Badge Boys were not required to strip and fold their bedding every day – meaning they did not compete for washroom space or ironing boards.

The food here was worse than the Annex. The CMG fed breakfast, dinner and supper for two thousand boys. It was mass production of largely tasteless and rubbery food. Eaten from steel compartment trays – served by uninterested chefs – most with tattoos of naked women and anchors on their arms. I never saw one smile. It was obvious the Navy chefs were more miserable than the boys and resented something, maybe their youth –there seemed no motivation whatsoever to cook good food. It was pure crap.

I found out on a subsequent work assignment that there was a large pen of pigs on the outskirts of the establishment that were fed almost exclusively on the waste food from the CMG.

Back in the mess we had an hour to ourselves – the first in four weeks. Most of the boys smoked and worked on kit and bedding. A few boys walked around eying up the others – nobody really said anything. Rocky Rooney and the Rat Starrat were in my mess. Boys in adjacent messes peered through their windows at us Nozzers.

At 1300 Doggy Bone and P.O. Stimpson returned. We were all assigned a watch, Port or Starboard and a "part of ship", which specified the area in the mess that was assigned as responsibility to upkeep.

Our first assignment was to scrub the entire floor, which was called the deck. We were given tubs of floor polish to be applied with our boot brushes. One line of eight scrubbers worked up the mess with another eight coming behind – buffing and shining. Behind them were two boys pushing heavy "bumpers" back and fro. These weighted blocks in a blanket put the final sheen on the floor. The rest were assigned to wet scrub the entire washroom and drying room. The night heads were painted red and green on the deck – we were instructed never to use them. During the process Doggy and P.O. Stimpson gave detailed instructions and assessed the efforts of each boy aloud.

On the way back to the mess after tea I followed the line of boys going into the NAAFI. This was the only shop available to boys at Ganges. NAAFI was the Navy Army Airforce Forces Institute – they handled all sales of incidentals in Navy ships and establishments. Another long line of boys snaked through the door and up to a counter with several servers. For sale were cigarettes, tobacco and rolling papers, sweets, washing powder, toothpaste and soap. That was it – one visit a week took about half the five-shillings pay for essentials and then you had to pay for fags. I decided to roll my own.

Back in the mess we cleaned up, laid our beds and worked on kit. Rocky Roony had his first fight in the washroom. The first I knew of it was Starrat running out of the washroom holding his nose gushing blood. Apparently he had got into an argument over splashing with Roony but before he could get in his classic head-butt Roony had landed two elbows to the face. It was game over. Starrat was again in the limelight for the wrong reasons.

Everyone pretty well knew that it was not a good idea to challenge Roony – I had known since the boxing final in the Annex. Starrat was proving he was a fool. When Roony emerged from the washroom he was bare chested and carrying his pajama top – on the back way to his bed space he drew up his chest to maximum and glared at each boy. No boy looked back at him defiantly – most looked away. Eventually about half way down the mess a boy stared back. It was Eason, a big boy from London, pushy and loud already. Roony kept stride, straight into Eason's bed space and beat him so badly in a matter of seconds Eason was sprawled on his bed bleeding from a hail of punches to his face. Looking on I noted Roony had not even used his head-butt – this was just a routine fight – just like smoking a cigarette. I was happy my bed space was at the end of the mess. All of a sudden there was a benefit from the inconvenience.

P.O. Stimpson returned to the mess at 2030 and ordered us to bed in fifteen minutes – he ignored the condition and appearance of Eason and Starrat and the blood still leaking from each of their faces. We laid there motionless until the Officer of the Day did rounds – checking that every bed had a boy in it. As the lights went out at 2100 P.O. Stimpson slammed the doors shut – screaming, "I'll be back soon – you better be ready Nozzers."

An uneasy atmosphere hung over the silent mess. Very few of us knew our new messmates – we were mostly from Annex classes that did not interact – it was a whole new Ganges experience.

As was the raid by Anson 24, the senior mess. These boys, a year and a half older, were about to pass out from Ganges. They were the elite communications class and bossed the establishment.

The doors to the mess burst open about fifteen minutes after lights out. An organized gang of raging older boys, in pajamas, destroyed the silence. In ten seconds a dozen beds had been overturned, with the boy underneath. The seniors formed a line across the mess as a few separated to grab two boys as they scrambled out from under their beds.

Once again I had benefited from being at the back of the mess. We all got out of bed and moved toward the back wall. Even Roony walked slowly back – not willing to take on twenty boys. I tried to fade into the background as they stripped the two boys from our mess. Both had their balls "blacked" – black boot polish applied with brushes.

Someone shouted, " fuck this – let's fight". Fight we did – there was so much built up anger of being put down for so long that on the first night of semi-freedom – being assaulted by seniority was the fuse that lit the bomb. Roony and I picked up a bed and threw it at oncoming gang – halting them immediately.

Buoyed by the change the rest of our boys charged toward the bed and the seniors trapped by it. We got in a lot of punches and kicks before, all of a sudden, they ran from the mess.

Someone switched on the lights as we stood around surveying the damage to our previously very organized and immaculate mess. Four Royal Marines entered the mess carrying batons. We were ordered to stand by our beds until a full count of all boys had been made. The marines didn't appear surprised, we were ordered to clean up and go back to bed. The marines left and the lights went out for the second time. Again the eerie, uneasy silence fell over the mess.

Dropping off to sleep I could feel my bed slightly shaking. The boy behind me, a skinny pockmarked lad from Cornwall was bashing the bishop. For me I had not even had the urge for a month. There was a rumor that saltpeter was added to our food because apparently it suppressed the sex urge. Maybe that was why the food tasted so chemical.

At 0500 P.O Stimpson returned in full nausea – banging the polished dustbin and screaming, "Roll out – Roll out - grab a towel and fall in outside – Move!" We formed our squad outside in the freezing and dark colonnade. P.O. Stimpson marched us about fifty yards to a shower building. Another long brick shed – this time with a line of thirty shower heads. "Strip off – Get in". Knowing the drill that a towel meant a shower I had grabbed my soap – some boys had not. We were given five minutes to shower in the steamy room and one minute to dry.

In ten minutes we were back outside and formed in our squad for the march back to the mess. A squad of twenty or so older boys came thundering past at the double – wearing tin helmets and oilskins. The marines from the night before were in charge of the squad. As they passed I recognized some of the faces of the class that raided us last night – they were being punished by the "Shotley Routine".

Back in the mess and folding my bedding I had another surprise. Garner, the tosser from last night had pissed the bed. I noticed it because he turned his mattress over – something we weren't required to do. Another thing about Garner I had noticed in the shower. He was a very skinny boy about five feet two or three like most of us – but his body was all bone – except this huge hanging sausage that almost reached the top of knee. It looked like I had drawn a shaky neighbor in the next bed space behind me.

In the bedspace in front of me was Lofty Brown from Brixton who was in my Annex mess. He was also very skinny and the only boy six feet tall. He was again assigned as our marker for all squad activity and parade drills. I had formed a friendship with Brown. He was a bit different – he didn't smoke or eat sweets. He saved as much of his pay as possible every week. We carried our cash in our money belts that was always worn regardless of rig. Lofty Brown was the only boy I had noticed who had notes in his money belt. The rest of us had five shillings in coins on payday only and it was soon gone.

At 0830 P.O.'s Stimpson and Bone marched us to the school block just outside the main gates. The colonnades and roadways were teeming with squads on their way to first classes of the day. All the class squads were about equal size of twenty-five to thirty and controlled by boys who wore the white gaiters – Badge Boys – the summit of power at Ganges.

In a school classroom we were given IQ tests, some arithmetic problems and a composition to write about why we joined the Royal Navy. I breezed through the tests and lied about why I had joined up. I had heard quite a few boys discussing trying to buy themselves out already. This notion was dashed by Doggy Bone who informed us there was no chance

We soon settled into a routine. There were two classes before dinner and one in the evening after tea. Classes were varied and included maths, English, science, seamanship, Naval History, ships and boats. The seaman boys had classes in gunnery and radar. In between we had three gym sessions a week, parade drills and rifle drills. We learned how to sail whalers and cutters and how to row them as a large crew – called boat-pulling. There were training sessions on the rifle ranges, also a full assault course.

In the afternoons we mustered at Anson Division Office - dressed in sports gear for Football, Rugby, Boxing, Sailing and Boat-pulling. There were two P.O. PTI's attached to our division. One of them, P.O. Price contacted me after a gym class of rope climbing, weight circuits and vaulting. "Hudson – we have you down as a possible for football, rugby, boxing and swimming - for the Division." I felt an immediate surge of energy. "Yes Sir". "O.k. Hudson following afternoon muster today report to me at the main sports field." "Yes Sir".

I was assigned to "higher" education class and separated from my messmates in school classes. One other boy from my mess was also assigned to the class. His name was Oakley and had already earned the nickname Annie, which he didn't like. Welcome to the club. He was from Birmingham and spoke as if he didn't know whether the sound should come from his mouth or his nose. Oakley was a chain-smoker. Before his feet hit the floor at 0500 he had lit a Weight and whenever he could throughout the day he would be dragging on one. His fingers on both hands were coated in nicotine. He received money in the post from his family so was able to buy a constant supply of Players Weights. Most boys had some money from home – or food parcels – the rest had to make it on five bob a week so it was four fags a day maximum ration.

Some boys could not hold to a set smoking amount and ran out after a few days. They tried to cadge drags off boys who still had smokes. Some boys borrowed money from other boys at interest. Lofty Brown had started loaning money for cigarettes at double back. So boys were paying two shillings to borrow a shilling before payday. He was making good profit – the chronic smokers seemed happy enough – until it came to forking over their pay on payday.

Another Nozzer class from our Entry moved into the mess next door, Anson 21. Among the boys were Jonah, Eddie Williams the boy from Wheatley on my first train and the big Geordie boy I beat in the boxing semi-finals. His name was Snodgrass, which was I thought only a name in books. He had a head that was as big as most boys chests. On it there was an almost flat face and a stack of ginger hair. His nose had obviously been broken a few times and scars on his forehead reminded me of his head-but. His massive chin reminded me of Desperate Dan from the Beano comic. We had passed a couple of times in squads since the Annex boxing and I noticed he appeared to be looking for someone and then when he saw me his gaze became fixed in a sneering stare into my face.

On the sports field after a week of trials P.O. Price told me I was in the Anson first team for football and rugby and a possibility for Ganges second team in Rugby. My assistant

Divisional Officer was a rugby man and wanted Anson boys playing for the ship. I achieved rugby second fifteen, playing at fly-half. It was a huge honor and an unexpected success. My scrum-half was also in my mess – a boy from Hull who was a natural. He was small in height but packed with muscle and one of the toughest boys I had ever met. His name was Catt so he got the nickname Korky.

It was go, go, and go from 0600 in the morning until 2100 lights out. There were a couple of other athletes in the mess. Roony was in boxing and rugby, Korky was in rugby. A welsh boy called Owen was in the other Nozzer class in the mess next to ours. He was already in the Ganges first fifteen rugby, playing wing forward. Jimmy Green proved to be a skilled coxswain and was soon given a cox's white sweater. I could tell we were being tested and evaluated as Badge Boy candidates.

There was a constant stream of parade and rifle drills – mostly instructed by Doggy. Two more swimming tests were given in the first month in the main establishment. The second required jumping from a high board in overalls, swimming two lengths and treading water for five minutes. A lot of boys failed – some afraid to jump in overalls. They were placed as backward swimmers and had to report to the pool at 0615 three days a week until they passed the test. Also they were singled out in musters and class assessments. "Backward swimmer" was "weak fool" in the minds of some boys.

There was a lot of arguing and swearing on the mess deck – particularly over the irons and ironing boards. Scuffles were expected every day and full-on fights were common. Rocky Roony was methodically working his way through the mess in one or two fights a week. I noticed he started to bait me a bit – especially when I was in charge of marching the squad. "Are you Doggy's boy then Rock?" he would say when the class was dismissed. The last thing I wanted was to fight Roony. It was bad enough in a ring wearing gloves – when he finished in a mess fight there was blood and scars.

I was having big problems getting by on the five bob a week. We were paid on Thursdays and normally by Monday most boys were broke. Only the few boys who didn't smoke or those getting pocket money from home had any money for fags.
Annie Oakley started selling single Weights at three pence each – to be paid next payday – a few boys started getting into serious debt because it was the only way to get a smoke.

Ganges wasn't like Oxford where you could just steal everything easily, including money. There was nothing to steal here – unless it was to break into the NAAFI or steal from your messmates. We had been brainwashed early on that a mess thief is an outcast – the worst form of human life – branded a "tea-leaf" in naval jargon – a despised hand on any ship.

By early December, apart from a couple of early departures, we had formed into a loosely connected group of twenty-three boys. A few cliques had developed. The boys from Scotland banded together, as did the boys from London and Liverpool areas. Boys from the South like me did not identify with anyone really. I connected with Lofty Brown and Korky Catt. Also a boy from Aberdeen who spoke so slowly and deliberately that you felt compelled to listen intently. His name was Jock Taggart. He was without doubt the best looking boy in the mess. A perfect specimen – everything about his face, hair, body, build and posture was eye-catching. He didn't seem to notice because he just did everything right – and every day kept a low profile.

Doggy Bone called me aside one morning before muster. "Hudson you've been selected as acting Leading Boy – well done". "Report to Commander's Orders at 1000". "Yes Sir". It was the best day of my life. I had a feeling that I had not experienced or anticipated before. All of a sudden I was elevated into an extremely coveted position. The "Badge Boy "in charge of my class and mess. Although I really wanted it, I never thought I would get it. That was not how my life normally worked. It was a big change – it felt good, very good.

As Badge Boy I was issued with white gaiters and a blue and white bed quilt. My bed was moved to the head of the mess and I was excused from daily stripping and folding. I became responsible for reporting the mess as secure to the Officer of Rounds at "pipe-down" or bed-time. I gave the orders to fall in and ordered the muster. At the CMG I no longer queued – walking straight to the servery – as did all Badge Boys. It was a huge surge of energy – a feeling of unexpected power. As Badge Boy I also earned sixpence a day extra.

I began to take pride in my kit and appearance – I wanted to stand out as a Badge Boy totally dedicated to the Ganges culture of spit and polish. The Dentist told me I needed to have "caps" applied to my front teeth or have them pulled out and have false teeth fitted. He didn't ask me which option I preferred and proceeded to use a miniature rotary saw on the drill to cut my front teeth into points. The pain was worse than I had experienced in Oxford – by far. After the sawing the Dentist glued a pair of caps over the points. I was amazed at the result. I no longer had to hide the stained and failing fillings in my front teeth – I could smile. I began to feel even more feelings of self worth.

In boxing training I was getting incredible support from PO Price and the other PTI's. They encouraged me to use the balance and speed of movement I'd developed in Judo – getting into better and unexpected positions to land hooks and overarm punches. In the Main establishment I was a weight under Rocky Roony so did not have to fight him for a team place. I did often spar with him in training. Occasionally at the end of a sparring round the PTI ordered thirty seconds of "let the gloves fly". Roony came after me like a charging bull in those seconds whenever he could. PO Price started to question me why I smoked – he said it didn't make sense for a boxer to smoke. I felt dejected – I had thought smoking was my main purpose in life.

Most of the boys in the mess accepted me as Badge Boy – all of them were jealous of my place. Some boys gave me a stiff stare or turn of the shoulder at orders. Only Roony and a boy from Plymouth – Jackson J. – nicknamed "Jan" gave me active opposition – attempting to goad me into a fight at least once a week. Jan Jackson was a very burly boy – he wanted to play rugby but lacked the speed and coordination. He also tried out as a coxswain and failed. In the gym he would stand next to me and make comments about how the instructors loved me. In the mess he was building a small group of dissenters – they were boys that were struggling to keep up with the stringent kit inspections and shirked duties or sports. One troubling point was that Jan Jackson was friends with Ginger Snodgrass as the Geordie had had become known. Snodgrass occupied the same position in Anson 21 as

Roony did in my mess, Anson 20. He was the street fighter to take on anyone – but unlike Roony he was a pure bully.

Christmas was approaching, with home leave for two weeks. I started to dread the release back to the outside world. All the boys were massively excited about going home. Bungy Williams asked me where I would be for Christmas – I told him I wasn't really sure yet. He said I could stay at his house in Wheatley – his Mum and Dad ran the Railway Hotel pub. Also Lofty Brown told me I could stay at his house in Brixton – both of them gave me their addresses – Bungy's house had a phone.

My competitive ability developed at the same pace as my physical growth and fitness. In rugby and football I was in the Division first team. I'd had four inter division bouts at eight-stone seven and won them all. I began to look forward to boxing training and the official bouts. I qualified as a coxswain and obtained the coveted white jersey and gold arm badge.

Before I knew it Christmas leave was the next morning. Stimp crashed through the mess at 0330 and herded us to the showers. We were all ready with towel and soap and I joined in the excitement of pending freedom. By 0430 we were mustered outside the mess in full number one uniform, wearing burberries and carrying kit bags. I marched the squad to the main parade ground and into lines moving into Nelson Hall. The vast indoor parade ground was packed with boys collecting their leave pay and travel warrants. Many desks were set up and manned by Writers doing the issuing. There were quite a few officers hovering around.

Eventually we collected our pay – mine was four pounds and three shillings – comprised of pay that had been withheld and "leave pay" to be given to parents or whoever is providing shelter and food during the leave period. My train warrant was to Oxford via London. We boarded a fleet of busses that delivered us at Ipswich Station for special trains to London, Liverpool Street. On the bus with Bungy Williams and Lofty Brown I sat in silence as we drove through the main gate and passed the road to the Annex. In fifteen weeks I had changed enormously without really noticing. In those fifteen weeks my transformation had been caused by a rigid hour-by-hour system of action. The action was demanded but I had learned that if you put in more effort than the basic demand – there were potential big rewards. Reflecting on the difference between Ganges and Oxford I recognized the Navy men were fairer and had no airs and graces – also not so many had nicotine stains and were clean and shiny.

The train to London was crammed with Ganges boys with some money and freedom rarely experienced. In the carriages there were games of 3-card brag that boys were loosing their leave pay on. I followed Lofty Brown through the train as he picked up his debts from loans and cigarette sales. His money belt was bulging. No boy complained, even those I knew were broke for leave – and Lofty never flinched when requiring and collecting payment – he was always ready to lend more at a higher rate.

Lofty Brown was adamant that I would be welcome at his home so I went with him to Brixton on the tube. His family were incredibly kind with one younger brother who was in awe of Lofty. He was also tall and gave me some of his old clothes that fit well. His Mum was suspicious that I had not gone to my own home right away and kept asking me why my parents weren't worried. So after three days Lofty escorted me to Paddington and I was on my way to Oxford – full of trepidation and really not knowing where I could stay.

I stood in the corridor as the train rolled through Hinksey – noting my house on Bertie Place and all the houses on Wytham Street, Haynes Icecream factory and the Bowls Club. It was a strange feeling to be back– an area where I had learned to be a tramp.

It was two days before Christmas and much too cold to camp out in the hills – all the churches were busy so all the secluded hiding places were vulnerable. After walking from the station to Queen Street I sat at a window table in Crawford's looking down on the afternoon shoppers. The queer manager came up to my table – "well look at you sailor – are you getting lots of fun"? I wanted to disappear from the embarrassment but he was in his element. "Have you seen the golden rivet yet?" I kept staring out of the window, avoiding eye contact. "Well you can always get some fun here if you like". I kept my head down as I put my cap on and picked up my kitbag.

I walked to Queen's Lane along High Street – passing all the shops I used to steal from and the entrances to the covered market – and by-passing all the Gentlemen's toilets I knew would be experiencing many visitors at this popular time. The bus to Wheatley took twenty minutes – the conductor gave me a free fare for being in uniform. I found the Railway Hotel, which was closed. The bell was answered by Bungy – "Fucking hell oppo – what are you doing here?"

There were five other children in the house. Two older sisters worked in the pub – the oldest, Bungy's brother was an apprentice bricklayer. A younger brother and sister made up the six. Bungy's Mum was a very attractive lady with very large tits and the main attraction at the pub. His Dad was a huge stone-faced, bald, vacant looking hulk that seemed incapable of conversation. Behind the bar though he was a jovial Landlord –"Jekyll and Hyde" was his reputation.

I slept in a sleeping bag on the floor of Bungy's bedroom – which he shared with his younger brother who was thirteen. I thought about going to my house. But I could not visualize my parents' faces any more – I just saw a blur that would not clear. My house was no longer a home. And it was a place that had punished me for all my life. Why would I want to go back there? I could not explain the feeling to myself. But after careful thought I decided there was nothing there for me except more hatred and abuse.

Bungy's sister started flirting with me and touching me every opportunity she had in the pub. One evening she followed me outside and I led her into the side garden. In an instant she kissed me so hard I almost fell over. After that we just rubbed against each other until it became impossible not to touch. The moment she cupped my balls I was shooting again. Her quim was the first I had really touched for a long time. Before I knew it Bungy's dad was rushing towards me with a torch. It was too late to cover up. He was half drunk and fully mad – his size and momentum flattened me on the ground. He kicked me in the ribs and the back of the head as I covered up. I scrambled up and ran into the pub as the girl screamed at her father. I thought he was going to come into Bungy's bedroom at any second as I picked up my kit bag and headed for the back door. Bungy was beside himself laughing. "See you on the train back to Ganges Rock".

Ganges would have been heaven at that moment. I tied my cap to the top of my kit bag and held it up to the traffic on London Road as I thumbed a lift back to Oxford. A lorry driver stopped and asked me where I was going. I told him Hinksey Park. He dropped me at Carfax. Looking up at the clock the hammers struck the outside bells ten times. It was New Years Eve tomorrow – I had to survive for three more days before I could board the train back to Ganges. Options were not coming into my thoughts – a frenzied mind was overwhelming me. I stared across at the elegantly dressed mannequins in the window of Pages. In one hand I held my kit bag, my future – the other was empty – Oxford had drained me again. I thought about my life back in the mess where I was the most important boy and didn't have to fend off queers and mad people.

Instinctively walking back to Hinksey I stopped at the Gentlemen's toilets on Blue Boar Street next to the Town Hall and Library. I dropped a penny into the slot and sat down to have a smoke. There were glory holes both sides and a lot of drawings of cocks shooting and ads for boys.

Pretty soon someone came in to the cubicle next to me. Right away his tapping foot was approaching the small gap at the bottom of the separating wall. A paper wad popped out from on of the smaller holes and I could see an eye looking through. Maybe I could make some money here – my stomach churned – and I sat trembling on the seat in this stinking place. I was totally confused – unable to accept or figure out why I was getting hard.

Another paper plug popped out and through the hole I saw a finger beckoning. I stood up and dropped my trousers and underpants – showing my stiffness. Then I chickened out and started to pull up my clothes.

The door shook as it was banged three times – "Oxford Police – open the door immediately – repeat Oxford Police – Open the door now". Before I could get my trousers up the door burst open and a policeman grabbed me and pulled me out. Another policeman stood by watching. The door to the next cubicle opened - a man walked out and began talking to the other policeman – who checked his watch and removed his notebook from his tunic pocket.

The policeman who had dragged me out asked my name and address. I gave him my home address on Bertie Place. "How old are you?" "Sixteen – I lied." "What are you doing here young man? "Nothing – having a smoke – on my way home on leave". "Did you just engage in lewd behavior young man?" 'No sir – the man next door did it". "The man next door young man, is a police constable and is giving his witness statement to my colleague." I was flabbergasted and stunned to silence. 'We will be in touch with your parents young man – you should warn them about this offense. Now get along and don't be using public lavatories in a perverted way."

Making my way back to Hinksey Park I could think of nothing but escape from Oxford – again. Why did Oxford always punish and reject me? Two options became apparent as I picked up yet another fish and chips in St.Ebbes.

After a freezing night sleeping on my kit bag, on the floor in an allotment shed, I was back at Oxford station Toilets washing my face and brushing my teeth.

I decided to go back to the Seaman's home in Guildford – my cash was almost out and I was determined not to steal again – no matter how hungry I was. The trains over to Guildford were slow and involved changes. All the time I reflected on my situation – would the Oxford Police summons me or would they drop it because I was at Ganges. I already had the three year suspended sentence on my juvenile offender record – hanging now was another unexpected cloud over my future.

The Seaman's Home manager had changed since January. I pleaded my case that I needed bed and food for three days and would work for it – I had nowhere else to go. The manager seemed sympathetic to my situation but said I would have to work eight hours a day in the Home for my board. Thank god this nightmare leave was almost over I thought as I lay down in a bed with clean bedding and a pillow. The work in the Home was not too bad. The galley was nothing like the grease pit and cockroaches of Ganges. The chefs were ladies and very nice to me. I spent most of my work time washing dishes. The ladies gave me cigarettes also.

I was down to about one and six in cash when I put on my perfectly prepared uniform to leave the Seaman's Home bound for Ganges – I discarded my threadbare civvy clothes in the dustbin – they were not allowed at Ganges. The trains to Ipswich were packed with Ganges boys returning. I started to feel relaxed again – there was a lot of banter and laughter – something I hadn't experienced for a while. There was intimidation and self-doubt in my mind surrounding this Oxford experience – I tried to bury it in determination to excel again in Ganges life.

My messmates slowly trickled back into the mess and started to get organized again. We were now "old hands" – a term which meant you had completed four months at Ganges. By teatime we were all back from leave. All the boys had food parcels and money from home except me and Annie Oakley. The boys shared their food but not their fags – it was time to stop smoking again. As I stood for Officer of the Day rounds it felt good to be back in my new life again.

At 0500 the next morning Stimp was beating the dustbin with broom shouting "your mum's not waking you up any more – get out of the rack Jack you're on duty". We doubled to the showers and woke up on the way.

Garner stood next to me. "Did you have a good leave Rock?" Nodding toward him I immediately noticed he was tossing off. I felt sad for Garner – he was a different queer – he wanted me to be his friend as well as sex. I turned my back on him but felt an arousal. This and other encounters were baffling - and why did these queers always think I was open for it?

The crisp-air stride to breakfast in faded 8's, mirror-shine boots and white gaiters was like going over for a try or smashing a goal, but constant, not over in a minute or so. My status in Ganges was special, and I had achieved it myself.

Boxing and rugby training started up again on the second day back from leave. By the third day I stopped smoking again. The CMG food was still as bad as ever but puddings and custard were somehow good and were available at dinner and tea. It became my main food source. Other boys had different likes. There was always plenty of marmalade put out in bowls at breakfast and tea. A lot of boys made marmalade sandwiches from the infinite supply of sliced white bread and margarine. The sandwiches were then smuggled out under shirts to be heated up with irons.

Anson rugby team was beating all other divisions - several boys were on the ship's teams – including myself at rugby and boxing. P.O. Price coached me three times a week – I felt like each session I grew in skill and stamina – I had never encountered any person before like this – all he wanted was total loyalty and in return you received total support.

My mess and Blake 4 mess were selected for the ceremonial man-the-mast coming up at the Parent's Day soon in the Summer. Korky was selected as Button Boy in the first trial, an amazing feat, one boy selected from two thousand. He was the perfect choice, with a fear-nothing attitude and an athletic body almost designed to stand on the button. As my scrum-half I was energized by his achievement and the sheer magnitude of it. Only a very small list of boys over the history of HMS Ganges had been "Button Boy" for the annual ceremonial event.

I was proud to be selected as one of two boys manning the half-moon – just two stands below the button. Every practice I looked up and saw Korky effortlessly salute and stand to attention in strong and eddying winds – 142 feet up on a wood disc about 18 inches wide – his slightly bent knees gripping the lightning conductor. On the Half-moon we held the ratlines with one hand and swung out during the ceremonial tune by the Royal Marine Band.

Serious training for upcoming seamanship exams was also underway. Doggy and Stimp led endless classes on rope work, boats, rules of the road, navigation and naval history. In a class one morning the Badge Boy on Commanders' Messenger for the week knocked and entered. "Yes?" Doggy enquired. "Leading Boy Hudson to report to the Main Gate Sir." "Roger that – Hudson off you go at the double". I ran up the long colonnade and over the Quarterdeck. Being called to the Main Gate usually meant trouble but I had done nothing wrong so an excitement came over me – maybe I was going to get my P.O. Boy rate – the ultimate as a Ganges Boy.

I reported to the Leading Patrolman at the Main Gate – he instructed me to report inside to the Regulating Petty Officer on duty. At the desk the R.P.O motioned me to follow him and led me to an office marked "Master At Arms". "Leading Boy Hudson R. – is that you Boy?" "Yes Sir". Turning to one of two other older men in civilian clothes the Master At Arms said "Hudson this is detective-sergeant Graham from Oxford Constabulary " and turning to the other "and this is Dr. Malcolm from Royal Navy recruitment services". My heart sank immediately and that old feeling of panic and confusion rushed in – to make it worse I recognized the doctor as the one that examined me in Portsmouth last year.

The Detective spoke "Are you Roy Hudson of Bertie Place, Oxford?" "Uh yes Sir that was my home address." "What do you mean "was" your home address Hudson?"
"I left there last year Sir". "Are you saying your home address is HMS Ganges?" "Yes Sir."
"Hudson that is not the case" interrupted the Master At Arms. "The Navy houses, feeds and pays you but your

home is where your family is Boy – do you have a family?"
"Yes Sir."

The Detective spoke again – "Roy Hudson, on December 30th 1954 you were apprehended for lewd behavior in a public place, namely the Gentlemen's Toilets at 17 Blue Boar Street, Oxford. The Oxford Police were unable to summons you at the address provided at the time of apprehension. You are hereby summonsed for lewd behavior in a public place and for absconding without informing the Police." He thrust a white envelope against my chest until I took it in my hands.

"Do you have anything to say Hudson?" The Master At Arms probed. My brain was so scrambled I could not think of anything except "I didn't mean anything bad Sir – it happened without me really knowing." "Why did your parents say that you did not live at home Hudson?" "I don't know Sir." "When did you last speak to your parents Hudson?" "Uh last year Sir." "Before you joined Ganges Hudson?" I felt as I was sinking in mud – "Uh yes Sir."

The Master expanded his chest and puffed his crimson streaked cheeks to order "Leading Boy Hudson Hhaww." I snapped to attention. "Left turn – quick march – report to the R.P.O." Outside the office the R.P.O. took my arm and escorted me to a small room with a steel cell door. "Hudson you are going to be charged with bringing disrepute on the Royal Navy. Strip off to your underwear and empty all contents of your clothes into the tray provided."

I felt degraded again – back in the land of punishment for punishment's sake – defeating my whole image of the Navy and my new life. It was gone in an instant and the unbelievable kept happening – Oxford was shadowing me and hunting me into as much punishment as they could bring.

I was given a cell uniform and locked up. There was nothing in the cell except a steel toilet and sink, and a cot bed with a straw mattress and hairy blanket. A bible was propped against the pillow. The thought occurred to me this was worse than my tramp camp in Chiswell Hills, much worse.

Soon I was escorted to an interview room with Dr. Malcolm. "Sit down Hudson let's see what is going on here. Are you a homosexual Hudson?" "No Sir." "Then why did you expose your erection to the undercover policeman?" "I didn't mean to Sir – it was a mistake – it wasn't meant to be homosexual Sir." "Have you done this before Hudson – this is not the first time you've visited these toilets is it?" "No Sir." "You knew the holes in the walls were there didn't you Hudson?" "Yes Sir but..". "Never mind but Hudson – you were there for a homosexual act weren't you Hudson?" "No Sir – for a smoke".

"Why did you not go home on leave Hudson?" "Sir I was not welcome there." "Why not Hudson?" "Because I did not get on with my parents Sir." "Or your brother either Hudson according to the reports." "Did you steal from your parents Hudson?" I remained silent. "Were you trying to prostitute yourself Hudson – hoping to trap a homosexual into paying you?"

The R.P.O. escorted me to the mess and stood over me as I put my toilet gear and a towel in my attaché case and got my paybook from the draw in my locker. "Get one set of underwear and one pair of socks Hudson."

Back in the cell I was dazed and confused – in slow motion. How had this happened to me? How had my new good world fallen apart in two hours? The sneers on the faces of the policemen, the doctor and the Master at Arms gnawed their way into my mind. I vomited in the steel toilet bolted to the cement floor. The door clanged open and a Leading Patrolman handed me a coil of coarse rope. "Start picking that apart Hudson." The door slammed shut like a steel trap.

In about an hour or so I was marched to Commander's Defaulters. "Leading Boy Hudson "Off-Caps". I removed my cap smartly and correctly as drilled. The Master At Arms read the charge. "Leading Boy Hudson committed a lewd act in public while on leave and was apprehended by the Oxford Police for same – having now been summonsed to appear before Oxford Court."

"What do you have to say Hudson?" My brain was overwhelmed. It seemed I should beg – but what about and for what? I had told the truth. I was trapped in a deliberate effort to punish me again. I knew it but not why or who was pursuing me to such lengths. "It was a mistake Sir" – my voice was trembling and hardly capable of mumbling. "Ordered to Captain's Defaulters as charged," the Commander sighed as if in disgust. "On-caps – right turn - quick march" bellowed the Master as the R.P.O. fell in alongside me in escort back to my cell.

In a few minutes the door clanged open and I was ordered back into Defaulter position. Soon I was facing the Captain behind the now familiar lectern. I was virtually unable to think or speak. Dr.Malcolm stood a little behind him to the side. "Leading Boy Hudson "Off-Caps". I removed my cap smartly and correctly as drilled. The Master At Arms read aloud "Leading Boy Hudson is charged with committing a lewd act in public while on leave and was apprehended by the Oxford Police for same – having now been summonsed to appear before Oxford Court."

"What do you have to say Hudson?" – the Captain's voice sounded vexed. "This is a very serious charge Hudson and has resulted in the Oxford Police serving a summons in HMS Ganges". "Do you have anything to say that might help you avoid the most serious punishment Hudson?" "It was a mistake Sir – I didn't mean anything bad." 'Well Hudson I'm afraid that is not good enough." "Dr. Malcolm can you advise here?"
The Doctor moved forward alongside the Captain. "Yes Sir – Hudson has shown erratic and reckless behavior in his short time in the Royal Navy. Including several encounters with Police. It appears Hudson is in denial about his homosexual leanings but is willing to engage in homosexual acts – to the extent that his activities were noticed by Oxford Police Sir."

"Thank you doctor" the Captain's eyes fixed on mine. "Leading Boy Hudson you have brought disrepute on the Royal Navy. The Royal Navy will not tolerate such behavior from a Boy Seaman entrant. You are herewith de-rated to Boy 2nd Class, ordered to receive 12 cuts per the Admiralty Punishment Code and discharged from the Royal Navy immediately thereafter. Do you understand the punishment Hudson?" For the first time I sobbed – I could not help it. I saw the look on the faces around me and realized it was hopeless. There was nobody in the world now remotely concerned about me – I was about to be flogged and thrown out of the Navy – my dream was gone forever.

For dinner and tea I had a meal of naval hard biscuits and water. During a sleepless night I thought up a survival plan – there was no other choice now. At 0500 the R.P.O. clanged open the door and ordered me into the shower cubicle. He stood and watched as I showered and dried. He then led me to a locker of civilian clothes and tossed me a pair of jeans, a grey shirt and a tweed jacket – all were threadbare and musty. "You will be wearing these when you are discharged today Hudson – take them to your cell."

By 0600 I stood in front of the Master At Arms desk. "These are your discharge papers Hudson – give them to your parents - we will also notify them directly. Your parents are responsible for you Hudson – not the Royal Navy anymore. Do you understand Hudson?" I stared back. "This is your pay that has accumulated in your savings account since joining HMS Ganges – there has been a deduction for the cost of the uniform you were issued with. There is a rail warrant to Oxford. Good luck Hudson."

In the cell I dressed in the junk civvies and thought about the ordeal coming up. I had seen Starrat's ass after 6 cuts – this would be the worst punishment yet – but then I remembered the worst was still to come. Starrat had survived 6 to brag about it almost. I would survive 12 cuts but the thought of total abandonment and isolation was an impossible problem to solve – the nightmare kept flashing in my mind.

At 0700 the R.P.O. marched me from the cell. I was dressed ready to be thrown out – except no underwear. In a large room off the cells I was led to vault-horse and stood to attention before it. The Master read out the charge and the punishment again. The R.P.O. then strapped me on in a bent over position. My trousers were stretched over my buttocks and the R.P.O.'s held my arms down. The Master-at-Arms picked up a four-foot wicker cane and flexed it to my side view. The Captain and Dr. Malcolm stood to one side and I noticed the Ship's Head Chaplain had joined the group witnessing my shaming.

"Permission requested for one Cut Sir" The Master upped his voice. "Yes please Master" the Captain's voice was terse.

Two seconds ticked before I heard a whoosh and then a razor sharp rip hit my ass. My legs kicked away involuntarily and I flailed like a fish on the vault-horse. A head jerk and shriek of pain caused me to bite on my tongue. The taste of fresh blood in my mouth was sickening and added to my despair. The second cut was delivered in the same way, with the same words and same timing. No one except the Master and the Captain spoke.

Each cut seemed to take forever before the deadly swoosh and slash. I managed to stifle my pain reactions by forcing my face into the vault-horse – trying to bite the thick hide. My knees would not stop shaking and as I was led away – wobbling and hopping – it was extremely difficult to stand up and walk normally. My entire lower body was numb.

Chapter 12.

On the Run

Detective-sergeant Graham escorted me back to Oxford. It felt like a mountain of dirt had buried me and each way I looked was completely dark and airless. At the Police Station in St. Aldates I was questioned again. "You will be released on remand Hudson and must return to Magistrates Court as summonsed. "Do you understand that homosexual behavior is against the law?" "I'm not homosexual Sir" "Then why were you apprehended for a homosexual act Hudson?" I had no answer anymore. "Now Sergeant Graham will escort you home Hudson". "I don't have a home Sir." "For our purposes Hudson you are a minor, your home is with your parents now that you are no longer in the Royal Navy."

As the police car pulled up outside my house my mother was looking through the window. Sergeant Graham told her I had been charged with lewd conduct and the Navy had discharged me for bringing disrepute. My mother's face was fierce and twisted in anger. "Can he not be put away?" "Not before he's tried Mrs. Hudson." "That's where he belongs Sergeant" she spat.

The sergeant left as soon as he could and I determined to be right behind him – I had an hour before my father would be home. I realized there was only one option left now – to run. I brushed past my mother and went to my bedroom. I heard her leave the house.

In my brother's room I took a few clothes that fit. In my parents' room I took all the money in the draw and a locked savings box from the Bank. I had nothing to lose now - I had been expelled from the High School and now the Navy - I knew I had to escape the world that continually flowed against - I had to run again, but this time far away.

Under Hinksey Lake bridge I recovered my sheath knife and fishing tackle. Up in Chiswell Hills I recovered my water bottle and cook-pan. My rucksack was still there concealed in a horse chestnut tree about twenty feet up – with my groundsheet and the rest of my fishing tackle.

I caught the bus at the bottom of Lake Street – next to the Gents Toilets. I noticed a couple of well-known queers get of the 13 Bus from Abingdon as I waited for the 8 into Carfax. As I walked passed the Gents Toilets in St. Giles there was a lot of men going down the stairs – a few were recognizable – this was always the busiest time here – with the Gown going to and fro to drink and dine – why not drop in to the Toilets in St. Giles for a little distractive fun, eh what chaps? I wondered if there were Police watching – waiting to pick some unfortunate tourist to go after. For sure it would not be a young man in college attire or a professor in tweed suit and brown trilby. Maybe that's why they called them "brown hatters" in the Navy.

Passing T.E. Lawrence's family home at 2 Polstead Road I thought about what my father said about him – that he was a queer who paid boys for sex and my Uncle had been his batman in the RAF. I entered the Judo Club building through the normal side window and removed all the cash in the box.

It was fully dark as I entered the cricket pavilion at my old school sports ground on Marston Ferry Road. There was nothing to steal here except a few bars of chocolate but my bike was still safely concealed in the attic. With a chisel from the toolbox I pried open the cash box. There was one pound sixteen shillings. This brought my total to almost ten pounds. There was absolutely no more in my foreseeable future

From there I cycled as far as Burford – I reckoned it was ten miles, which was half my day's goal. At the Burford roundabout I followed the signs to Cheltenham until about 0500 when, exhausted, I made a shelter in the bushes close to a layby.

It took four days to cycle from Oxford to Penygraig. I followed the coach route – sleeping in lay-by's – stopping in Cheltenham, Gloucester, Ross-on-Wye, Monmouth and eventually at Pontypridd and the Rhondda. I cycled along dark and deserted roads at night and hid beside them during the day – the dawn was always welcome – time to collapse into a fitful sleep as the day's traffic commenced.

Needing to buy new tires and food along the route I was depleting my funds fast. My body was almost skeletal – living on raw vegetables, thankfully in season, fish and chips and occasional meat pies and crisps. Anger was building daily – I began to imagine killing my brother – then my father – then all the perverts that had hounded me.

At 0900 the fourth day I was in Pontypridd at the market place. In South Wales – no one cared who you were but if you spoke with an English accent you were viewed suspiciously. I started practicing my welsh accent again.

Around 1200 I stopped at the Porth Public Swimming Pool and paid three pence to get in. The showers were cold but washing five days of road dust and sweat from my body felt good. As I set out over the mountain heading for Tonypandy a feeling of freedom and accomplishment overcame the fear of my failure.

Dropping down through Pandy into Penygraig I first went to the tip behind Aunt Joy's house. Nothing had changed except the tip was much steeper and longer. The house was quiet as I eased the door in the back garden wall and peered in. The pantry was still almost empty, as I remembered it – no food was visible, and no movement detectable.

From there I went to the hill above Lyn's family flat and watched for any sign of him. It was getting late in the afternoon – if he was still in school he would be coming home soon. If he was already working shifts in the pits, as likely, who knew when he would be home?

After an hour I decided to approach the flat and knock on the door. I was quite positive no one would recognize me as I practiced my welsh accent. Lyn's mother opened the door slightly and peered out. "What?" she exhaled in a boozy breath. "Is Lyn Home Mrs.?" "He doesn't live here anymore – who are you?" This lady was nothing like I remembered. "I'm a friend from school." "He's up in the mountains somewhere – his father won't have him in the house anymore – nobody wants him." This sounded very familiar to me but I had not expected Lyn to be in the same position.

I checked in the snooker hall and the Plaza but no sign of Lyn or any boy I knew. My hunger was extreme by dinnertime when I bought faggots, peas and chips at the chip shop in Pandy. I was down to less than five pounds now – still a lot of money but without any paydays in sight it would soon be gone.

That night I slept in the Trealaw cemetery against the stone wall looking down on the railway. The railway would be my way out of Penygraig if I couldn't find Lyn. I would then have to get to Cardiff as the only possible way to survive. I had heard at Ganges that some merchant ships from Cardiff would take on seaman without identity papers.

In the morning I was in Pandy Square just after dawn and got a cup of tea from the Brachy's as soon as they opened. I waited – looking up the mountains – hoping to see Lyn coming to the boxing gym. If he was still alive and still the Lyn I knew and loved he would still be boxing. Soon a boy I knew, Gareth Evans, walked toward the gym. Evans told me Lyn was sometimes at a gypsy camp on Nantgwyn – he didn't know the location. "He was banned from training." "Why?" "He beat up his father."

After trekking back up the mountain for my bike and gear I dropped down again into Penygraig, along Nantgwyn to Gilfach Road and up into the mountains again following the miners paths over to the Gilfach colliery.

It was getting colder by the minute as I climbed the hilly paths leading to a thickly wooded copse halfway up the mountain. Coming toward the copse I could see whitish smoke rising on the far side. I circled round and all of a sudden three Jack Russell terriers were going berserk in front of me. Soon on the scene was a young boy followed by a man that could be his father. They were both dressed like travellers that I knew worked and lived in the mountains.

"I'm Tudor - are you lost Dai?" "No I'm looking for my butty Lyn – I heard he may be up here." "Who wants to know Dai?" "Just me – we're friends – like brothers – I've come from Oxford to find him."

Lyn jumped out of the bushes – "Rock is that yew?" he screamed. For the first time - in a very long time – I felt a sense of belonging somewhere. "What are you doing here Rock?" "I got kicked out of the Navy after five months and before that I was kicked out of my house – this is the only place I know that I could hide from the Oxford Police." "What did you do?" "Nothing much – bit of stealing."

Tudor eyed me suspiciously. "Can Rock stay here in my tent tonight? " "Are the Coppers after you Dai?" "Not here I don't think sir." "How did you get here?" "I came on my bike sir – I hid myself most of the way." "Well you can stay tonight but we can't hide anyone that the coppers are chasing." I realized the lie had backfired on me. I was not a burglar or thief – nor was I a queer. I was running from the constant hatred and punishment – not from any crimes.

Lyn was living in a small tent hidden in the bushes about fifty yards from the traveller's encampment. The smoke I'd seen was from several open fires of logs and coal. Over each fire were sturdy iron poles driven into the ground, with a hook at the end. On the hooks hung various types of pots and kettles. Chickens were scratching the dirt and several ponies were tethered to a rail and feed trough.

Traveller families were gathered around the stairs to their carts. A long arched tent with a gap at the opening for a fire, was opposite each cart. All the children and their mothers looked closely at me as we made our way to Lyn's tent. It was bare – just a covered sleeping place that required your own groundsheet and sleeping bag. A candle gave enough light to see inside.

Lyn, like me, had changed. He was taller but seemed less robust – he was now seventeen and yet, still before my sixteenth birthday, I sensed I was stronger and fitter. Late into the night we told each other of our experiences since we parted five years ago.

My story was wide, zigzag and rollercoaster where Lyn's was still all focused on his family and the Valley. He was kicked out of his house for stabbing his father with a pair of scissors as he was raping his younger brother. His brother's screams had wakened the whole house – his mother had a nervous breakdown over the incident and was now an alcoholic recluse. He said he was drinking any alcohol he could get and was planning a burglary in Pandy to steal wine and cigarettes from a Chemist's shop.

Lyn had found his current shelter by meeting Tudor at a miner's fair. Tudor was fighting bare-knuckle – all comers about the same weight – for two shillings a round of two minutes. If you did not survive the two-minute round you lost your two shillings – if you won you were paid four shillings. There were several takers. Lyn was one, at sixteen and fighting fit, boxing for Pontypridd. The pair fought three rounds before both conceding - a true draw. Since then Lyn was like a younger brother to Tudor. He abandoned the disciplined path of amateur boxing that he was doing well in to follow the bare-knuckle route of getting paid to fight – for food and survival.

The next morning Tudor told me to leave his camp because he would not harbor a runner – he just wanted me gone. So I left – and Lyn came with me, which Tudor didn't expect. Surprisingly he didn't react badly. It became clear why when Tudor's twelve year old daughter Vivian appeared from their cart as we were getting ready to leave. She had simply the most perfect face I had ever seen. It wasn't only the loveliness or the magnetism of her eyes and smile, or the movement of head and her hair – there was some other magic about this girl.

We moved out of Tudor's encampment – about a mile over the mountain to an abandoned old shack. With the weather now warming there were small rock outcrops that could easily accommodate lean-to tents for shelter. Also there was usually a well-established fire-pit with kettle props in these mountain dweller campsites. The plan was that Lyn would maintain contact with Tudor and the Travellers – I would stay out of sight. It was up to me to make a way for myself – working any jobs that came up and helping in burglaries, and stealing food and sheep.

I could not get the image of Vivian out of my mind. In Oxford I had seen many images of the Mona Lisa but never could see the beauty they raved about. I pictured Vivian in the same portrait and it stuck in my mind like a tattoo. That night I used those thoughts to fall asleep. Before that we had talked about our plans to make a life. We also talked about punishing our punishers. Lyn was ready to kill his father and go to prison. I convinced him that would be just more for him to bear and would consume his entire life. I also wanted my father dead – but I would not deliberately kill him myself. My desire for revenge was so intense I felt the rage taking over my mind sometimes. We decided to put revenge aside for now and use our energy and brains to build a life. My thoughts of Vivian somehow made that a more attractive path.

We talked about fighting and boxing. I described the training at Ganges and how I had grown bigger and stronger – my prior life had been stunting me. Eventually a training plan developed and we set a date to start on the next Sunday as we hiked down into Pandy to stake out the chemist's shop for the pending break-in. I waited in the queue while Lyn stood next to an open door to the storeroom. As instructed I bought a small jar of Vaseline. Lyn said it was the cheapest thing in the shop and we needed it to fight bareknuckle.

We went into Woolworths in Penygraig to shoplift clothes and soap and into the cobblers where I found used miner's boots, newly studded that had never been picked up. Maybe the miner died underground or in the cage going up or down. There were accidents in the Pits and the workings every day. Next stop was the Naval Colliery yard to steal some hundredweight sacks. Back in the camp we half-filled two with stones and slag coal – these would be our training sacks for the miners' coal carrying competitions. That night at dusk we followed Tudor on a search for stray sheep. The small dogs trotted quietly just ahead of us.

The mountain soon was blacker than ever, except for a faint tinge of orange moonlight. An eerie silence was broken only by a distant bleating – Tudor following the sound and looking at us with a finger pointing to his lips for silence. He began to unfurl a rope net from his shoulder and with a faint snap of his fingers the dogs heeled behind him. Crouching now we followed him up a small rise toward the sound of the sheep. He waved us to the ground as he peered over the top of the rise. Ducking down he snapped his fingers again and waved his arm in a circular motion – the dogs looked at him for a split second then darted off as if to outflank the sheep.

That's exactly what happened in the next ten seconds. Running over the top of the rise we saw a straggly sheep running toward us – away from the dogs that were closing in. The sheep veered away but not fast enough to avoid Tudors rope net tangling its feet and legs. In an amazing flow of movement Tudor released a twelve-inch sheath knife, grasped the sheep's nose, pulling it back to expose the neck – which he sliced to the bone. He then wrenched the head to one side and with a loud snap the sheep's spine was completely severed. The sheep's bleating scream ended instantly as Lyn threw a sack onto the spurting fountain of blood.

From out of the blackness emerged two more travellers – pulling a handcart. The sheep was quickly loaded and we set off at brisk trot down the mountain. Above Nantgwyn we dropped down to a tip and then to the nearest row of miner's cottages. A back gate opened and we entered a typical backyard with a coalbunker.

This coalbunker was different. Along one side of the wooden shed was a long butchers bench at waist height. Hanging on the wall behind it was an array of knives, saws, cleavers and mallets. Tudor waved us back out of the gate and we were soon up the mountain again and circling toward our camp.

We stopped at a feeder pond, stripped naked and washed our clothes, then our bodies, before putting the wet clothes back on. Tudor dunked the three terriers a few times each. He said it was to remove any scent of the sheep from their coats. We jogged back to the campsite

179

and hung up the wet clothes to dry. That night Lyn brought back food from Tudor's family. There was rabbit stew with vegetables I'd never seen before – and bread sticks toasted with cheese to perfection. I felt a new sense of energy.

At dusk the next day Lyn and I retraced the route over to Nantgwyn and down to the butcher's coalbunker. We were loaded with a sack each of mutton and offal – weighing about three stones each. We set off back up and around the mountain at a brisk pace. My used miner's boots were rubbing hard on the back of my heels. Tudor was waiting for the sacks and before long some of the offal was boiling for dog-food and another traveller had shown up with bags of eggs, potatoes and peas. A trade for half a sack of mutton took place. The rest of the meat was placed in an underground oven fired with coal started hours before. The ground was covered in fresh soil and then scrub – to the newcomer it was invisible. The traveller life was becoming more appealing. Specially as Vivian was part of that world.

A few nights later we did the chemist burglary. We left the camp at 0200 and met with two boys behind the Plaza at 0230. I was posted as lookout on Tylacalyn Road as the others entered via a roof window over the storeroom in the lane at the back of the shop. They were in the shop for ten minutes and lifted all the cigarettes, tobacco and snuff they could find into sacks carried out the now open back door. On the way out Lyn grabbed a few bottles of "medicinal wine". The roads were deserted and not a single dog barked as we got back over Nantgwyn. The spoils were viewed and portioned back in our camp tent. We had bagged six thousand cigarettes, over a hundred packets of tobacco and tins of snuff. It was divided into three except Lyn kept the wine. I was given a "nod" from each of the others for helping. They gave me two hundred cigarettes each and a few packets of tobacco and snuff.

The next day I asked Lyn how I could sell my "nods" seeing I didn't smoke or sniff snuff. He made a "gypsy deal" for me with Tudor. For all my nods I would get a pair of trousers, a jacket and a scarf – that was it. The Navy had taught me the logic of hard, work and training brings rewards – this way of surviving was opposite to that.

I decided to train myself for fighting and miner sports. Everything I needed was right here on the mountain. The Ganges assault course was a mere hillock when compared to the strength and stamina challenges on the mountain every day. All I needed was a shelter and food plan – and some clothes.

I remembered all the tales Uncle Dai had told me about the miners sports – specially the coal-carrying races. I remembered all his musings on the right boots and sack harness – the fit of the vest and the material of the shirt and sweatbands for the head and wrists – the application of vaseline under the arms where the leather sack harness interlocked. The sack harness was a key element. A lightweight, flexible back carrier – capable of securely slinging a hundredweight sack.

Next morning Lyn couldn't remember a thing after passing out drinking a bottle of the wine. He immediately started drinking the other bottle. I suggested he stop and sober up – he ignored me. I asked him why he was getting drunk as it just was changing him so much. He said, "I don't care – I just want that place – where I can feel better." "Are you

ready to start training like we planned?" I asked him.
"Who knows?" he replied tersely.

So now it was really down to me to go it alone – there was
no one else except me now. I'd found my brother but he
was not the same brother I was searching for. By
afternoon he was drunk again with a few swigs still left in
the bottle.

I left and hiked over to Clydach to retrieve my bike and
rucksack. Walking through Penygraig and Tonypandy the
smell of lamb roasting for Sunday dinner was everywhere.
The miners with clean and shiny faces above white shirts
were smiling their way to the Pub, or the Club. The smell
of beer wafted from their doors and mixed well in the
atmosphere of a day's freedom from the pit. There were
children playing on all the streets and wild daffodils were
growing on the mountain slopes.

The thought of Vivian made it all perfect. The chip shop
was closed so I had to find something I could afford in the
Brachi's. I got a ham sandwich for nine pence – it was days
old. Food was now a problem for sure. I needed a new
plan to feed myself.

I slept the night back in the Trealaw cemetery - got up as
dawn broke and went down to
the snooker hall in Pandy. At the desk I asked if there were
any casual jobs going. The manager asked me if would
empty ashtrays and clean up after players for sixpence an
hour – I agreed and started right there. Four hours later I
had two bob in my pocket only to be spent on fish and
chips. By the time I got back to my camp in the cemetery I
was hungry again.

Trying to reason with Lyn had been impossible. The Navy
had taught me at least two important lessons. One was

that individual effort could bring satisfaction and two, never take anything for granted. Lyn had given up on trying it seemed – he was giving in to savage thoughts put in his mind by his evil father. He didn't care about his own life anymore.

Realizing that Lyn was likely to get me into serious trouble I began thinking about ways to put distance between us. The sense of loyalty was still strong but a more powerful sense of survival was pushing it aside. It was also obvious that I needed to get away from Penygraig and Tonypandy before one of my father's relatives got word of my whereabouts. I was still very worried about the chemist's shop burglary – if the police traced me to it via one of the other boys I would soon be facing Reform School again and the old charges from Oxford would all be brought back against me as well.

I decided to run to Pontypridd. On my cycle journey I had stopped at the Ponty market, prominent in the Rhondda area. I'd noticed some stalls with boys working and thought I may be able to find a job. My sixteenth birthday was coming up – most boys in the Rhondda started work at fourteen or fifteen.

Tudor cracked a rare smile when I pushed my bike into his campsite and asked him what he would pay for it. I think he was smiling at the thought I was leaving. Vivian was also smiling at me from their caravan window – but not because I was leaving I thought. Tudor gave me four pounds for my bike and threw in a used flat cap to assist my disguise as a traveler boy. My hair was now long enough to brush over my forehead and three weeks of constant physical intensity I was stronger and fitter.

A penny platform ticket was all I needed at the Penygraig station to get me on the train to Porth and Ponty. Arriving at Ponty I went to the Gents toilets and waited for ten minutes until the passengers had all filed through the gates and the inspector was back in his ticket office. Then I walked up to the end of the platform and out into the car park through a dislodged spike in the iron fence.

It was mid-afternoon and the market was winding down. I tried all the stalls that were idle – asking the owner in my best welsh accent if there was any casual work available. A fishmonger told me if I was here at 0700 in the morning he could give me an hours work for nine pence. A grocer told me I could work for two hours now for nine pence an hour. My job was to clean out the workroom behind the stall, scraping old vegetable cuttings off the worktable and the floor – then scrubbing down both – the Owner gave me a trial on the spot.

I remembered that Jonah at Ganges had told me he boxed at the Pontypridd YMCA before joining the Navy. At about 1700 I walked up to the desk in the YMCA building in the centre of town. I enquired in my best welsh accent if there were beds available. "So you're travelling are you Dai?" the young man asked. "Aye I'm here for a few days – looking for work." "Where are you from Dai?" "I'm from Monmouth" I lied. How old are you Dai?" "Seventeen" I lied. "Well you can get a bed for a shilling a night up to five nights – you can't come back for two weeks, but if we have beds we can do it on a night by night basis sometimes."

I signed in as Dai Jones and gave my address as 25 Barnes Road, Monmouth. There was a shower in the washroom and a gym with weights and ropes. As I lay my face on a pillow for the first time in weeks I saw some daylight appearing on my horizon. The bed was in a dormitory of twelve – kind of like a small Ganges mess. Young men were sitting on the beds when I was shown in. They all just stared until I nodded – most looked away. After a while a few conversations started – I was so exhausted I paid no attention – besides I needed to be at Ponty market by 0700. I stashed my money in my socks and wore them in bed.

The smell of laundered sheets and a constant flow of nightmares kept interrupting my sleep so I was still groggy as the cool morning air gave me energy on the way to the market. On time at 0700 the owner was surprised to see me. My first task was to load sacks of ice off a lorry and into big insulated drums at the back of the stall. Then I scrubbed down the two marble slabs in the front and washed down the path between them. Next came the fish delivery at 0730. The owner and I carried the tin trays to the back worktable.

I was given a tray of a green, slimy mixture called lava bread, made from seaweed and told to portion and wrap it in greaseproof paper. I watched in awe as the owner sharpened his knives and dissected the fish to be laid out. Herrings were gutted in seconds and arranged on a bed of ice – the same for mackerel and cod. Bowls of cockles, whelks and mussels were placed out with crabs and lobsters at the rear in straight rows.

Mr. Jenkins, the owner, was a very big man – he looked like a mountain – as wide as he was high. His face was blue and red-veined under his cream fishmonger boater-hat. He was jovial to a tee – his wide smile spoiled by a deep brown groove in his front teeth – from gripping a smoldering pipe for forty years. The only other exposed part of him was his hands. They were the same look as his face – swollen shades of scarlet with spider web veins. He liked my work and paid me one and sixpence for two hours.

At 0900 I walked down a few stalls and reported to the grocer – Mr. Buller. He set me to work immediately. I carried in sacks of potatoes, cabbages, cauliflowers and carrots. Mr. Buller showed me how to cut the loose stuff of the vegetables and place them on the stall in the most pleasing way. He was very different from Mr.Jenkins. He was wiry and serious without much of a smile. His face was fresh and glowing – his look accommodating but at arms length – all business. I kept the stall stocked as Mr.Buller and his wife served. It was a natural job for me and I applied my method of maximum effort.

At the YMCA I went straight to the gym and did a routine of ropes and weights I learned at Ganges. This entailed climbing ropes, a weight circuit and twenty pushups. Then ten deep breaths and do it again.

After that I ran from the hostel up the street until a side road led up toward the mountains. I ran up as far as the grass went – the rocks after that were not to be tackled at this time – they were in the future as P.O. Price used to say "the pain hasn't started yet." Coming back down the slope I turned backwards – forcing myself to balance in retreat on the grassy hill. From the hostel I reckoned the run was thirty minutes round trip – that was my goal for now. I kept my mind on the end goal though – but for now like the Navy had taught me – going up and over the mast – take one step at a time.

On Wednesday evening the Pontypridd Boxing Club was training at the YMCA Gym - I went down to take a look. There was temporary ring set up on floor mats and the boxers were going through drills. A coach came over to me and asked me if was interested in boxing. I told him yes and he invited me to join in the training. My rope work and fitness impressed the coach – he got more interested when he saw me working on the punch bag. "Where have you boxed before Dai? Are you from Ponty?" "No I'm from Monmouth I lied." "Were you boxing there Dai?" "Just a bit in school." I lied again. He looked at me suspiciously. "Well you can train here with us Dai – it's five shillings a month – we train Monday, Wednesday and Friday. If you do well Dai we may be able to get you a sponsor but we're strictly amateur of course." "Yes Sir, thank you Sir – I would like to join please." "O.k. Dai we'll see you here Friday at six." "Yes Sir – thank you Sir".

For the next four days I repeated the same tasks except my time at Mr.Buller's stall was increased to four hours a day at ten pence an hour. Mr.Jenkins increased my pay to ten pence an hour too – so I was making five shillings a day by Friday. Also Mrs. Jenkins brought food leftovers from their home for me. So soon I was doing well for work and food but I would have to be out of the YMCA in a day.

Each day I ran the mountain track – getting a bit faster and fitter each time. The atmosphere in the dormitory was strange – no one knew each other and there was a constant flow of new young men. But unlike Ganges there was no tension in the air. A vicar came around each evening and chatted for a few minutes. He asked me about my family. I made up a story that my parents had recently died in a car accident. "Do you have a place to live besides here?" "No Sir" I said truthfully. "Where is the rest of your family?" "Ah well Sir there's only my grandmother." "No aunts and uncles?" "Ah no Sir." "Do you have a birth certificate?" "Ah no Sir." "Mm what about school report or pay receipt from work." "Well Sir I have two jobs at the market – Mr.Buller the grocer and Mr. Jenkins the fishmonger." "How long have you worked there Jones?" "One week Sir" "Alright Jones we'll start there and I'll see what I can do."

So it looked like Rock Hudson was a boy from the past now. Dai Jones was in his place –and with a new name came a new chance I thought. Even more promising was the end of the Rock Hudson life completely. At the gym that evening the coach handed me a pair of plimsoles, a pair of shorts and a singlet when I handed over my five shillings. I went to the dorm to change and felt really good in the gym.

There were about a dozen boys training – ranging in age from about ten to seventeen. Soon I was getting the odd good comment from the coach – noting my effort in the drills and ropes. After a half hour workout we gloved up and sparred, shadow boxed and punched the bags for another half hour – the coach circling, urging and commenting. The last half hour was in the ring. It felt really good to put up a real stance and face an opponent.

My round was against a boy my age but very strong and wild. I used a left stab and right hook combination – mostly to his stomach and ribs that were permanently exposed when I moved inside his flailing arms. He was happy to end the two-minute round.

The coach took me aside – "That was well boxed Dai - you've been trained haven't you Dai? Where have you been boxing Dai?" He wanted an answer. I decided to use Lyn's story – they thought I was seventeen anyway. "I've been travelling for a year - fighting bareknuckle Sir. That's how I've trained Sir – for bareknuckle boxing Sir." "O.k. Dai I'll take you at your word. Keep your nose clean and keep up the work – you could do well Dai – we'll see but there will be no bareknuckle while you're boxing here Dai."

The vicar came back and explained that the YMCA would extend my stay for ten days. But at that time I would need some kind of letter from a family member or guardian confirming my name, date of birth and former address. I was relieved and worried at the same time. But at least I had ten days to find a place to live – first I needed more work and more money.

Sunday was my sixteenth birthday. If I had still been at Ganges I would have manned the mast for parents day – even if my parents would not have been there. I would have been completing my basic training and passing for Ordinary Seaman upon reaching seventeen and a half. Then soon on my way to Gunnery School – and then a ship. Being in Pontypridd I remembered Jonah again – he would be on leave soon – maybe he would come here.

My clothes were quite ragged and my boots were falling apart – I felt out of place and shamed. The pride I had in my Navy uniform and the credit it drew were distant, but clear memories. I remembered P.O. Price's instructions – "plan your work – work your plan" and "be patient." I went into the newsagents to get some crisps and asked if there were any morning paper-rounds available. He asked me I was willing to learn a round with a boy who was leaving – it would mean two days walking with him at no pay. The pay was one pound per week after that – six days a week starting at 0600 in the shop. I took the job – starting tomorrow – now I had three jobs and I needed new boots badly. That became more pressing as I completed my mountain track run in the evening – so far I had not missed one day of my training plan.

Next morning was raining hard at 0600 at the newsagents. A boy also named Dai showed me his list of papers and addresses. He showed me how to fold and stack the papers in a large canvas shoulder bag. We set off in the rain and delivered about fifty papers in the same area as the road I took on my mountain track – all to miner's cottages in lanes and small roads ending on the mountain slopes. I quickly realized I could use this job to add to my strength – if I ran the round it would be like a coal-carrying training race every day.

At the market after six hours work I bought a new pair of boots – the cheapest black boots that all the poor families and miners wore. The price was nineteen shillings – a big slice of my pocket. The cobbler charged three shillings and sixpence to hammer steel studs into the soles and heels. The bite of the studs created a metallic warning of my approach but protected the leather soles and heels from the biting stone of the valleys.

Boxing training that evening was different. Two older boys about eighteen, and bigger than the rest of us joined the group. I anticipated that the coach was going to put me up against one or both during the session. Sure enough I was paired to spar with one – getting the idea of the power of his punches. Predictably the coach put me up against the other big lad in the final one round free-for-all of the session.

"Where are you living Dai?" "Here at the YMCA coach". "Do you have other options Dai – for the future." "Not really coach – I was hoping to get enough work to pay for a bed somewhere – maybe a hostel." "Are you serious about boxing Dai – can you keep it up – what you're doing?" "Yes coach I want to box more than anything"."O.K. Dai I may have a sponsor for you to meet."

Work the next two days flashed by. My bosses were giving me more to do and more hours. It would have been so easy to steal from them and from many of the old ladies who would hand over their purse for the boss or his wife to take the money for their purchase. Everything was on a personal trust basis and the Buller and Jenkins families knew all the other families in Pontypridd and surrounding towns.

At training coach told me to meet him at the gym tomorrow for an introduction to a possible sponsor. I had no idea what a sponsor was but I knew the coach thought it was very important. The sponsor turned out to be Mr. Madog Jeffries, a boxing Booth owner and boxing trainer. He stood about six feet in a smart suit with gold chains on the pockets of his waistcoat. He pulled one and a gold watch slid out into his hand glancing down at it he said "Where is your father Dai? "He's dead Sir"." "And where have you been living then Dai?" "In Monmouth Sir." It was a last ditch lie.

"O.k. look Dai the coach here thinks you have some talent but there is some question about your background – you've come from nowhere and no family. Your parents passed away is that right?" "Yes Sir." "O.K. lets see you train a bit and we'll decide what to do." Mr. Jeffries was a very intimidating man. Besides his stature his face was large and square with a massive and thick black moustache that completely covered his mouth. After speaking he licked his lips to brush away the hairs that had fallen over them.

There was expectation in the gym as we stood round the temporary ring. I was gloved first and paired with the senior boxer. He was much warier this time so I was forced to attack to show some intent and ambition to Mr. Jeffries. I decided to switch to southpaw and use the right jab to set up a left hook – he had not seen those punches from me before.

"Well done Dai – very well boxed – Mr. Jeffries wants to give you a trial if you're interested." "This is how it works – you'll be an apprentice in Mr. Jeffries stable of boxers. You'll train here and at Mr. Jeffries yard – every day for two hours in the evening. If you do well you'll start sparring with the Booth boxers – who mostly came from our club - it's up to you how quickly you progress." I was very excited and it felt like I had been accepted in Pontypridd – my welsh accent intensified.

At Mr. Jeffries yard next afternoon I was rotated among the smaller Booth boxers for shadow practice and sparring. These young men were in their twenties which seemed very old to me. A lot of them smoked which was normal but there were a few quietly confident men who stood out as boxers. The coach had told me the Jeffries Booth – known as Madog's Men were some of the best fighters in South Wales and had bred champions through his system of training and boxing.

The last half of the session was a rotation into the ring for a minute or less. Madog directed the session – ordering boxers in and out of the ring – setting different opponents at different levels of skill and fatigue. I was in the ring for four stints – each time against different boxers until the last one. I was matched against an experienced Booth boxer – very muscular and lily-white skinned. His punches were like getting kicked by a horse – each one making me move back as I fended them off with my forearms. This was the most deliberate and menacing boxer I had met to date. His blond hair had a curl over his forehead – I later learned his name was "Pretty Boy" Joe Hand. Mr. Jeffries only kept me in with him for a half a minute.

Sticking to my work and training I was further rewarded when Coach Alby told me he had found a room for me in Trehafod. It was with a miner and his wife who had lost their only son in a mine accident. The boy had been a year older than me and was crushed between two drams when a chain parted on the underground track. The wife was crippled with arthritis so needed help around the house – that was part of my lodging requirement – to make and clean the fires and empty the chamber pots. I knew the routine well from my grandparents' house. Now I had a bit of a home and my three jobs were paying enough to cover my rent and food.

The miner's name was also Jones, Trefor Jones. The first thing you noticed about him was his enormous nose. At the pit he was known as "Conk" Jones. His nose was not only big but had been battered and broken many times it appeared. So it covered half his face – laying on it like a big piece of cauliflower. But it would take a brave man to make fun of Conk Jones. At forty-one he had worked underground for twenty-eight years. Starting as a pony driver he was now the underground leadman on his shift, on his knees, cutting at a four-foot high seam of steam coal with a crew of twenty miners.

Conk quietly ruled by his presence and knowledge. His arms, exposed by rolled up, ragged shirt sleeves, were covered in blue and black scars from cuts inflicted by sharp shards and edges as the coal face - six hundred yards beneath the black, grinding machinery at the pithead. The scarred forearms were proof that muscles expand and bulge with repetitive flexing. They were the size of most men's legs and one reason no one made fun of Conk Jones. He didn't care about the nickname and his standard line was if you think my snoring-organ is big Dai you should see the daddy down here – pointing to his crotch. His gigantic thighs were developed playing prop forward for Trehafod Rugby Club. He had no discernable neck – his massive round head sat on top of a chest that was almost touching your face when you looked him in the eyes – which were bright blue and crystal clear.

Mrs. Jones was elf-like – the complete opposite to Conk and much older. Her fragile looking body was twisted at the hips, sitting awkwardly in her chair. She reached slowly to a table next to her and picked up a package of ten Players. "Would you light one for me please Dai." I put one between her lips and struck a match. That set off a coughing bout for a while. Automatically I looked on the table for a jam-jar and soon had it open in front of her mouth. Bubbly phlegm dribbled out – I dabbed at it with the hanky on her lap. This was exactly like my grandmother – but this lady was younger – nevertheless crippled by tobacco and arthritis so bad her hands looked like crab claws.

"I miss our Dafydd – he was such a nice boy he was aye". I waited but she said no more and drifted off into her cigarette smoke haze. "Tell me if you want something Mrs. Jones – anything I can do – let me know O.K? "Can you fill in the football pools Dai?" "Yes Mrs. Jones where's your coupon?"

Mrs. Jones first husband had been killed in a mine accident fifteen years after their marriage. There had been no children and as a result the couple were almost recluse. Being a middle-aged widow was onerous and finding a new husband was essential as it was the only means of survival in the valley community. Trefor Jones was a virile young miner and rugby player fifteen years younger and challenged with a face that young women found unattractive. But Enid and Trefor were sparked by a meeting at the Baptist Church that led to a courtship and marriage in six months. Equally quick and even more shocking to the neighbors was Enid's pregnancy and birth of a son, Dafydd.

The late birth almost killed Enid who was in labor for two days before an old lady - a gypsy midwife from Aberdare, was bought in by Trefor. The gypsy midwife delivered Dafydd in two hours – even more attention was noted by the community. Trefor doted on his son, perched him on his giant biceps after rugby matches and brought him up to be a miner, play rugby and drink beer. Dafydd was a chosen boy with loving and doting parents who never expected a child. In the valleys this was unusual and people watched Dafydd's progress via the gossip channels.

Dafydd followed his father down the pit and onto the rugby field. He was an image of his father without the nose which was silently blessed by Trefor and Enid. He also followed his father in taking on the local bullies from around the valleys. On a day that started perfectly, almost seventeen, he ate welsh cakes baked by his Mam with bacon done in the oven over the fire. Dad would soon be home from his morning shift.

Trefor often relived the walk home over the mountain that day. How could he know the uplifting thoughts of Dafydd would be on the last day of his son's life? With half the ten-hour shift done, a link pin on the dram drive chain failed, releasing the dram to careen back into the one behind. Dafydd was crossing the track where the two drams collided - crushing his abdomen and ribcage – killing him instantly.

Trefor answered the door that afternoon – they never had many visitors. He noticed the pit manager immediately. "Trefor we have some tragic news." "Dafydd?" Trefor wailed.
The pit manager nodded – tears running freely over his cheeks. They stared at each other for a long time until Trefor beckoned the manager in, leading him to the back kitchen. Enid collapsed on the terrible news and never totally recovered from the shock and grief. The pit manager went to lengths to explain that Dafydd died instantly. The joy in their life also died instantly.

I was given a small bedroom with a dresser and chamber pot. The toilet was called old "ty bach" and was a little shed over a hole at the bottom of the back garden. The seat was a plank with a hole – but there was toilet paper. Mr. Jones tended to his wife's needs for the ty bach in their bedroom and deposited a newspaper package alongside the chamber pot for me to take down to the ty bach when necessary. The smell coming from their bedroom was as bad as the ty bach smell. They didn't seem to notice.

There was also a place at the table for me. I brought home food from the market every day – Mrs. Buller was very generous, often bringing left overs from their home meals. Mr. Buller gave me first choice of any fruit about to spoil and cutting from the greens I prepared for the stall. Once a week Mr. Jenkins gave me a piece of lava bread. I gagged at the texture of it so never tasted it really, but Mr. and Mrs. Jones couldn't get enough of it. We ate mostly lamb mince, corned beef and potatoes, bread, margarine, bacon and baked beans. There weren't many eggs and meat was scarce. However the traditional Sunday dinner welsh lamb was never missed.

During the next six weeks I stuck to my training program like glue. Each day I felt stronger, faster and more determined. Madog coached me at each session as did coach Alby at the YMCA. A routine to build power into my punches was ordered by Madog and followed to the tee by coach Alby. It involved doing a hundred push-ups three times a day. I still kept my running paper round which built strength and stamina in my legs plus the lung capacity to box three, three-minute rounds easily. I was keenly aware of the edge that endurance gave – I began to think that stopping smoking was the best thing I had ever done for myself.

I was entered in a local tournament – representing Pontypridd boxing club as a 10 stone novice. The bouts started on Friday evening and went all through the day Saturday to the finals that night.

The tournament was staged at Ponty Town Hall and brought together boxing clubs from throughout the Valleys. Conk Jones was in the audience on Friday evening for my first bout. His presence was immense – not only to me but to many of the others in the audience. He was a legend in his own time in the Valleys – first for his physical invincibility and now as a hardened underground leader with a heart of gold.

Coach Alby was in my corner, and mentally so was P.O.Price. My opponent was a muscular, strong boy about eighteen with a height advantage. He was very wary to come in and stood off stabbing high jabs to my head. His guard was high and rigid so I knew that the inside uppercut under the ribs, the Jonah punch, would work at some point. Using a fake side-move and plant I got in two rapid left jabs to his nose – as he moved away I jumped in with the right overhand cross. The power of my punch, increased greatly by my body momentum forward, rocked his head sideways and distorted his face and then down – I had knocked him out. Madog nodded at me as I left the ring.

At home that night Mr. Jones was very pleased. Sitting in the kitchen smoking his pipe – drinking tea with Mrs. Jones hanging on his every word – him stopping to accommodate her coughing episodes. But they both were smiling and happy. I suddenly realized that I was feeling the same. Again, the spirit of the Valleys had lifted me.

Saturday I boxed at 1200 against a miner from Porth Boxing Club – this time about nineteen and rippling with upper body muscle, built crouched at the coal face, constantly hacking, hammering and chiseling.

This boxer was a scrapper, throwing wild punch after wild punch – which I took on my guard for two minutes. Countering with jabs and hooks as I led him in different directions. In the third minute I heard coach Alby "Rev it up Dai". With my confidence building and my opponent tiring I was able to land combinations Madog had taught me and then moved in with the Jonah punches – hurting him with every one.

A technical knockout put me into the final in my class. Again the nods were coming from Madog and coach Alby – these men had put trust in me.

The final was at 1800 – the hall was packed – smoky and buzzing. "In the blue, boxing for Pontypridd Boxing Club - Dai Jones." – the announcer silenced the hall. My opponent stared at me across the ring – I looked around and back and he was still staring hard. Coach Alby had taught me this ploy – "Just look away and around." He was much tougher and rougher but I kept boxing defensively to survive two rounds. In the third round he still kept coming – he was a like a machine – my counter punches were just bouncing off him. I took a real beating but stayed standing – the relief when the final bell went was incredible – I thought I was going to cry – I could see the concern on coach Alby's face. The referee didn't hesitate to raise my opponent's arm.

At the end of the tournament Madog took me aside. "Well fought Dai – a good tournament for you. In that final you fought a very good boxer who is well established. As a novice you really shouldn't have been in there but we thought you were ready and you were. How do you feel Dai?" "Pretty well beat up Sir." "Aye – get used to it Dai – if you're going to box in my Booth."

That night Mrs. Jones baked welsh cakes. The smell from the oven over the fire mingling with the tobacco smoke and fresh tea was exactly as it was in my grandparent's house. But here there was no tension – I had a proper place to live – I could hardly believe it.

Mr. Jones was happy when I told him I wanted to compete in the coal-carrying races at the miners' mountain fairs. He provided me a harness and new pair of football boots that he assured me would work best on the damp grassy slopes. Madog and Alby kept the pressure on me to work hard in training.

At this time I had a growth spurt. It happened so fast I didn't notice it until my trousers were half way up my shins and were flapping about like most of the other youths from poor valley families. Madog was watching closely as he was expecting to try me out in the boxing Booth after my eighteenth birthday – which would actually be my seventeenth.

We boxed regularly against other clubs in South Wales. The Rhondda and the valleys produced boys that fought by nature. Fighting at ten stone ten I won all my bouts during the summer and approaching Christmas. I kept my head down and trained hard. Each bout and win brought more encouragement and advice from Madog who tested me against all his Booth fighters around my weight. His message was you needed three things in your favour – "Brains, a knock-out punch and Brains." He ran the hardest and toughest apprentice Booth boxer program in the valleys.

During the summer I went to the miners fairs and sports-days on the surrounding mountains. There were lots of young girls and some not so young interested in my friendship. Another Madog's tenets were "Don't let the trouser-trout out" but my thoughts of affection were all for Vivian. At each gathering I looked for Tudor and his family, Lyn and any other familiar faces. There were none. I competed in the coal-carrying races – running a three-mile circuit up and down the mountain carrying half a hundredweight of coal. Finishing in the first three in all and winning two races I became a bookies favorite.

At one gathering on the mountain at Tylerstown, Tudor was there fighting bareknuckle. I watched as the miners and travellers fought viciously – the bookies taking bets on each fight. I wanted to fight – in my mind a constant repetitive thought was "I can fight!" – it was in me – part of me. Tudor was a gypsy. I liked Gypsies, they were different in just about everything – they had their own creed and rules – they always seemed to be stronger and tougher – they used what ever was available and made do with what they had. His wife and children were there – along with his group of travellers.

His wife was selling herb bunches and fortune telling. Their Tinker was there doing amazing repairs to knives, daggers and belts. Several of the men were fighting. But for sure every man and boys' eyes were on Vivian. In the year since I had seen her last she had become even more luscious. Her face was even more irresistible – dark brown eyes with black eyelashes and eyebrows – a flawless nose above the most hypnotizing pink lips and mouth imaginable. My whole being stopped and stared -then my stomach knotted up.

That Christmas at sixteen, I felt seventeen, in Trehavod with my new family and future. The punishment and discrimination was history – faded and papered over by my new life and outlook. The year started well – Mr. and Mrs. Jones watched over me like a new son. They were very frugal – their only luxury was pipe tobacco and cigarettes. In the evenings we listened to the wireless, Dick Barton and the Archers. On Fridays I bathed in the tin bath. We had roast lamb on Sunday – the valley life was hard but bearable.

We never went to church – I had no wish to hear that tripe anymore anyway. Mrs. Jones lamented her absence and believed in Jesus as her savior. "What has he saved you from my love?" 'I don't know but he will." Their banter was good-natured – so different from the tense, stiff conversation of my parents. The Jones' liked each other.

My mother and father didn't like each other like the Jones' did. They feared the gossip of the long-term Oxford Town residents so they kept a low profile. Unlike the Valleys the atmosphere in Oxford was one of suppression – keep things hidden and don't voice an opinion – on anything.

Things were going well in all respects – until the club boxed Porth, Tonypandy and Pontyclun at the Naval Club in Tonypandy. It was a Saturday afternoon and evening in spring. With six wins, my progress was perfect according to Madog. My bout was at 1900 in the ten stone ten class.

My opponent from Pandy Boxing Club was a determined and stylish boxer. I fought defensively at the start but soon realized this opponent did not have a strong punch. He threw punches from the shoulder – almost without any chest or back power – like a cat pawing at you. But like most cats occasionally he surprised me with a different punch – one was a body uppercut like the Jonah punch. In the corner coach Alby urged me to attack - show a bit more aggression." "Yes Sir."

The second and third rounds went to plan – it was by no means a pushover but my training, strength and fitness were too much for my opponent to counter and he was happy to hear the bell. The bright lights over the ring hindered the boxers' view of the audience sat in a dim, smoky haze. As the lights came back up for the decision, the referee raised my arm immediately – the crowd was standing and clapping. I turned to all sides of the ring with my arm raised. This was always the best feeling – of winning and getting recognition.

I noticed a man sitting in the middle rows – staring but not moving – he seemed out of place. It was hard to draw my look away – and then I realized why. The hunched over rat-faced man, with a cigarette hanging limp from his mouth, was my father.

The surge of excitement turned to instant dread. I saw my father stand and start making his way out – the gait and hunched body were unmistakable. I was back in the changing room as quickly as possible. What to do now – I began to panic. Why was he here – did he know I was boxing? I hoped it was just coincidence and he was visiting his parents. What would he do now? Between the panic surges I also realized no matter why or how, he now knew where I was and his next move would be to get me into custody.

I was quickly on the first train to Ponty and to my house in Trehafod. The Jones' were excited to hear my good news but very soon knew I was in a state of panic. "What is it Dai?" Mr. Jones peered at me and Mrs. tilted her head in concern. These two were my best friends in the world – they had shown me unconditional trust and security like never before. I could not lie anymore – there were no lies left in me – the lies had caught up like they always did.

"Sir, Mrs. Jones I have been telling you lies about my life." "We know that Dai." Smiled Mrs. Jones "We don't care where you came from anymore." A lump came to my throat. "Well it's more than that – I'm on the run from the police and they know where I am as of tonight – I need to leave." "What are you running from Dai?" Mr. Jones was shaking his head. "It's a long story Sir – I didn't do anything wrong – I didn't want to run - but I knew they would punish me and put me away." "But for what Dai?" "They said I did lewd behavior." "Did you?" "No Sir – it was a police trap." "Where?" "Oxford Sir". "Oxford! – Why there?" "That's where I'm from Sir – my father was at the boxing tonight – he will try to get me arrested – I know that Sir." 'Why Dai?" "He wants me shamed and locked up so he can disown me Sir." Mrs. Jones drew in a sharp breath – shaking her head.

As if on cue there was a knock at the front door. Mr. Jones motioned me upstairs and went to answer. "Good evening Mr. Jones – My name is Detective Constable Gibbons of Glamorgan Police – this is Mr. Hudson from Oxford. He believes his son Roy is here would that be right Mr. Jones?" "Not to my knowledge Constable." "Well the Pontypridd Boxing Club have informed us that a boy staying with you could be Roy Hudson." "His father here has identified him as his son – is he here Mr. Jones?" "If you are referring to Dai Jones he is not here – Dai is from Monmouth anyway." "Do you know where he might be

Mr. Jones?" "Probably at the dance in Trealaw". "When he comes home please ask him to contact Pontypridd police station. Mr. Jones I should add that if Dai Jones is Roy Hudson he is sixteen and a juvenile in the charge of his father." "Dai is seventeen then so it's not him is it?" "Thank you Mr. Jones."

They did not ask to come in – attest to the menacing appearance of Conk Jones – he would have killed my father with one backhand across the side of the head. "What a mess Dai – you should have told us before – now what do we do?" "I'll get ready to leave Sir." "Where will you go?" wailed Mrs. Jones. "I'll survive – you've given me the best home I ever had." "You are welcome back any time Son."

I asked Mr. Jones to tell my bosses at the market that I had to leave in emergency – I felt huge guilt for letting them down. There were tears from them both as Conk slipped a white folded note into my hand – it was five pounds – a huge amount to boost my survival funds. "Be careful Son – we'll be here for you when this all ends." I left by the back door and over the wall at the bottom of the garden. At about 2230 I was lucky to get a bed at the YMCA in Ponty. Lying down, exhausted and depleted, my spirits descended into despair. I had to keep moving or automatically go to borstal for two years. There were no choices.

At 0600 I informed the newsagent this would have to be my last day. He was not well pleased but accepted my story that I was a runaway and my father was coming for me. Then on to Madog's yard where the early training would soon start and he would be there checking his fighters in. "What are you doing here Dai?" 'Can I speak to you Sir?" In his office I came completely clean – Oxford,

Penygraig, Ganges and Ponty - everything. Madog sat silent – smoking and refilling his pipe. "What do you want from me Dai?" "Nothing Sir – I came here because you gave me a chance – I wanted to tell you the truth about me before I leave." "Where are you going Dai?" "Back up the mountain Sir – at the moment". "Why not give yourself in and tell your story?" "Because I've told it so many times, to so many people and it's never made a difference - my story is buried under their dirt."

Getting up to leave Madog stopped me. 'Look Dai – you can box – nothing will change that." 'When this dies down come back and see me O.K.?" "Thank you Sir."

Chapter 13.

Conversion to Traveller

Tudor's camp looked somewhat the same except there were several more caravans and cooking fires – more dogs, chickens, children running around and a pen with more horses. It was bigger but the same picture. Tudor eyed me suspiciously as usual. "Hello Dai – haven't seen you for a while." "Aye I've been working in Ponty – lost my job – I'm looking for Lyn." "Lyn's locked up Dai – will be for a long time." "Why?" "Breaking into shops in town and stabbing his father again." I kicked him out of here because he was drinking meths." "Are you on the run again Dai?" "Kind of – more bad luck than anything." "What can I do for you Dai?" "Could you let me stay in my tent close by – I'll do the same stuff for you that Lyn did – even more." "I seen you coal racing Dai – and heard you were boxing for Ponty."

"What did you do?" "It was an old offense for stealing from shops." I lied – I just could not bring myself to tell him about the lewd conduct charge – the shame was simply too much – I would have preferred to die.

Spreading my groundsheet in the musty tent reminded me of my days as a tramp in Chiswell Hills. At least I had a new identity in Wales and had proven to myself that no matter the odds I could make a life by doing my best and fighting for myself when the odds were stacked against me. Now coming up for my seventeenth birthday I had learned the hard way that dishonesty ends in misery and stomach-wrenching guilt.

Punishment left my life when I left Oxford. The harshness of my current daily existence was not punishment. I was not inflicted by people who were relentless to see me suffer – school masters, church leaders, crooked police and limitless twisted neighbors couldn't reach me here.

The people of the Valleys were different. There was no Gown here – it was inconceivable the Gown mentality could survive here. People here were all in the same boat – there was no privilege afforded anyone and no one wanted it. The tough life created a level community who cared for each other. In Oxford there were no mine disasters – no tips – no pits. A bad experience was when it rained on Mayday and one's gown got a little wet.

That night I vowed to stick with my plan to fight – it was my only worthwhile path – the only thing I could do naturally. Next morning I went down to Tudor's camp and asked if he needed any work done. He directed me to clean out the campfires and the cooking pots. It wasn't long before I saw Vivian. An image of her was permanently transfixed in my mind. But each time I saw the feelings of mesmerism took over again – for a day I could not eat or sleep.

My chores in Tudor's camp were traded for food and shelter – but he made it clear my shelter did not include coming and going from the encampment. He had established himself as the local Rom Baro – the dominant Gypsy of the area. Everyone knew that his group could probably steal from the area – but not in when Tudor's camp was located in it – so tolerance bought protection and peace to the mountain area.

Tudor was fighting bareknuckle several times a month but was not training much. He had a punch bag set up and a couple of sparring partners. The fights were at miners gatherings in summer and arranged on the mountains. Gypsy traveller fighters came up against miners – they were mismatched in their ways of life but not in their instinctive compulsion to fight.

I tended to the vegetable garden and mucked out the pony enclosure. I dug the dirt ovens for cooking the stolen sheep and made the runs to the illicit butcher and back. At the quarry where Lyn and I had made a camp I rigged a course of lifting rocks and carrying them at the double up and down the rock outcrop. I shadow boxed for half an hour and ran a coal-carry circuit every day. This was all I knew for three months, while I kept my head down - constant training and strengthening. Ganges had taught me the simple rule that hard work and ambition paid off.

As Christmas approached again there had been no police at the camp – no-one had been looking for me and Tudor was getting used to seeing me – although he rarely spoke. I was very anxious to please him – for security but mostly to have the chance of seeing Vivian. As I passed seventeen, eighteen as Dai Jones, it was obvious to me one day that my body was literally bristling with aggression. My first thought every morning was "I can fight – I want to fight"- there was no deliberate thought, it was just there in my mind as soon as I woke – and I tried to prove it to myself every day.

By Christmas I was established with Tudor as a reliable worker - and confidant to some extent. I had been in on two more sheep kills and had become a trusted apprentice. This meant I had gained approval from other travellers in Tudor's group. I saw each approval as a move forward and a closer connection with Vivian, who was constantly at the front of my mind.

Tudor often dispatched me with messages to Porth and Aberdare – and sometimes instructed me to go back and pick up messages from the same places. I knew I was being tested. Each successful task and test produced more trust and acceptance. On Christmas Day I was invited to eat at his cart that he called the vardo. But not at the family table – instead a stool was provided in the spotless kitchen. From there I could see Vivian and found it impossible to take my eyes off her – to the point of Tudor noticing. He was not well pleased I could tell when he said, "Are you dicking at my daughter Dai?"– so I ate the delicious cockerel dinner and excused myself with great thanks.

At a Boxing Day gathering in Tylerstown I entered the coal-carrying race – winning easily and making two pounds-ten shillings. Conk Jones was there to see if I had come out of hiding. His voice was unmistakable behind me "The harness works well then son." I almost collapsed at his closeness and cried when he hugged me. He looked around "You can come home anytime son – no one has been looking for you and everyone in Trehavod and Ponty misses you. "How is Mrs. Jones"? His mangled face cracked a smile, nodding "She's lovely Dai" and hugged me again. I slumped into his hug, seventeen years of humiliation had come to an end."

We went to the bareknuckle fighting location - a round ring was formed with rope held by a circle of men. Around the ring was a thick crowd. Jugs of ale were everywhere and the vapored breath mixed with a haze of tobacco smoke hovering above the crowd. They were all miners from the Rhondda – dressed in their best suits with waistcoats and gold watch chains – all but a few were mustachioed and wore flat caps. A bookie was taking bets as a pair of fighters were introduced.

An enormous, tattooed traveller wearing black leather knee-breeches and black boots paced back and forth on the sawdust surface inside the ring. His opponent was mustachioed miner with a white rippling body – swollen with protruding veins. He stood motionless with an unblinking stare straight ahead. He was the example of a stern and instinctive tough man - a man that could be relied on underground.

Each fighter had a fair-play handler to intervene if the rules were infringed. No biting, head butting, gouging, kicking or hitting a man on the ground was allowed. If a fighter is beaten to the ground the other will wait thirty seconds until a recovery is made or a submission is given.

The traveller was taking on all-comers at two pounds per round – if you lasted a round you got a pound back – if you defeated the traveller you got four pounds back. There was an excited atmosphere as the traveller known as Tiny Mont had already beaten six men in succession, all of them in the first round. But gradually the competition was increasing and now one of the local strongman miners was in the ring with him. It was a brutal contest with blood and sweat spraying onto the fair-play men. The miner was fitter and more of a boxer – but not enough to withstand the brawling steamroller that took punch after punch in the face without blinking. It looked like the miner would get a pound back but just before the bell a head-butt broke his nose and knocked him out.

The miner crowd went berserk with the fair-play men calling it accidental. Tiny Mont stepped out of the ring as the miner was supported out by his fair-play man. Into the ring stepped a young miner about twenty-five – much bigger than me.

He had supporters in the crowd and was introduced as the Tonypandy Tiger. He was asking three pounds to fight three rounds, and offering return of the entry fee plus five pounds for anyone that could stop him. A round was to end when a boxer took the knee or was beaten to the ground. Then he was given thirty seconds to come to the center of the ring, ready to fight on. If he failed to come to the center of the ring the fight was awarded against him.

The first challenger was an older miner, about thirty, quite a bit heavier with enormous arms and shoulders. The older man was the aggressor for a minute before the Tiger started connecting with counter combinations. In less than another minute the older miner had taken the knee.

Coming to the centre for round two the older miner barged into Tiger – trying to knock him over. The crowd jeered but need not have because Tiger sidestepped the charge and delivered an overhand right to the jaw that sent the older man crashing to the ground. The first fight was over.

Turning to Trefor "I think I may have a go at him Sir." "That's up to you Dai." "Will you fair-play for me Sir." "Of course son." We approached the sponsor and I over handed three pounds to fight. "What's your name Dai"? "Dai Jones". "Where you from Dai?" "From Trehavod." "Okay let me see your hands Dai."

I was very soon in the ring and squared up. The fights moved along continuously until a new sponsored boxer entered the ring. The Tonypandy Tiger was aptly named. He attacked from the first second. It felt good to be back where I wanted to be – in a place where I could fight.

My ring skills were rusty so I stumbled on the sawdust a few times as I sidestepped lunges and swings. Tiger landed a few good hooks but was easy to evade for the most part. The round drew to the two-minute limit without much excitement for the crowd. I heard a few shouts of "Conk is this your boy?" – followed by laughter. Centering for the second round I knew that Tiger was susceptible to the Jonah punch. A swing from his right turned his left torso toward me so perfectly I could see his rib cage outlining the target area. The punch came from the height of my crouched knee - up under his ribs. I felt blow land hard and continue into his stomach. He let out a loud screech – he was hurt, totally winded and gasping for breath. The Tonypandy Tiger had been defanged. Afterwards he said, "I've never been stopped by a body punch Dai."

Collecting eight pounds from the sponsor was terrific – the training and discipline had paid off again. Plus the police had not been around – so apparently my father had been unsuccessful in getting the Glamorgan police to take up his persecution of me. Mr. Jones told me they had not been round again and the whole street and market were behind me – Conk had influence.

Word of my wins had reached Tudor before I saw him at my chores the next day. "Heard you won a few quid Dai – and stopped the Tonypandy Tiger." "Yes Sir – well I did stop him." "I've fought that boy Dai – few times – he must have had a cold."

"Well you'll be able to pay some rent then Dai." 'If I could have a bender tent in your camp Sir, I would pay rent." "And do the chores Dai?" "Yes Sir – but I can't be involved in sheep stealing." "Why not Dai?" "Well Sir I want to be finished with police and punishment – I want to be a boxer." Tudor eyed me like a hawk – distrust of the "muskers", the police, was universal among the gypsies. He turned and walked away without an answer.

I rarely saw Vivian. She was kept busy by her mother cleaning and polishing the immaculate vardo and learning to crochet. Her mother was a "ducker" at the fairs and miners events, telling fortunes from palm reading and tealeaves. As the daughter Vivian sat beside her mother – learning the trade. In the vardo and the camp there was a strict code of behavior for the "shavers", as Tudor called all children. Girls were not allowed alone with boys – ever – and a boy could not enter a vardo or tent without the permission of the Dad.

Children sometimes went to school but all left at age eleven to start work for the family. Their language was a pidgin English mixed with gypsy and welsh words. Although the tents and vardos were spotless the shavers and their parents had a look of shabbiness about them. They rarely bathed or washed their hair after age eleven. Their skin was swarthy olive, their hair black and unruly – the eyes deep brown and always staring. This made Vivian stand out even more than her natural lusciousness – men and boys could not resist her fair skin, lustrous chocolate hair and luminous hazel eyes– they became stunned as soon as she came into view.

Tudor surprised me a few days later. "Do you want to train a bit with me Dai – do some sparring?" He had not talked to me in days. "What like shadow or tapping?" "Aye". I agreed and went down to the camp in the afternoon. Tudor had obtained some boxing gloves I was glad to see. He led me through an elaborate warm-up routine – using language that was sometimes hard to follow. Every muscle, tendon and ligament was stretched and loosened. Ten minutes punching the heavy bag came after a hundred push-ups.

With the gloves on Tudor scripted a fight – coming at me aggressively but not punching – just tapping or feinting. He was faster than I had estimated. But at thirty he was getting to the end of his prime. I found him predictable – his moves were embedded, mechanical and telegraphed. Using the P.O. Price plan I slipped past the half-punches and tapped at his torso from inside – digs and stabs. "You box well Dai – you've been training seriously Dai." "Yes Sir." "Where were you first trained then Dai?" "HMS Ganges Sir – the Royal Navy." "O.k. so are you on the run from the Navy?" "No Sir I was kicked out for my offenses in Oxford when they caught up with me." "How long did you do Dai?" "Half a year Sir." "Did you want to stay in?" "Yes Sir."

Soon after Tudor allocated me a tent pitch on the edge of the expanding camp. Several of the other gypsies cut the wood and carved the pieces for my bender tent – a rounded arch frame covered by brown, thick raw wool blankets. This was not a tramp camp – this was a home – again I felt the strange feeling of belonging – whatever it was it made me feel good – instead of guilty. My rent was one pound ten shillings a week. On top of that there was three shillings a week to pay off the cost of my tent. My savings were mounting a bit – I needed to build a safe somewhere to hide it.

At Easter there were miners gatherings and sports events everywhere in the valleys. Tudor and two of his group prepared and rigged their vardos to travel. The horses were harnessed into the shafts with the feedbags stored under. Inside the pristine, glossy surroundings were tied down by the family.

On top of the mountain above Llantrissant a thousand miners gathered on Good Friday at 1000 – all clean and shiny in their best clothes. The weather was perfect to watch their fellow miners in prizefights and strongman competitions. The travellers were there in force selling leather gear for underground and cheap jewelry for the drunken miners to take home for their wives. The ale was flowing, the snuff was being snorted and the cash was changing hands with the bookies. Tudor was there with his group – his wife telling fortunes and the gorgeous Vivian, now fourteen, turning every man's head in sight and luring them toward the tent.

There was a very strong field for the coal race. Miners from throughout the valleys came out for this popular Easter event - one of the few days the pits stopped producing. The favorite was a nineteen year old from the huge colliery at Cwmparc, Treorchy. He was also a marathon runner. Pretty soon Trefor Jones and his group from Trehavod and Ponty arrived. A buzz went round the crowd "Conk Jones" and his boys were about – his name and reputation strong even this far from Ponty.

He gave me a bear hug – lifting me off the ground like a leaf. His butties patted me on the back. I noticed Tudor paying attention. Hoping the same would be the case for Vivian, I was disappointed her head was turned away – it was deliberate I thought. For weeks now I had been trying to make eye contact with her – but to no avail – she showed no interest in me at all – it was starting to gnaw away at my gut. Maybe I should just give in and look elsewhere to calm the emotions that were rampant inside me – but no – this girl was the only girl that interested me – to the point of obsession.

The coal race was very fast and grueling. The favorite streaked away up straight up the mountain – a runner could choose his path as long as three check points were made on the way up and on the way down. In fine weather with good visibility, strong runners would sometimes attempt a straight climb as opposed to following the trodden paths of the colliers. I followed the leader, along with a few other strong contenders. Settling into my pace the leader pulled further ahead – but I knew it was the last quarter of the race that was most critical. On this course it meant you had to run all the way down the mountain to the outskirts of Llantrissant – then back up the steep slopes to finish going uphill. Conk Jones had warned me to conserve energy for that final quarter.

Coming back up the mountain, about a quarter mile to the finish there were only three of us in the running. The leader was twenty-five yards in front of me. I shrugged the harness up on my back – setting the coal sack as high as I could to spread the weight to my shoulders. A hundred yards from the line it was me and the leader fighting it out. I was right on his shoulder when he suddenly lunged across, tripping me and tangling his own legs. We both went down and the third man staggered past. The miner from Cwmparc was up first and it seemed that the third man slowed down a bit until Cwmparc caught up. All three of us collapsed, exhausted, over the line. The crowd erupted – they had all seen the collision and finish. Cwmparc claimed he had stumbled over a rock and it was a complete accident. Then why did his butty slow down to let him win? Several scuffles were breaking out and the bookies were surrounded by waving tickets. Many were looking at Conk – expecting he might have a word. He did. 'It's Good Friday boys – let it go for now – we can sort it out later if needs be – O.K.?"

The crowd of a thousand excited, intoxicated miners came together and let it go. Not all were happy but Conk Jones was not a man to be dismissed. "I think that was deliberate Sir – he cut straight across me." 'Yes that's true Dai – but why were you so close to him – basic mistake that close to the finish." "You had him beat why get so close?" I had no good answer. "Look son – never get that close to a man with a coal sack on your back – one good nudge and your over. You just learned that it takes more than strength and stamina to win here. Are you up for boxing today son." "Yes Sir – I need the money now I lost the coal race and my three pound entry ticket." "O.k. son – take a breather for an hour.

The boxing ring was a bit more elaborate due to an event of this size. Round poles used underground were sunk into the ground with three strands of rope connecting them for a fifteen-foot square. The sponsors were lined up with their fighters and fair-play men – each had a favored bookie to place bets on their fighter. Tudor had a group of supporters – he kept eyeing me through the crowd. Finally I saw Vivian look over at me – following The Dad's gaze – her face more alluring than ever, despite the blank stare. Mr. Jones noticed my reaction – his look said enough but his voice made sure "No time for hanky-panky now Dai – you'll be in the ring before long and it won't do you a bit of good then – will it son?" "No Sir." "Alright son – now let's get you a rub down."

Two of Conk's corner men washed my body and toweled me dry. A liniment was rubbed into my back and shoulders – petroleum jelly applied to my face. I put on my knee breaches and boxing shoes. A rag soaked in vinegar was rubbed into my knuckles. I would be ready to fight after a bit more rest.

The fighters were mostly miners – but a good few gypsies and some iron workers were lining up. Among them were some very skilled and experienced fighters – not to say some of the most brutal men in the valleys. Most were fighting for reputation and free ale – some were deadly serious and set on winning every fight. Many were hoping to make it into a Booth like Madog's Men. Madog was here – with an entourage of fighters – I wondered if he would allow any to fight bareknuckle. But he did not. All his boxers wrapped a bandage over their knuckles and wore a thick cotton glove over. Madog wanted to test his fighters but not break their hands in doing so.

For two hours the fights went on one after another. The only break was when a sponsored fighter retired or was beaten – which was very rare. With Madog's men here that could happen. Some of the biggest and heaviest fighters boxed two or three opponents in a row – none of them were beaten – and few opponents lasted more than the one round minimum to get back half the entry price.

Tudor was sponsored by a group of travellers – the Tinker that lived in his campsite was his fair-play man. In Tudor's group his name was simply "Tinker". I had seen this man do amazing things with the myriad of tools hung on his cart. From shoeing horses to repairing chains and harnesses – shaping kettle props over his outside anvil – and building a whole new vardo wheel from scratch. Tinker shouted, "Tudor of Gilfach will fight all-comers of his size for one round at three pounds a fighter. Round ends when either fighter fails to come up to scratch or is knocked out. Challenger will receive ten pounds if he can stop Tudor of Gilfach."

Tudor was far too strong and experienced for me – but I also knew I was fitter and faster. But for now it would have been man versus boy – not a good decision. He stopped the two opponents who stepped up.

The next fighter was from the Blaencwm pits – sponsored by the colliers there. He was about twenty – the miner's lily-white muscle mass of an upper body standing on spindly legs. His calves looked like a ballerina's. Tref folded his massive arms and nodded at me – meaning he thought I should fight this man. The word was passed to him that this fighter was dirty and had a reputation of clashing heads deliberately. He was one of the Treorchy toughs – ready to fight anyone in the street. His sponsors wanted three pounds for three rounds - anyone stopping him would get eight pounds back. I was already out three pounds for the day.

Entering the ring the miner got a great cheer from his supporters. Conk got a bigger shout than I did. He applied petroleum jelly to my eyebrows, nose and lips. "Just box your normal opening Dai – watch out for this boy's head – he'll try to put the nut on you." "Yes Sir." To the back of the crowd I saw Tudor, watching intently – so was Vivian – she didn't turn her head away. A surge of excitement invigorated me.

Conk was right – the Blaencwm man came in head first – both arms swinging – ending each charge with an elbow jag. His forehead was thrusting out from a bulging neck – just looking for me to lean in and fight. Conk's arms separated us after each clash.

After a minute the forward thrusts slowed – he realized I was side slipping each one - countering with body stabs and hooks as he turned back. This miner had a fighting instinct that I'd seen before in the valleys – loosing was not a reason to give-in – it was a reason to get more intense. All my trainers from P.O. Price to Madog had emphasized that same tenet. "That is when you box the way you've been trained – that is why you train – never panic!" Madog would preach.

This fighter's style made it hard to set up the liver punch – getting inside was difficult because his low elbows followed every swing. I knew it was time to change tactics. I noticed he kept his jaw thrust forward when his charge ended before stepping back. I exploded out of a crouch the next time he stepped back and landed a full-on overhand smash to his exposed jaw. It worked – the miner was stunned by the speed and power the punch. The crowd quieted a bit, and then erupted as he took the knee.

Waiting in the centre Tref told me "If he comes back – he'll be after you with the nut. Start off defensive again. The Blaencwm man raised a loud roar from his supporters when he came back to the middle. Sure enough he openly tried to head-but me from the start – much to the delight of the crowd.

My opponent flagged after another two minutes – by which time I was beginning to get into a confident stance and looking for a punch to end it. I could hear a cheer coming from the crowd – I imagined Vivian looking. I finally caught him with a vicious liver punch and a right uppercut to follow – his eyes rolled as he fell back. A huge cheer came up – Tref hugged me "Well done my son, well done." As soon as I could I looked up into the crowd – she was gone – the travellers had left.

The campsite was quiet – the evening fires dwindling. Tudor's vardo and bender tent were still – the voices of the younger children could be heard now and again. Tinker was repairing his grinder barrow with his wife helping him. They had no children – the only couple like that in the campsite. He nodded at me as I walked toward my tent "Kushti fight Boyo." He raised his hammer in salute. I knew the meaning was good.

The next day I was summoned to Tudor's vardo. "Heard you lost the coal race Dai – I thought you were the best." "Well Sir I wouldn't say that but I should have won – I made a big mistake." He gave me one of his long quiet stares. "The mush from Blaecwm is a tough gorga aye." I knew gorga was a name he used for anyone who was not a gypsy traveller, not necessarily a slur.

"Yes Sir he was a strong fighter." "You boxed him very well Dai – that's two well backed gorgas you've nobbled. What's next Dai?" "Just keep training and fighting when I can – try to make a living from fighting and save some money." "Is the Rom Baro from Trehavod your backer?" "Not really he's my fair-play man and like my family." "I have a job if you're interested Dai. My third boy is eleven and has left school now – I have two others already out of school – twelve and thirteen. I was thinking you might teach them more schooling after they've finished work for the day."

"I don't want them to be like me – it don't make sense anymore. But we need them to pay their way in the family." "I think I could do that Sir – what did you have in mind?" "O.k. Dai I was thinking one hour a day – except Saturday and Sunday – five hours a week. For that there's no rent on your tent anymore and the tent is yours. Will that be kushti? "I think so Sir." "O.K. Dai – now don't call me sir anymore." " How should I call you?" "Call me Mr. Tudor Dai – is that O.K.? "Yes Mr. Tudor – when should I start?" "Tomorrow Dai – after training." "Yes Sir – I mean Mr. Tudor – do you have some paper and pencils?" "It'll be here in the vardo tomorrow Dai."

That night in my tent I thought back to all the schooling I had received in my life – I realized it had been exactly that – all my life had been schooling – either in a school or a church. Only since I was kicked out of the Navy was I not in school. And all my life in school I had been punished and hounded – even in the churches. The memory of my first Latin, Greek and French classes flooded back.

There were no books that I'd seen anywhere in the camp – the travellers were not much for reading or writing. Travellers were more interested in acquiring artisan skills rather than formal education – Tudor was breaking the mold. But only boys were to be given lessons – the girls would continue with no schooling.

Girls were taught home skills like crocheting hats and scarves, sewing and knitting. The eldest girl was trained in dukkerin and hawking jewelry and leather items - this was Vivian's future. Most of the girls, I had learned, were married at sixteen – the boys usually seventeen or eighteen. I knew that Vivian would soon be married and she would leave to live with her new husband's family and traveller group – that's the way it worked. They would then start a family right away. I felt useless – powerless to explore the possibilities with Vivian – Tudor would not hear of it for sure.

Later that day I ran down into Penygraig to the Woolworth's where I bought a set of color pencils and then to the Brachi's where I bought the South Wales Echo newspaper. Back in my tent I found welsh cakes left for me by someone – that unfamiliar feeling of family and belonging returned unexpectedly.

After training and sparring the next day I ran up to the feeder and bathed before showing up at Tudor's vardo. The boys were sat at the immaculate oak dining table – flanked on both sides by elaborate china cabinets holding sparkling crystal glassware and the best crockery. They looked the same – just three different sizes. Their clothes were similar and each had a flat cap deposited on the table. They looked dirty around the ears and eyes – they always did in a way – even after the weekly tin bath dip. Their hair was straggly and long.

Unfolding the Echo I laid the front page out in front of them. "Can you read this?" They stared back – shaking their heads – the younger one took a little longer. "I know some of them words Dai." "O.k. show me what you mean." There was a picture of a horse-drawn hearse with a story the undertaker was retiring the horse for a motor hearse. Pointing to the word horse he said "orse" in their blend of welsh and gypsy accent. He couldn't recognize many other words except Wales, train and cars. The older boys did not recognize any words except Wales.

Starting with the oldest I asked him to recite the alphabet – he got as far as "g" and then skipped a few letters here and there, ending in "x". The two other boys had a better grip on it – but at least I had a place to start – the alphabet – it was unbelievable that these boys were so behind the main stream. "O.K. take an exercise book and pencil – write your name at the top of the front cover. They all wrote the same "Tudor". "What's your christian name?" I asked – finally determining they were Vano, Chik and Jal. I explained in detail how to write each name fully and properly.

The first exercise was writing out the alphabet and repeating it five times – this took half the lesson but I could see it was making them concentrate. The same results came from an attempt at the two-times-table. We had a starting point.

On May Day there was a street fair in Pontypridd. Madog's Boxing Booth was a prominent show. I met up with Trefor at the Booth – it had been a while since I saw him. He gave me his usual bear hug but I could see he was preoccupied. "Are you o.k. Tref?" "Well Enid has taken a turn for the worse Dai – the nurse is at the house – I must get back now." "Tref you should have sent one of the boys to tell me." "She's going to die very soon son – I wanted you to know." In a second he was off on his way to the station for a taxi.

I joined the crowd around Madog's Booth – pulling my cap a bit lower. Madog called me over. "Nice fight at Llantrissant Dai – where are you training?" "With Mr.

Tudor of Clydach Sir " "Why not move back in with Conk and train with us Dai – the rozzers aren't after you now." "Thank you Sir."

First in the ring was a featherweight for Madog's Men – Vince "Shock "Volt of Porth. The boxers wore gloves and some had bandages wrapped around their knuckles. Shock knocked out his first three contenders in less than a minute each.

Then what Tref had said sunk in "Enid was dying." I ran from the Booth to their house in Trehavod. The hope of seeing her alive drove me to almost sprint the three miles. Tref answered the door. There was a strange bad smell in the house – not like the ty bach wrapped in newspaper – this was different. It was a smell I could not turn away from – it was everywhere in the house. It was the smell of Enid's dying.

She lay under a mound of bedding – her head almost bald now except a few wisps of white. Her eyes were closed. When I touched her forehead she opened her eyes to reveal dark holes – Tref wiped a dribble from her mouth – her false teeth were long gone.

I felt very sad as I left the house – sad for Tref in his loss that few could appreciate – sad that I was leaving him at a moment he needed me. It would be foolish for me to risk staying – it could mean my freedom and my whole life. But inside I knew it was Vivian that was drawing me back to Gilfach.

After a couple of weeks I asked Tudor how he liked the lessons I had given his sons. "Why are they drawin orses and vardos?" "Because they're interested in that and gives us something to learn about and read about." "In the paper?" "Why not it's full of reading and it's all we have for now. Do you like what they're learning?" "Maybe."

I decided to make my proposal to Tudor. "Mr. Tudor – I could teach the boys more if I had some books – from the Penygraig Library. If I had an address and a job I could get those books." "What are you saying Dai?" "If I could give my address as here and be an apprentice to Tinker – I could get books and make some money too." "You want to be a Tinker?" "Yes Mr. Tudor – I'd like to be able to be a Tinker." "What about all that learning you got?" "Maybe it could help me be a good Tinker Mr. Tudor." Giving me a suspicious eye he murmured, "Let me think."

Whenever I could, after sparring and training, if Tinker was at his vardo and workspace, I stood to one side and watched his every move. He didn't mind – even telling me about what he was doing. It was fascinating to see him make a horseshoe to fit so perfectly or to make a steel ring for a horse tether out of scrap metal. Travellers from the Rhondda and valleys came to see him to repair or make new parts for their vardos, harnesses, and horse and pony tack. He was an expert at sharpening knives and swords – he made brass earrings out of old taps and delicate bracelets and necklaces out of wire and seashells.

Tinker was also an old bare-knuckle fighter and Tudor's fair play man. He was well known at the fairs and miner community gatherings. One for being able to separate any fighters – due to his enormous arm strength. And two because of his metal work and jewelry. Tinker was also a partner in a fair show with an escape artist and another strongman. In a tent they would sit twenty-five people and entertain them by tearing apart telephone directories, bending steel bars and escaping from shackles and handcuffs while sealed and locked in a large sack. He was the senior traveller under Tudor and commanded respect from everyone in the gypsy and valley traveller community.

The sessions with Tudor took on more intensity – he was also benefiting from the repetitive training. He pulled me aside as I knocked at his vardo for the boys' lessons. "I talked to Tinker and we'll take you on as his apprentice and helper. But you're a gorga and that spot is reserved for Jal – so it can only be for two years until he turns thirteen."

The realization that I was accepted by Tudor as almost an equal flashed in my mind – he trusted me to teach and watch over his sons – and now adding a trusted position in the campsite and the traveller group that was reserved for his son.

Tudor and his group were very trustworthy. There didn't appear to be anything bad happening in the camp or among the group. All the shavers were well behaved – even if they all smoked from about age ten. Occasionally a young man would marry a girl from another traveller group and a new vardo and bender tent would be added for them. There didn't seem to be any queers around either – for the first time I didn't notice a man trying to lure me into a public lavatory or behind a bush.

Each day was full of work and effort. The campsite was completely cleaned up every morning and the horses tended to – new fires were set and stoked. School attendance was not a high priority for Tudor and the travellers – but their loyalty was stronger than I had ever met before. They were equally observant for the wellbeing of their animals.

Most days I saw Vivian and hoped she would notice me – once in a while she smiled a little, but never a word or wave. I fantasized she was watching me train and spar – through a crack in the vardo curtains.

Each day she looked more perfect – her features and lips were constant images in my mind. Sometimes I felt a sense of panic if I could not instantly recall those pictures – but when I could it was enough to drive me day after day – to do my best.

Tudor's sons taught me about handling and grooming horses – how to talk to them and ride them bareback. We rode out up the mountain and cantered over the short grass slopes – chasing retired pit-ponies that had been released to fend for themselves – something a traveller or gypsy would never even think of doing. The boys showed me how to catch rabbits, they called shoshoi, using the dogs and nets. Shoshoi stew was cooking somewhere in the campsite every day – as was the delicious breads the women produced in earth ovens.

If not training for boxing or involved in work for Tudor and his family, I spent my spare time with Tinker. He gave me tasks and instructions – they involved setting, boosting and cleaning up his coke furnace and blacksmith tools – sorting scrap metal – polishing the ornamental brass decorating his vardo. Tinker was also a Rom Baro, a Big Man in the traveller community. He was counseled by the group on many matters affecting the harmony and organization of the camp, and others throughout the valleys.

Tinker was also a teacher – a teacher of traveller culture and a teacher of bareknuckle boxing. While I worked, watched or assisted him Tinker commented continuously. It could be about my last sparring session with Tudor and how I was leaving myself open, or my balance in a counter combination. It could be about the exact color he was seeking when heating a horseshoe – or how he was sharpening a drill-bit on one of the grindstones I powered, by turning a massive handle driving the belts.

Occasionally he would ask me about my education. He was very interested in my experiences taking religious exams in Oxford and in my knowledge of the Bible, Latin, Greek and French. Tinker dressed the same every day – black knee breeches over black ankle boots and socks – held up by thick leather suspenders with silver hardware. His thick upper body – covered in black hair wore only a white singlet. A red neck-scarf sat under a huge, tweed flat cap – black curls fell down and around his bull neck. When he smiled, which was not often, a few blackened and irregular teeth spoiled his rugged, swarthy and healthy face. Most travellers, and most valley men for that matter, paid little heed to their teeth. Some brushed with charcoal or salt – not many used toothpaste – it was a matter of time before their teeth started rotting.

Tinker was a skilled gypsy Dandor too. His set of tools for pulling teeth was impressive and housed in an intricately carved wood box, with draws lined in green felt. At the back of his tent there was a curtained off area where a traveller would sit, have a stiff jolt of rum, lean back and open up. Tinker was a swift and ruthless tooth extractor – he did not rely on a client holding still. Instead he pressed his massive forearm into the client's turned head – gently to begin, but increasing as necessary to totally still the head and neck. Then in went the thrust of the steel pliers – crushing the tooth enamel until stopped by the core of the tooth – a deft twist of the wrist and the dand is handed to its owner. I observed these procedures closely – Tinkers's wife holding the patient's hand, and collecting the fee first.

Over the next year and a half I became more like a traveller than a gorga. My clothes were all traveller made – my hair long and plaited under a flat cap – my skin becoming more dark and swarthy with the continuous outdoors activity. Between eighteen and nineteen everyone including me was surprised at a growth spurt which took me to five feet eleven and eleven stone ten. My speech was different also – all hint of an Oxford yokel accent replaced with the melody of the welsh dialect – mixed with traveller words of pidgin English.

My reputation as a valley sportsman was building. I was a frequent competitor and a first three finisher in most of the Rhondda mountains coal-carrying races. Often at weekends I stayed at Trefor's house in Trehavod. He and his butties sponsored me in the races and Tref was my fair-play man in all-comer mountain boxing meets. Madog and other promoters' prevailed in the use of bandaged knuckles and padded gloves. I trained regularly with Madog's men and got the nickname Gypsy Dai Jones. The name appealed to me but rankled Tudor a bit. Tinker defended it saying I had earned the name even if was sometimes considered a slur on the traveller community. The travellers still settled arguments in bare-knuckle fights and when strong fighters emerged on the scene they were often paired in a dawn prizefight for a purse collected among the valley travellers.

The constant battering had flattened my nose and cauliflowered my left ear – my forehead was permanently swollen with scar tissue. In three years I had become almost unrecognizable from Roy Hudson – except for the red-welt scars left from the glass lacerations on my left arm. Tinker occasionally commented that he could disguise the scars with tattoos – he drew a tiger's head with snakes intertwined around it.

One wintery Friday night I sat in his Dandor's chair – he slipped me the customary tot of rum and before long the scars were completely and permanently covered. To balance the body Tinker tattooed a male lion's head on my other forearm. My physical connections and history with Oxford were effectively all gone now.

My friendship with Tudor's sons grew stronger. Each had special talents that were being developed by the traveller group. I sparked an interest in drawing horses and campsite scenes in Vano – Chik liked drawing too, showing talent for designing vardos and horse brasses. Jal the youngest and keenest was reading everything I could obtain from the Penygraig library – he loved the tales of King Arthur. None had any interest in mathematics except to add up the parts of a horse trade to make sure the full and correct amount was charged. But often the trade had future outcomes attached – like the first foal or a breeding opportunity. Everything was verbal and personally witnessed by all parties to the trade – nothing written down. It became clear that Tudor had in mind a son who could write his trades down and record the details. He asked me to assist him with this and train Jal to write letters for signing by all travellers involved in a trade. Tudor's group was growing – he needed more organization and was relying on me to help.

In physical stature now I was almost equal to Tudor – except for his muscle thickness. In sparring I could avoid all his moves quite easily – but hurting him with a devastating punch was much harder – I still needed more power to stop a fighter of Tudor's strength and experience. Fighting in Madog's Booth every week would take me to the level I wanted to be. The urge to fight was relentless – as relentless as my obsession with Vivian. In a grotesque way the urges were working against each other. My physical mind wanted to explode and reek violence and revenge – my emotional mind wanted to succeed in a normal life – where peace exists.

Experiencing the way Tudor led his family and his group was a life lesson. The difference in the loyalty, trust, self-discipline and respect for each other was so clear and the results proved well. There were no sexual predators in the traveller community – no thievery or exploitation – no upper class – no lower class - no poverty to degrade you. The notion of incest and family molestation was the most abhorrent action in the traveller culture – so it didn't happen – children born outside marriage were non-existent. There was a genetic factor of goodness embedded in the culture. In the Valleys and Oxford you'd be hard pressed to find this – let alone embedded in the entire community.

Two girls in Tudor's kampania married at sixteen – one to a boy younger than me from another group in the valleys – and one from the kampania aged seventeen. The couple from the kampania still stayed with their families but were allowed to court after the wedding. The weddings were meetings between the girl's and boy's fathers and involved paying the girl's father a sum of money for the loss of his daughter. A glass of wine was shared and after two days the couple were allowed to court – but not live together.

A girl marrying a boy from another kampania moved in with his family after the wedding. By Vano's account all the marriages were planned by the parents and sometimes involved the King and Queen of the valleys. At fifteen he was being encouraged by Tudor and his mother to look at eligible girls in the traveller community. As their eldest son he was a ranking prospect among other prominent traveller families seeking to arrange marriages for their daughters.

Soon Vivian would be married too. The thought brought panic and nausea – I knew that unless I at least made a play there would never be another chance and I would have to live the rest of my life without her. Although I could not touch her – and never would without her permission anyway – I was able to see her almost daily. And each day my obsession and feelings for her grew stronger.

Among the many things taught me by Tinker was how to make gypsy jewelry. I wanted to give Vivian a sign that I was in love with her. It was also becoming obvious to Tudor and Vivian's mother. We did not miss an opportunity to watch each other and look for eye contact. Vano was jibing me about his princess sister and all the valley traveller boys pursuing her. It made me sick to my stomach and often unable to eat.

Tinker produced a small bar of silver alloy in a crucible buried in the white-hot core of the coke furnace. I watched and listened intently as he worked it into a long thin, flat wire. His ferari skills so evident to produce this fine wire. Taking small pieces of the wire he made them into circles of different sizes – closing each one with a delicate silver solder. I kept the tools and materials hot or warm according to Tinker's stream of instructions. Amazingly in between the apprentice training he talked of the importance of the circles in the bracelet we were making. How the circles stood for an endless loop of love and that circles within circles were wishes for children.

Over three months Tinker watched over my progress and repaired my mistakes as the bracelet took shape. A three strand interconnected filigree of circles and connecting arcs. A true symbol of gypsy love and commitment – so delicate to be almost invisible on the wrist but markedly noticeable when drawn to the flawless skin beneath it.

Tinker and his wife became like uncle and aunt – I felt the same connection of support that Aunt Daisy and Uncle Dai had given me. A feeling that they were on my side – a feeling that I mattered at times. Tinker knew that I was in love with Vivian and the bracelet was about her.

Without saying it he was supporting my instinct and attempting to guide me in the ways a gypsy boy would handle the situation. But I was nineteen and didn't feel like a boy – I was financially independent and on an upward curve in the valley sports events. My following among the miners connected with Conk Jones was unique for a gypsy competitor – even if I wasn't a kaule I was living like one. My early life situations had taught me to defend and stand up for myself when needed. The kaule life had taught me fairness and trust - and a life without the perpetual crime raging in the gorga community.

Tudor, Tinker and the travellers never isolated or snubbed me. They weren't infected by personality problems. In the kampania travellers were open and positive. Outside they became closed and suspicious – knowing the gorgas hated them. They hardly ever said it – but it was as obvious as the massive pyramids of coal waste lingering menacingly above the villages throughout the valleys.

Of real interest to Tinker was my early boyhood - because I knew so much more about life outside the traveller kamapanias, and was educated beyond his imagination. I told him of the tobacco stained tweedy school masters who relished the caning and detention of boys for minor infringements – heaping punishment upon punishment on vulnerable boys from the Town – while coddling and cheating for the sons of their Gown friends.

Tinker told me of the traveller rituals and rules, saying that punishment like this had never been heard of. Because the Dad disciplined a son for breaking the rules from birth - and the kampania social cohesiveness took care of cementing it into the daily culture. I told them of the extreme caning of boys in the Navy and the underground network of queers stalking and raping boys in Oxford. He had never heard of such things – they did not exist in the traveller community.

With my new brothers I talked about how we could take revenge on people like my father and Dumbo – the church caretaker and the judo master. The angst raged among them as much as me – the mere notion was enough to bring violent and vengeful consequences into their thoughts. For me the rage was persistent and gave rise to malicious ideas of retaliation – I wanted to hurt them.

One of Madog's Booth fighters was making a big name for himself in the valleys – John Stone of Ton Pentre – known as Stone John. His record of wins and knockouts was drawing crowds, bookies and challengers to Madog's Booth wherever the fair was on.

Time was running out on any chance of marrying Vivian. Now sixteen she was loveliness personified - monopolizing my thoughts, driving my ambition and hostility. It was time to make a move – I had been defending too long. We saw each other daily and often spoke in groups – she now looked into my eyes for a few seconds and held her head a certain way when I was talking. I could not take my eyes off her. Everyone in the kampania knew I was in love with her.

Tudor was not well pleased and stopped talking to me – even when he sat watching me teach his sons to read, write and draw - in his own vardo. Vivian's mother was more flexible it seemed. She smiled when talking to me and gave me equal meals to the rest of the family. Most of the families travelled in their vardos from Easter to September. They worked all the town and village fairs and the miners outings – each family or two covering different parts of the valleys. They traded horses and ponies, sold jewelry and gypsy clothes. The mothers told fortunes and read palms. Some had sideshow acts like the escape artist and a full-body tattooed man who stripped of in a tent while customers filed through.

But by far the most popular attraction at the valley fairs was the Boxing Booth, and in this world Madog Jeffries was king. As was the case when the annual Pontypridd Fair was held in the centre of town that year. A large group of travellers was there involved from setting up the fair to hawking sideshows and standing guard at vardos and tents. Madog's Booth was next to a haunted-house ride and a dodgem ride. Madog barked over the fair noise easily, as the fighters lined up on the stage facing the crowd.

"Come on men – step into the ring with a boxer of your choice men – who do you think you can beat up here men?" The fighters flexed and swiveled – bobbing heads and shoulders in intimidation. That was all most of the half-intoxicated miners needed to start lining up for a round or two. "Come on you local boxers – you local boys – you local strongmen – test yourself against these boxers – all fair bouts – all fair refereeing – give it a try – your girlfriend will like it." Stone John was in the middle of three boxers standing at the front of the stage. He was eying me and bobbing – a bit of a snigger on his face. From training, he knew as well as I did that we would eventually meet in the ring for proper fight. I looked at Tref and raised my eyebrows – expecting him to shake his head as he had at other fairs – he nodded – it was time to go all in.

Madog was barking "Come on you Ponty fighters – you men of the fighting Town – the Town of Freddie Welsh – a World Champion – he fought in the streets and the mountains in the valleys and took on the world – Come on boys – who will take on these boxers?"

The big crowd murmured and joked. Fighters from among them could earn two pounds for every round completed up to three but most were dispatched in the first round and left with nothing. If you could stop Stone John there was a fifteen pounds bonus. Madog needed to get some men to step forward. "No entry charge if you box John

Stone." Two men stepped forward at the notion of fifteen pounds for a fight.

Fifteen pounds was a lot of money – two or three weeks wages down the pits – but the money was less important in my plan. I stepped up behind the other two men. Madog was not surprised – one of his rules was any boxer in training could challenge a boxer already established at the Booth. Madog called us up on the stage and asking for names he introduced us to the crowd "Gypsy Dai Jones of Trehavod" I looked over at Tref – a faint smile on his face. Stripped to the waist we bandaged and gloved as the crowd filed in to the marquee tent.

For months, at the library, I had been reading about Sugar Ray Robinson challenging again for the World middleweight championship. I learned his double bolo punch combination – a high left-hook, a liver punch and a right hook delivered in two seconds with stinging power by the twist of his body just before each impact.

Stone John dealt with the first two challengers swiftly – almost sparring with them before ending each bout in round one with technical knockouts. The audience of well over two hundred crammed around the elevated ring – murmuring discontent at the lack of a fight. Tref stood in front of me in the corner of the ring – his huge head and bull neck breathing in my face. "Three two minute rounds on the clock Dai – not up at referee's count of ten stops the bout - right Dai? "O.K. Tref." "Box him now Dai." I nodded.

Stone John was angry when he came out at the bell – lunging at me with his head and shoulders. I remembered the Sugar Ray model – the goal not to knock him out at this stage but to wear him out while not getting hurt. For the first round I evaded all his power punches but got a severe jostling from his head and shoulders.

I could tell he was getting frustrated when he threw wild swing after wild swing at me toward the end of the round – trying to finish it. He nearly did when he caught me with a blow to my left temple. For a second I saw black – then flashes – blinking as he hit me on the back of the head going down. I heard the referee shout "four" before the bell sounded.

The cold sponge soon cleared my head. "Keep boxing Dai – you've got him worried – I can see it in his eyes – there's two more rounds yet – he'll tire out soon – when he does, come inside – hurt his body Dai." I took a deep breath and nodded as the bell went.

Looking across at Stone and Madog from my corner after round two I could tell there was concern in their camp. Madog was waving his hands as if to say "get going man" – Stone was not hearing it – he was exhausted. He was now retreating – wanting no more of the fight – I started looking to for a knock-out as I sensed the crowd getting behind me, when he was parallel with my body I hit him with a liver punch – that stopped him cold – leaving me time to hit him twice on the jaw as he folded.

The Booth erupted – cheered on by Tref and his boys who had bet their wages. As I looked around I saw Mr. Jenkins from the market and coach Alby. At the back I saw Tudor and his family – a stern look on his face. Tinker and his wife stood next to them – obviously elated.

The Tudor boys were waving and cheering – Vivian smiled – and waved – my heart lifted off. My plan had taken a turn to the positive – I was willing to fight forever to keep it going.

Madog offered us a cup of tea as Tref and I sat down with him at the back of the tent.

A few days later, after lessons with the boys I asked Tudor for a word. As always he was accommodating but stern and silent as I looked squarely at him – an hour before I had sparred with him in training. The same combinations I had used against Stone John that I had been practicing with Tudor for two years. But still there was the barrier of kaule to gorga – I could never be kaule.

I asked to him listen to me as a man – regardless of kaule or gorga. I told him I was in love with his daughter and wanted his permission to court with her. "That's impossible – you're gorga – we don't marry outside." "I'm asking you to accept me as known to the kaule – I want to be as much kaule as I can – I promise total loyalty to the kaule and your group Mr. Tudor." I offer all my earnings for one year as a darro to you for this honor Mr. Tudor. I have secured a boxing contract with Madog Jeffries of Pontypridd. I will be Dai Jones of Trehavod, an equal, and prepared to protect your daughter with my life, forever. I don't care what you call me or say about me – unless you offend me for no reason – then I will challenge you Mr. Tudor. Would you expect less of a man asking to court your daughter? Tudor was not happy to be in this situation but I persisted.

"Tinker has said he will sponsor me for acceptance and a vardo in the group if you are agreeable Mr. Tudor. He has said I am fully trained for some of his trades now and he would allow me to pitch up next to the ferari's shop. I have made a bracelet for Vivian Mr. Tudor – could I have your permission to give it to her. "I'm knowin Tinker's thinking. Vivian is a kaule Dai – she's not to marry a gorga Dai." "Mr. Tudor if you will accept Tinker's standing for me then I could be accepted as equal over time – that's all I ask. Of course if Vivian is not agreeable then there's nothing to talk about Sir."

"It's me that will decide Dai – not my daughter. How much lovo are you giving for her?" "I expect wages about seven pounds a week – I would offer four pounds a week to your family for one year – to be allowed to court Vivian and be accepted into the group Mr. Tudor." "So what will you do Dai if I say no?" "Mr. Tudor if you or Vivian reject my proposal I'll leave the camp and move to Trehavod with my guardian." "Conk Jones – he's a baro gorga." "Yes Sir he is." "O.k. Dai let me think about this – it's not easy."

Standing to leave I took the bracelet from my pocket – now in a soft leather purse I had made to Tinker's instructions. As I placed it on the table as Tudor's wife walked in. She smiled and nodded toward my gift. Leaving, I was so relieved I wanted to scream.
But not for long when Vivian came out of the tent – I passed closer to her than ever, inhaling the air around her. She looked straight at me and smiled – a little laugh on her hypnotizing lips.

Tudor kept me waiting for a week – despite sparring and training and occasionally watching me teach his sons. After a session he called me over, placing the bracelet on the table. "Aye Dai you've turned a few heads – seems like some would have you in the kampania." Possibly for the first time I saw Tudor crack a smile "I don't think I should but I'm goin to give in on this – we'll have to talk about how it can work – for that I need to be talking to your family – but you don't have one – so Tinker will be your kaule family and will meet with me to decide on the courtship. "Thank you Mr. Tudor – I won't let you down Sir." "Go ask Tinker to come 'ere." "Yes Mr. Tudor." "You can speak to me as Tudor now."

I floated back to my tent and started to collect my sparse belongings – my plan was coming together. Feelings stirred everywhere in my body – the worst that Vivian would reject me – the best was that I may be on a path to kissing her – my body trembled spontaneously. For three years I had watched her from a distance – hardly speaking until a year ago. I knew she was watching me too, as I was craving her attention.

Later in the evening Tinker came to my tent – a broad smile on his face. "So Tudor has given his permission – but a few points need to be organized." "Do you a have birth papers Dai?" I was ready for this thanks to Tref. He had confided a year ago that I could adopt his son Dafydd Jones' name – because he considered me as his son. He had shown me Dafydd's birth certificate and where he kept it in the front room china cabinet. "I do Tinker – it's at my guardian's house in Trehavod. "Good Tudor is worried you are not a proper citizen – will you be called up for National Service?" "I don't think so – my welsh name is Dafydd or Dai Jones – if the papers came to Tref Jones he would return them as his son no longer living – killed in the mine." "O.K. we know that method – a few of our boys have gorga birth papers that way – so many boys killed in the pits we could all have gorga names! By the way Dai we would like you to take a Rom name when you live inside the kampania." "Thank you Tinker for all the many special things you have done for me." "You have earned them all Danior." "Danior?" "Aye, Danior is your Rom name – it means good teeth - from now on, for me you will be Dani – is that fine?" "Yes Tinker that is fantastic."

Tinker explained my responsibilities in detail. I was to move my tent into his pitch area, which was the second largest in the campsite. During the next year it would be doubled in size and a new fire pit built at one end. I must pay the darro promised to Tudor – full payment of the traveller dowry was critical. The lovo was to be in cash every week, on Saturday morning. After three months if the betrothal is going well I will be allowed to visit Vivian once a week with her mother present. Following another three successful months, two visits a week were allowed. Another six months, provided I had paid Tudor the full darro of two hundred and eight pounds - a wedding date would be arranged. At that time I must have a respectable tent with a cooking and heating fire for my wife to move in. I would then be expected to start acquiring a vardo – either building with the group help or buying from another group or family. Either way the money was my responsibility – these were the normal expectations placed on young men marrying in the traveller tradition. Any failure would be public and embarrassing in the kampania.

Under my contract with Madog Jeffries I was required to train two days a week and box two days a week – to whatever the schedule Madog demanded. When travelling overnight from Ponty I would be paid subsistence for lodging and food. My pay was guaranteed at seven pounds a week – bonuses were earned at each Booth appearance. – depending on the number of challengers defeated. Any losses were to be charged back directly to the boxer's account – that could mean losing two weeks wages in one fight. I was barred from competing as an individual in miner's events and from any bare-knuckle boxing of any kind. I hoped I would not find myself in a traveller bare-knuckle contest – used to settle internal disputes within the groups and community.

The time began running fast. Most Friday afternoons I reported to Madog's yard to travel to a fair location. Madog's men usually numbered about four to six boxers at different weights - all in top fighting fitness. Other members of the Booth crew drove the lorries, erected the Booth frontage, tent, ring and stands to house the audience. All were boxing trainees in the stable and ready to go into the ring if Madog wanted. I noticed occasionally he would send one or two of the crew into the crowd. If challengers were sparse he nodded for them to come forward as contenders – "to get the tempo up", as he liked to say.

I continued to out-train any fighter in sight. I kept up my daily training with Tudor and now, his three sons – my pupils rapidly becoming my brothers. All three displayed natural fighting ability – showing no fear to hold up their fists to anyone. At night we sat in my tent and told stories about our lives and ambitions – them chain smoking rolled up tobacco or pipes – and me distracted by my thoughts of Vivian. A band of brothers grew naturally – we all lived equally but had our individual standing in the kampania – earned by supporting the community first – before self.

Tudor was rarely boxing any more – he still trained some days but was becoming more involved with the broader traveller community. He was on a panel of judges that resolved any, very rare, serious matters in the traveller community. Adultery, theft and fraud were the most serious wrongdoings and were extremely rare – no instances at all in Tudor's group. He began to rely on me for reading and explaining letters that were delivered to him – and writing his comments for return. These experiences of the traveller justice system made me wonder why it was not applied in the gorga community. The only serious crimes were in tales told around the campfires. It seemed any traveller who committed one and repeated it was banished from the community – but it was speculated that banishing involved the offender disappearing one night on the mountain – never to be seen or heard of again. All other disagreements or vocal arguments were settled by the men in bare knuckle fights - once the contest was over the men shook hands, and the slate was wiped clean of any lingering issues. It was impossible for a traveller boy or girl to be molested or abused – unless by a gorga.

My first courting time with Vivian was a Saturday evening following my first darro payment. I had prepared obsessively – using all the skills the navy had taught me I sat in a chair with her next to me – close enough to sense her breath and see the fine dark hair at her temples. I was utterly unable to speak without my lips trembling and my voice cracking. She just sat and smiled – it was enough. Her mother sat at the other end of the vardo – out of sight in the kitchen but heard occasionally to move or cough – to confirm her presence.

Eventually I picked up enough courage. Taking the bracelet from the table I touched the purse to my lips and placed it in her lap. Looking at me eye-to-eye for the first time I saw a full smile – her blushing pink lips parting invitingly. This girl had completely immobilized me – just by her aura.

"Thank you Danior – is it o.k for me to call you Dani?" I could only nod in a breathless stare. "This is a kushti bracelet Dani – I like it a lot. Do you want to put it on me?"

From Spring to Autumn we attended all the major town fairs, jubilees and miner events. Boxing was the sport of the valleys along with rugby and strongman contests. As soon as we returned to Ponty I left for the kampania and my other life. I began to realize the kampania was really where I wanted to be. As one of Madog's Men I was doing well in my trade, being matched against the toughest and strongest boxers and mountain fighters in the valleys. On some weekends I boxed ten bouts a day - every miner in the valleys was a fighter of some type.

My fascination with Vivian grew – in or away from the kampania I craved the sight of her. Our affection was growing – courting twice a week and talking quietly about our interests and hopes. Vivian was a virgin to life outside the kaule - as well as literally a virgin within its strict courting culture. Her knowledge of the gorga world amounted to the immediate local environment and geography of the valleys they travelled. She couldn't read or write but had an amazing hand at drawing, sewing and knitting – could ride horses like a jockey and recite and sing kaule poetry, stories and fortune telling myths. I hung on her every word. When I left her vardo or their tent after a courting she would touch the back of my hand with hers – we were forbidden to touch so this moment was the most special.

Madog started signing me for local professional bouts at middleweight – boxing at the lower end of the night's card. I was boxing so much that I hardly needed to train –

but I knew my edge was due to the extra work in training – specially the mountain running.

I won every bout in my first year signed for Madog Jeffries – in the Booth and in the South Wales professional rings. Each and every day I looked up and thanked fate for bringing me here. I noticed the relentless urge to fight was giving way to a more mindful view of my situation and future.

As a year of courtship approached everything was going to plan. Vivian's upcoming sixteenth birthday marked the beginning of our betrothal week. My earnings from boxing were twice what I had expected. Tinker and my traveller brothers extended my tent and built the new fire-pit. Tinker and I made a kettle and prop, a stew pot and a meat roasting spit. Vivian's mother and families in the kampania made quilts and bedding – my brothers carved a Romani mask from a piece of oak – to hang on the entrance of our family tent. I placed my savings in Tinker's care and under his guidance. With Chik drawing and designing, I planned the building of my own vardo.

Without noticing the change taking place, it was now obvious to me that my life with the kaule was everything I wanted – not only for the privilege of marrying Vivian – but for the unconditional acceptance as an equal – based on nothing else except good will, simple rules and true character. It didn't matter a farthing who you were – there were no comparisons going on – like in the Oxford Town and Gown.

Every week something for our betrothal was donated by the families in the kampania, and others in the valleys. Vano and Jal now seventeen and fourteen were very promising boxers. Both were apprentices with Madog's

Men and travelled with the Booth. They trained with me every day except Saturday and Sunday when we usually travelled with the Booth to a town or village in the Rhondda. I spent so much time with them, Tinker, Tudor and the kampania, my speech and appearance were very similar. I noticed in some villages and towns, further up the valleys where we were strangers, some locals gawked at us and muttered insults about gypsies.

Later when they saw me and Vano on the Booth stage with the other fighters, they were not as brave. We punished these ruffians if they came into the ring. Good fighters who knew of me in the valleys did not get into the ring with me lightly. Some fighters travelled the fairs and regularly challenged us – specially up and coming boxers like Vano and Jal. These challengers were vitally aware of my liver punch and it's devastating effect if I landed it perfectly. But local tough-guys were not clued in to it, so my Booth bouts often ended in the first round.

Chapter 14

Fair Boxing Booth

After dismantling the Booth at a fair in Porth, Madog called a meeting at the yard when everything was parked-up. He announced a contract he had made with a travelling fair group, to join them in their annual tour of the Valleys, Monmouthshire, Gloucestershire and Oxfordshire. My temples pulsed at the thought of Oxfordshire – St. Giles fair immediately pictured in my mind. Madog announced that fighters and staff to travel with the Booth would be informed in a few weeks. The tour was to start July 1st and end September 15th back in Ponty.

Taking me aside Madog told me I was his first pick for the summer fair tour – and my brothers Vano, Chik and Jal were hired as back-up fighters and Booth hands. We would have a caravan to travel and live in on the fair sites. That evening I talked it over with Tudor and Tinker. Soon my full year of darro payments would be completed and our marriage could proceed. The first Monday in June was chosen as the wedding day. A week before the wedding day I was to be accepted into the tribe as Tudor's intended zamutro – his son-in-law – there was to be a ritual where I would have to drink a special potion. Tinker said If I survived the effects of the potion I would be accepted – he didn't say what happened if I failed.

The tribal acceptance ritual was simple enough – although the foul potion almost made me vomit. Tinker, Tudor and other rom baros watched me drain the goblet and gaped at me after as I fought to hold it down – which I did with great difficulty. After there were laughs all round at my expense – the potion had a definite odour of goat-piss.

Our wedding a week later was just as simple and did not include any vile potions. It was more like a business meeting than a wedding. First Tinker and Tudor sat alone together and drank a glass of wine – from a bottle specially procured for the purpose and adorned with a gold chain – a purse of gold sovereigns was attached to it – a gift from the families to start the couple on a prosperous path. Then Vivian's mother and Tinker's wife joined them for a glass of the wine. Finally Vivian and I joined them and were also given a glass of wine. We exchanged gold rings – made from coins melted down and fashioned in Tinkers shop. Tinker tied a headscarf, made by his wife, around Vivian's neck. That was it – then for the first time we were allowed to walk together.

Although we were now husband and wife I felt awkward reaching for her hand. Walking with her up the mountain on a perfect, warm, early summer evening, I was so charged with feelings – passion, protection, affection, accomplishment – infatuation. Above all I was thankful to the people who had trusted me and allowed me into the Valley Gypsy community.

Picking up courage I put my arm around her back and let my hand fall on her shoulder. Her reaction was immediate, and exciting, when she slipped her arm around my lower back – I felt her fingers through the cloth of my shirt. She was waiting for me to take the lead but was willing once I did. The immense silence of the mountain was like a dream substance. Moving in front of her I held her shoulders and drew her in. Her thrusting mouth found mine instantly. This was my first kiss in four years but it was like the first kiss ever – it will be available for instant recall the rest of my life and I will think of it every day forever. There was a feeling behind her kiss that was as different as she was – the most lasting and deep impression possible.

We stayed locked in that embrace for an hour at least, as darkness fell – a thousand kisses transpired – each one craving the next. All these months spent imagining her kiss were eclipsed by the real kiss. A feeling of optimism flooded over me. I finally had a life with a future - no one was trying to attack or punish me.

We drew smiles and good wishes when we returned to the kampania for a celebration of the marriage. A whole sheep was roasted on a ceremonial fire-pit. Jugs of wine and beer were passed around the families with an accordion player leading rom songs about prosperity and a large family.

Tinker had advised me of the important customs I should adhere to. Vivian and I were expected to live somewhat separately until our first child was born – that child was expected to be born in a year. Until then Vivian was to sleep in a space in Tinker's vardo or his extended tent. I was to sleep in my tent in Tinker's area of the kampania. We could not sleep together until our first child was born.

Tinker talked about the duties of a husband and a wife. I should be protective, loyal and industrious. In courting I should be gentle and loving. When pregnant the husband was responsible for all duties. At the birth Vivian would be taken to a special tent and remain there for a month – during this time I would not be able to see them. Following the month of isolation and recovery from the birth my wife and baby would move into our permanent family dwelling. Tinker stressed the importance of owning a vardo by that time – legitimizing the family within the kampania and the traveller group.

The next six weeks was as if I had died and went to heaven. Every day we took our time to walk up the mountain together – the day skipped by in anticipation of this special time we would spend laying on the cool grass slope – my shirt under her back. Looking into her eyes and saying 'I love you." Gradually each day parting her blouse to see her breasts pushing against the bodice – lifting it to see her nipples – each time like the first time. Vivian was like a silent virgin of perfection – yet as soon as I released her inhibition she became thrusting and lustful. My mouth over her nipples gave way to a torrent of release – hidden in this shy and innocent virgin was a full-blooded woman capable of giving and receiving. Every day was a revelation, our lovemaking created a bond of genuine affection. These were not hurried, fumbling encounters in the church boiler room or crèche – followed by embarrassment, reticence and shaming gossip. These were gifts beyond all expectation.

As the date of Madog's Booth departure for the summer fairs approached I became anxious at the thought that I could be detained by my enemies in Oxford. I was still a juvenile at twenty but could be sent to prison – now with a long record of absconding to add to my offending record. Thoughts of this predicament invaded my mind and angered me to the point of physical reaction. No matter how much I tried I couldn't reduce the drive for revenge. It was even stronger now that the role models of Tinker, Tudor, Tref and Madog shaped my future as a man. The previous dark figures of my father, brother, Dumbo, the queers who pursued me lurked in my mind – entering my thoughts without warning.

Vivian listened to my ranting but convinced me that finding and hurting them would get me into deeper trouble. Now five years of change and growth had healed me a little – I had a life now. I reflected on the hatred that had pushed Lyn to a life of permanent misery. In our campfire discussions of revenge we changed from ideas of torture, mutilation and live cremation toward public exposure and humiliation. But inside I still wanted to make them really hurt – something they could never forget – like the sentence they imposed on me for ten years.

Two weeks before we were to leave there was a coal-miner disaster on our planned route through Monmouth – forty-six miners were killed. A dark mist descended on the valleys – yet another massive loss due to the lust for money. It was another reminder that the gorga life was one of being controlled – if you were born in the valleys there was little else except to go underground to work at fourteen – no one was going to feed you except yourself at that point.

Leaving Vivian was a hard and most dismaying event, with tears and reluctance to let go of each other. For a while it was difficult to concentrate and I was permanently sad. Six of us from the kampania left in a lorry towing a caravan – Tinker driving, with his sharpening and repair stand loaded on the back. Next to him Patrin, his fair partner and the escape artist – the tent and the escape paraphernalia all loaded in the back of the lorry. My brothers and myself sat in the caravan under tow. We were pensive and concerned about leaving the security of our families – but Tinker was with us and we had a plan.

Our first fair was in Caerphilly where Magog's' Boxing Booth was well known. As usual we arrived at the fair site late in the afternoon before the first day. We met up with Madog and the rest of the crew, and in three hours had the Booth unloaded and assembled. The electricity was connected, fans were positioned to ventilate the tent, the ring was rigged and the microphone tested. Tinker's escapist tent and sharpening stand stood directly next to the Booth, our caravan parked behind. My brothers and I were assigned to help other shows and rides to get set-up – by midnight the area had been transformed into a fairground. The fish and chip stall started up and the whole fair crew were fed.

It was a peculiar group. The Dodgems, Waltzer and big rides had their own crews of labourers and mechanics –

254

these were all roughly dressed and greasy characters with many tattoos. There was a bearded woman, a man with a head like a goat, midget triplets, a man and woman with completely tattooed bodies and many performers and sideshow proprietors. There were other travellers there too – all of who were known by Tinker. Some of them operated labour gangs – following the travelling fairs and contracting for set-up, tear-down and clean up. They also collected scrap metal and rags, sold clothes pegs and told fortunes among the fairgoers.

At nine in the morning the fair opened and crowds began arriving. The familiar sights, sounds and smells of the fairground created a holiday atmosphere. Tinker, Jal and I manned the Sharpening and Repair stand. Soon we had scissors, knives and cleavers going through the grinders and stones. Leaks in copper jugs and solder repairs to jewellery were all handled on the spot or left with a tag bearing the owner's name. Vano and Chik were working the helter skelter for a morning's wages before the Booth opened.

At one o'clock we stepped out of the curtains and onto the stage in front of the Booth. Madog had already drawn a crowd as he introduced three fighters. Myself billed as Dai "the Dynamo" Jones, Stone John and a heavyweight billed as The Hammer. We were dressed to box except for gloves and expected to flex and bob up and down occasionally. First day there was no charge to challengers with a five shillings entry fee charged each spectator to watch six bouts with scheduled three rounds each.
All challengers lasting three rounds were to collect five pounds - stopping or knocking out the Booth fighter was worth fifteen pounds. There were lot of tough looking men and boys in the crowd – a few making eye contact and

gesturing. We were trained not to react to crowd taunts – "leave it for ring" was Madog's order. In a few minutes a group of men were assembled below the stage – offering to box. Madog picked six of them – brought them up on stage and introduced them – then the turnstile opened and the crowd of about a hundred and fifty walked through.

Two challengers were matched with each of us. If the first survived three rounds the other would wait – otherwise the Booth fighter would take on the second challenger to complete three rounds.

My first challenger was obviously a boxer with experience – probably in the local amateur ranks. He was cautious but looked poised as the first bell went. Thicker and taller than me, he was a bigger target in the body. For the first two minutes I led with body stabs, then move inside with speed and power – hammering at the stomach – two or three staccato punches each move. In Sugar Ray way I swayed away or ducked each punch until some frustration showed and my opponent started swinging. That was the opening I needed to floor him with an uppercut to his unprotected liver. His squeal and wincing face as he hit the canvas signalled this bout was over. I would have a rest now for two bouts and then face the second challenger. Between rounds and bouts Madog was out on stage with the microphone – urging new crowds to form and listen to his pitches. "Test your boxing skill against the Rhondda Dynamo - Dai Jones – the pride of Trehavod – the prince of the valleys. Stop him and earn fifteen pounds cash."

The show was repeated every two hours with last bouts starting at nine o'clock – when the crowd was at it's peak and most inebriated. The Booth fighters were occasionally rotated but I boxed three or four times a day at most fairs – then worked the Tinker's stand and escapist show. I never lost a fight and had no intention of doing so – the desire to fight had become an obsession with winning. First among my recurring thoughts was retaliation. If I didn't retaliate now, the chance would be lost forever - the evil would be buried inside me– to ferment and erupt in a sea of puss on my life.

At night in the cramped caravan Tinker counted up our take for the day – we were all paid on a per-day basis for our various jobs – including boxing – except boxing had bonuses and possible losses. All the lovo went into a single pot for the tour – we were expected to live frugally – no alcohol – cost of tobacco was to be born by individual's using it. Tinker paid out amounts on account for each traveller, each day – I was instructed to keep an account of the cash and became the scribe for the traveller community following the fairs. Our collective goal was to take as much lovo back the kampania as possible – every penny was important. I imagined this type of life was similar to serving on a Navy ship – putting in frugal time and effort to get back home with some reward.

The travelling fair moved on every few days and did the same show all over. Vano was getting some fights in the Booth and was excelling – Chik boxed young men on Saturday mornings at some fairs – but Jal had to be content with his role as the constant sparring partner with speed and amazing talent.

Through Newport, Chepstow and Monmouth a blanket of sorrow hung over the fairs. Miners from the Six Bells Colliery where forty-six of their brothers died were furious – as were all the miners in the valleys. How many more family men needed to die to command a Government response to underground safety. Not enough it would seem as the accidents mounted in proportion to the height of the waste coal tips hovering over the colliery villages. The only thing that mattered was the tonnage of coal produced every day – that was the only measure recorded or pursued. Even miners going underground with smoking materials were going undetected due to ill will between miners and management. But still the fairs were supported – there was nothing else to relieve the routine toil and boredom of the valleys.

The tour rolled on until we reached Gloucester and the big annual fair. To our surprise Tinker had arranged for letters to come to a local address from Vivian and the family. My letter from Vivian became the lifeline of my life – there were few words but many illustrations in the three pages – I could smell and almost touch her through the messages of love and distance. It was what I needed to keep going – to keep fighting – I kept it in my shirt pocket and looked at it many, many times a day.

We had become bonded with the rest of the travelling fair group. No one went without good food, a clean bed and a safe place to sleep. Breakdown of rides and equipment called for all hands on deck – there were always enough willing workers to help in a situation unplanned or unfortunate. Throughout the fairground an informal communication system kept everyone aware and attentive to the day and it's events. Madog gave me a raise and suggested he would act as my agent and promoter if I signed to box professionally with him. I had made it I thought – now I could see a clear path to my ambition of championship boxing – almost five years of hard labour and sweat had paid off.

Chapter 15

Oxford Revisited

Pulling into a lay-by on the Oxford southern bypass on Saturday night before St. Giles fair was history repeating in six years. Back then I was desperate to escape my existence – now I wanted to preserve it. Purging my obsession with revenge felt essential. We huddled in the caravan and went over the plan again, checking each other's complete understanding of their role – checking and rechecking the tools, devices and disguises. As dusk fell it was time to act.

My brothers and I left the caravan in total darkness. I led them through the fields to Hinksey Lake Bridge, through the railings at Hinksey Park and to a place where we could observe the Gents Toilets on Abingdon Road. We could see our small lorry parked in the farm lay-by – Tinker at the wheel. We settled down to observe the entry to the toilets and the Vicarage fifty yards further up Abingdon Road. As usual there was plenty of queer action going on. Chinks of light sometimes blinked through the Vicarage curtains – men and youths, on bikes and on foot, were stopping at the toilets. We waited patiently – the action was sure to continue – we expected certain visitors.

I recognized the queer stalker from Sunningwell Road who had pursued me relentlessly as a boy – he locked his bike to the park railings. Before long a youth walked in – the queer followed him – I signalled my brothers to pull on their balaclavas and gloves and follow me. I waved at Tinker as we silently entered the toilets - I saw the lorry door swing open.

Inside two adjoining cubicles were occupied – "engaged" showing in the penny entry lock - the other two were "vacant" – I led my brothers into the end one – we exchanged silent glances and waited. They looked at the walls covered in drawings of naked men and women in various sexual positions and acts. There were two glory holes about two inches wide and several other smaller viewing holes. I signalled my brothers to look through and see the holes in the wall of the next cubicle, giving access to the one next to it.

I heard Tinker clear his throat outside – the signal that someone had left the Vicarage and was approaching the toilets. My brothers perched on the toilet seat so their feet would not show in the three-inch gap between the floor and the walls. We waited. Soon some feet passed by and a penny dropped into the lock of the cubicle next door. The feet entered – we moved so fast that before the door was closed Vano and Chik had wedged it open and bundled the figure inside.

Jal slipped a jimmy tool in the far cubicle lock and pushed open the door – the youth was standing with his trousers around his ankles and a hard-on beginning to droop. Patrin entered and blocked the exit from the next cubicle as Jal and I slipped a self-locking chain around and between the youth's ankles and fed an extension under the wall. Patrin moved away as we jimmied the lock on the next cubicle and pushed open the door.

The pathetic queer from Sunningwell Road, who had frighteningly harassed me at will, was standing in a similar state. We slipped another ankle chain on him and joined it with the youth's under the wall. A panicked low sound was coming from the next cubicle – a pleading Gown voice

260

asking to be let go, as it was "all a mistake". Not one word had passed between us.

The cloaked figure from the Vicarage and the queer in the next cubicle were handcuffed in chains made by Tinker to snap on and be impossible to remove. A steel bar was passed through one glory hole and the handcuff chains were locked to each end – forcing the men to stand against the wall with their noses touching it They would get to spend the next few hours, shackled and staring up close to their artwork, reflecting on their evil – in a place where they plied perversion on young boys. Boys so young as to be oblivious or even capable of indulging willingly in such a perversion. As a parting gesture we pulled their trousers and underpants down around their ankles and pinned a sign on their backs "NONCE".

In less than three minutes we had shackled the queers through and under the walls – without a word being spoken. These visitors to the Gents Toilets that night will have a hard time explaining themselves.

We left silently and waved to Tinker and Patrin as they moved down Abingdon Road to the phone booth. Tinker called 999 and reported an assault taking place at the toilets – we walked casually down Lake Street and back over the bridge. My brothers were elated at our victory – we laughed mightily at the images left of the queers – not a one putting up a fight or an argument – they knew they were exposed. Walking through South Hinksey the customers were leaving the General Elliot pub – they paid no attention to a quiet group of boys walking home. Back at the caravan Tinker and Patrin were soon back with fish and chips. They had waited no more than five minutes before a police car arrived and cordoned off the toilets.

Part one of our plan was almost finished – a phone call to the Oxford Mail early in the morning would complete it.

At dawn we were up cleaning and preparing the Booth, and maintaining the ring and the tent rigging. An air of confidence was good but we had much more to do in the next two days – let alone taking on all-comers at the Booth starting at 1300 tomorrow. By 1100 we were pitching in St. Giles – about fifty yards from the corner of Beaumont Street – opposite St. John's College. Rigging the Booth I pointed out the underground Gents toilets, in the middle of the road opposite the Ashmoleam Museum. All Sunday afternoon there was a procession of men down the stairs and back up sometime after – some only to cross St. Giles to the other side and come back again via Martyr's Memorial – and down the stairs again for another go-around. The absence of traffic during the fair assembly aided a flow of new and recurring visitors – some openly chatting on the pavement before going down again for another random encounter or to watch one.

At 2000 we left the caravan behind the Booth, and in the back of the lorry Tinker took us to Hinksey Park. We crossed the Hinksey Lake bridge again and through the fields and shunt yards to get behind the Baptist Church on Wytham Street. The church was closed and locked after Sunday evening service by the time we arrived at 2045. As anticipated there was a light showing in the Gents toilets window and occasionally a shadow movement behind the opaque glass.

In balaclavas and gloves I led my brothers across Hinksey Stream, retrieved the key from it's hiding place in the boiler room and opened the back door to the church. Inside we moved silently to the Gents Toilets – a chink of light showing under the door. We waited in stillness. Before long there was a sound of toilets flushing and taps flowing in the hand basin. The door opened and out stepped Dumbo and Bert West – Chik handcuffed Dumbo as I held an eight-inch screwdriver sharpened to a needlepoint under is chin –pushed into his neck just deep enough for fold of fat to fall around it. "What's this all about?" he squealed until I quieted him with a tilt of the screwdriver. Vano had Bert West up against the door. The wretched, weak and winded church caretaker had a look of shock and panic. I snapped a chain shackle over both his ankles as Vano handcuffed him.

We placed rag gags tightly across the mouths of Dumbo and West. The look of terror in Dumbo's eyes immediately changed my hatred of him to disdain – a piece of shit at best. He will not be visiting the Gents at this church any more – that's for sure. We led them into the sanctuary – shuffling in chains and pleading through the gags. Dumbo was chained to the organ and West chained to the lectern on the pulpit. The film screen, projector and reels, were left in the vestry as the perverts were last viewing.

Returning to the toilets Jal was still holding the door against a third man who was knocking from the inside "What's going on – open the door please." My father's voice was unmistakable – even after six years – but his begging tone was new – gone was the sneering, sadistic tenor.

When he stepped out he looked pathetic – aged in spades. His mouth was collapsed like the rest of the family – his cheeks creased and yellow. A few straggly white hairs fell over his ears – he appeared miserably shrunk. We handcuffed and shackled him to the steel toilet cubicle frames and gagged him. My brothers were watching me closely – I'm sure wondering if I would now inflict a punishment that we had talked of around the campfire. They knew I had the razor sharp needle screwdriver I carried for emergencies – I considered extracting my father's cock and skewering it through the middle – watching him suffer before slowly pulling it back.

We quietly left the church and Wytham Street – retreading our path through the fields, out of sight to all. In St.Aldates we took different routes back to St. Giles – meeting up at the caravan. At 2200 Tinker went to the phone booth by Martyr's Memorial and telephoned the Oxford Police to report homosexual debauchery taking place at the church. He also telephoned the Oxford Mail and gave the same message to the night watchman on duty – adding the Oxford Police were looking into it. A notable sense of hatred began draining from my mind and body – replaced with a feeling of calm.

At 1130 on Monday I was central on the stage in front of the Booth. Madog was priming the big crowd "Dai Jones – the Rhondda Dynamo – Stone John of Ton Pentre – Harry the Hammer of Tonypandy – Vano the Travelling Tudor of Penygraig – Chik the Travelling Painter of Penygraig". Looking out on the early afternoon crowd – the fair in full swing on a fine day did little to encourage a longer stay than necessary. I recognized some people in the crowd – from Hinksey, from old schools and sports – people of all ages but specially boys in my age group when I left home at fourteen.

On both days of the fair we put on ten shows – badgering thirty challengers a day to enter the ring with Madog's Men. I hoped some of the older boys who bullied me, now in their mid-twenties, would step-up and put the gloves on. I relished the thought of taunting and stinging them with counter punches for two minutes – then finishing them with my feared, but unknown to these Oxford boys, paralysing liver punch. I also fantasized meeting my brother in the ring and torturing him for two minutes before knocking him out cold. But the bouts were all routine – there were very few students "up" and punting was more their style than boxing anyway.

Later in the afternoon on Tuesday a seller walking through was touting the final edition of the Oxford Mail. "Perverts shackled in Hinksey – Read about it" was his repeated squawk. The story on the front page described Police attending the Hinksey Park Gents Toilets and the Baptist Church on Wytham Street following emergency telephone calls. In both locations there were men shackled in chains and handcuffs with evidence of homosexual pornography and paedophilia. Police were continuing their investigation.

There was freedom and a sense of retribution in the air as we packed up the Booth to move on to Witney Feast until Sunday and then we would be on the way back home. Tinker, Patrin and my brothers had not only allowed me to join the tribe but had accepted me as family and supported me to the hilt. As family and kaule they came to my side in setting the record straight and dealing out suitable kaule justice for those that had made me suffer for so long.

We bought the News of the World on Sunday as we left Witney for home. The front-page headline read "Oxford Pervert Ring Under Police Investigation."

I swore this was my last exit from Oxford – vowing never to return. Now it was time to put that entire old life behind me and return to my new life with a family who appreciated me for myself and loved me in spite of my history. It was now time to build a new future with Vivian, my kaule family and championship boxing.

ACKNOWLEDGEMENTS

Welsh Romani and Gypsy Traveller background from:
Stef Bate UK Vardo Heritage (www.gypsywaggons.co.uk)

Town & Gown Boy

A Novel
by Jonah West

The story is told through the eyes and mind of a boy growing up in Oxford during
the 1940/50's. It is a time when homosexuality was criminal but the University –
"The Gown" flouted the law with impunity and the law itself sent the "Town" local
homosexuals underground. This silence created perfect cover for homosexual
paedophile men to exploit vulnerable boys of whom there were many – created by
the time and by the Oxford hybrid culture "Town and Gown".

A few Town boys crossed to the Gown world via the 11-Plus intelligence screening
that took place during the time. Some of these boys became vulnerable due to the
vast differences they encountered between home and school during early teenage
years. These boys presented a target for paedophiles from both Town and Gown –
out looking for them in the streets of central Oxford.

Could one of these abused boys fully survive this experience?

Seaman Boys – HMS Ganges

Made in the USA
Middletown, DE
25 July 2020